UNNATURAL CAUSES

An Egret's Loft Murder Mystery

T.E. HARKINS

CHARLES
FORT
PRESS

First paperback edition September 2022

Cover design by Joe Montgomery

ISBN 979-8-9868874-0-1(paperback)
ISBN 979-8-9868874-1-8 (ebook)

PROLOGUE

The day Ritchie moved me into Egret's Loft, I thought that was it, I was done for. In for life, with no possibility of parole. Extradition to a luxurious kind of prison where I, and all my new neighbors, were just waiting to die.

That might sound a touch melodramatic, but there's a pretty compelling reason people joke about Florida being God's waiting room.

Not the parts of the state furthest south, like the Florida Keys or Miami, where it's all surf, sun, and another three-letter "s" word that people of my generation don't like to use in mixed company.

No, I'm talking about the parts of the state where every restaurant has an early bird special and there are no cars on the road after eight o'clock in the evening. The kinds of places where the only children you see around town are the ones visiting their grandparents and the obituaries take up more space than the sports pages in the local newspaper.

A kind of place like Calusa, Florida—a small Gulf Coast town nestled comfortably between Fort Myers and Naples.

Population: 2,473.

Average Age: 75.

And Calusa was going to be my new home.

It was for the best.

At least, that's what Ritchie and Eliza had agreed before even bothering to broach the subject with me—their own mother. By the time I was brought into the conversation, they'd already picked out a high-end, low-crime community with guarded gates, loads of golf, and more activities than anyone over sixty-five could possibly have the energy for. But best of all, they said, I'd be around lots of people my own age.

I remember telling the kids, when they were little, that they should go play outside to be around people their own age. It didn't matter so much to me whom they socialized with, I just wanted to get them out from underfoot. This phrase has now, decades later, come back to bite me.

My outlook and attitude were grim as I packed my bags and prepared for the move to Cypress Point Avenue.

Little did I know then, the day I moved into Egret's Loft was the beginning of the most exciting chapter of my life…and the most dangerous.

CHAPTER ONE

Egret's Loft. A silly name for a retirement community, if you ask me. I mean, egrets are primarily wading birds. They nest in shrubs, close to the ground. And none of the houses here even have second floors, let alone lofts. A design choice probably made by wise architects who realized that stairs and dodgy hips can be a deadly combination.

Not that anyone who lives here would dare to call Egret's Loft a "retirement community." Ritchie warned me that the sales team had strongly encouraged him to never use the "r" word around the new neighbors.

You can't say "seniors," either. Or "old." The acceptable terms, I've been told, are "people with advanced life experience" or "active elders." That last one can be tricky, though, because slipping and saying "elderly" is the quickest way, I hear, to get kicked off the pickleball team.

As cynical as I am about the whole thing, I do have to admit that the people here seem really happy. Everyone we passed on the drive in was smiling and laughing. It felt a little like stumbling onto the set of a new Netflix series—*Stepford Seniors*.

I said as much to Ritchie as he stopped every few hundred feet for another golf cart crossing. He said it wasn't a good sign that I had violated the no "seniors" rule on my very first day.

Ritchie is leaving now. I'm waving to him as he drives away in the rented SUV that will take him back to the airport in Tampa.

"Mind your speed and try not to run over any golf carts on your way out," I call to him, trying to stem the tide of tears that are turning my eyes into overfilled water balloons.

He laughs and revs the engine. "The local rush hour doesn't stand a chance against this beast."

"Text me that you made it back safely," I say, using my most authoritative tone.

"I will. Eliza will be over this weekend, but if you need anything before then, give one of us a shout. Love you, lady!"

"Love you, too, Ritchie."

I'm not sure if he hears me. He's already reversing out of the driveway.

I wish Ritchie could stay a little longer.

He could only come down for the day to help me move in. If you could even call it that.

The house came fully furnished and decorated. "Curated distinctly to your taste" the brochure had said. The only things I had to fill were the closet—which reminds me, I need more warm-weather clothes—and the medicine cabinet.

My personal pharmacy of prescriptions filled that one easily enough.

I stand in the driveway long after Ritchie's car is out of sight. Until I remember I'm not wearing a hat. My dermatologist told me I always need to wear a hat. The sun is different down in Florida, she'd said.

Drink a lot of water too. That from my general doctor.

Ritchie had put some coconut water in the refrigerator for me. It seems like the appropriate thing to drink in the tropical November heat. My taste buds activate as I cross the foyer, past the study, a guest bedroom, and the dining room, and into the kitchen, where I find myself confronted by some kind of touch-panel screen on the sleek metal panel doors of the refrigerator.

Not a problem. Ritchie showed me how to use an iPad. I can handle this.

A big red box in the upper left-hand corner reads, "Life Alert: In Case of Emergency Press Here."

Another box in the center of the screen asks me if I want to "continue setup." Setup?

4

I hit "yes," mostly out of curiosity. The refrigerator then asks me if my doctor has me on a diet and would I like to set up an alarm to prevent overeating.

My finger finds the "no" option, smiling at how well I'm settling in.

But the fridge is just getting warmed up. Am I storing refrigerated medicine? Would I like menu options based on my insulin or cholesterol levels? Do I want to scan grocery items to get alerts about impending expirations? Would I like to upload recipes and sync them to my grocery list?

I start hitting buttons to make it stop, but that only makes things worse. The fridge starts talking to me instead, asking all of its questions with a computerized British accent.

I want to call Ritchie or Eliza for help but know I can't.

I told them I was perfectly capable of taking care of myself. If I called them, five minutes after moving in, to tell them I couldn't figure out the refrigerator, I'd never live it down.

I wish Clint was here. He would know what to do, he always knew what to do.

In my frustration, my hand slips, and I hit the "Life Alert" button.

Oh no!

Phones I didn't even know were in the house start ringing from every room, and speakers built into the walls come to life.

"Please remain calm. Help is on the way."

"No! I'm fine. I don't need help," I say loudly. Maybe the speakers can hear me too.

The phones keep ringing, and the walls won't stop talking. I can feel my blood pressure skyrocketing.

I run outside, into the fresh air, forgetting my hat.

My dermatologist is going to be so upset with me.

Just then, a golf cart with a tinny-sounding siren and a red cross stenciled above the rear tires pulls up. A red-faced young man jumps out, medical bag in hand.

"Everything is going to be fine. Help is here," he assures me.

"It was an accident, I'm so sorry," I try to explain.

"You were in accident? Are you hurt? Can you remember your name?"

"My name? Of course, I remember my name—"

"Are you experiencing any hip pain?"

"No, no! I wasn't in an accident. The appliances were asking me questions, and I hit a button by accident. I didn't know how to make it stop."

"You're sure you're not hurt?" He doesn't seem convinced.

"*Tranquilo*, Jimmy. She just moved in," a sultry female voice says from off to my left.

I turn and see an impeccably dressed woman with shoulder-length, dyed brown hair, heavy eyeliner, and gorgeous olive skin.

"Let me guess." She winks. "The refrigerator?"

"How did you know?" I ask, wondering if I fell asleep and this is all a dream.

"I know everything that happens in this place." She smiles before turning to address the medic. "Jimmy, *cariño*, I told you we need to have someone explain the appliances when new residents move in."

"Don't look at me! I told the board that smart refrigerators were a dumb idea." Jimmy shakes his head.

"I know, I know." The mystery woman waves her hand as if she's already bored with the conversation. "I'll talk to Victor about this. I know he just wants to help Stan, but this has really gone too far. Stan's little project must be stopped. This poor dear could have been killed by her ice box!"

"My name is Madeline. Madeline Delarouse. And it really wasn't that bad—"

"Nonsense, Madeline. Those things are a menace. Something needs to be done. In the meantime, Jimmy, can you be a darling and shut off all the alarms inside? I'm going to take our new friend here on a tour of the property. Have you had a tour yet?"

6

"Not yet, I was only just getting settled in. A tour would be lovely. Can I grab my hat?"

The mystery woman grabs my elbow and starts walking me across the gravel garden that separates my house from the neighboring property.

"No need. I have spares in my garage. It's only just next door. Come, come."

"Thank you for your help. I didn't catch your name."

She stops abruptly. "*Dios mio*, where are my manners? But then I just assumed your handsome son would have filled you in. He is such a lovely boy, your Ritchie. We had many conversations before you moved in. I am Carlota Morena Hernandez. I'm President of the Board of Directors for Egret's Loft."

"Oh, yes, Ritchie did mention you." He didn't, but I don't want to appear rude or, worse, uninformed. "It's a pleasure to meet you. How long have you lived here?"

"Since the day the property opened. I helped build this place. In fact, the name, Egret's Loft? It was my idea. It's a very powerful name, no?"

I keep my smile fixed. "It's definitely something, yes."

"Here we are. Jump in. There is so much to see. I'm very excited you are here! We're going to be the best of friends; I can feel it already!"

CHAPTER TWO

"We designed all the streets in circles. Active elders wandering can sometimes get lost. In circles they will always find their way home, yes?"

I nod, a borrowed Prada sun visor, that probably cost more than the average car, perched on top of my whitish-blond hair, as Carlota reverses the golf cart out of her driveway.

"Wave to Phyllis," she instructs, holding up her own hand, as we pass the house across the street from mine.

"I don't see anyone—"

"*No importa*. She can see you. I guarantee."

Feeling a bit foolish, I raise my arm and wave. No one appears at the window to return the wave, but I swear I see a light flash on and off in one of the back rooms.

"Phyllis is one of our residents with the most advanced life experience. She stays inside mostly, but sometimes she drives to the River Club for a drink. There have been a few incidents with mailboxes, but nothing serious. We have a repairman on standby. Hello, Helen!"

This to a heavily botoxed woman in a tennis skirt and designer sneakers, carrying weights as she powerwalks.

"Howdy, Carlota," Helen says. "Who's your friend?"

"Our newest neighbor. Madeline, this is Helen. She lives just up the road."

"Very nice to meet you," I call out, but we're already driving away, as Helen continues walking in the opposite direction.

"*Pobrecita*. Her latest husband died last year. It was very sad for her."

"Latest husband?"

8

"Yes, I think he was number six. Maybe seven. All dead. Helen has very bad luck with men. Anyway, in this house are George and Jinny. Jinny with an 'i.' She is very particular about that. She'll be knocking on your door tomorrow with a welcome basket. You'll recognize her because she only wears pink."

"I'm partial to green myself," I offer.

"Yes, green would suit you. Matches your eyes. The woman who lives here—" she points to a house three doors up from mine on the other side of the road, "—only wears black."

"Is she in mourning?"

"No one knows. *Pero* no, we suspect someone has told her black is slimming. Still, it's only a color, it cannot perform magic. Selena is her name. That's pretty much all we know about her. She doesn't talk much, except to the gardeners. And this house belongs to 'Raging Roy.' You have heard of him, no?"

I wonder if this is something else Ritchie failed to mention. "The name doesn't ring any bells. Should it?"

"Only if you like American football. Roy Everhard. He played for many teams. In Super Bowls and everything, though he doesn't like to talk about that. Oh. *Hola*, Roy!"

Almost as if he heard us talking about him, a large man—not fat, but large—emerges from his house. His remaining hair forms a kind of wreath around the sides of his head, and the short sleeves of his flowered shirt are clearly struggling under the weight of too much pressure.

"Hey, Carlota. Who's that beautiful, young thing sitting next to you?"

"Our newest neighbor. Sorry, no time to chat. See you later." She adds in a whisper to me, "Watch out for that one. He cheats at Scrabble and his hands are gropey."

"You play Scrabble? I love Scrabble!"

"Do I play Scrabble? I'm only the Egret's Loft champion five years in a row!"

There is genuine delight on her face. English is clearly her second language, so she must have to work twice as hard for that title.

"Champion? Oh, I'm not sure you should play with me then. It wouldn't be much of a challenge for you."

"*Ridículo*! We will play. Maybe I let you win the first game." She winks conspiratorially.

"You'll do no such thing," I playfully admonish. "I've never been a charity case, and I don't intend to start now!"

Smiles all around.

Her energy, at first intimidating, is quickly becoming infectious. This place may not be so bad after all. If only I had Clint to share it with.

Just then, a car races past in a storm of squealing tires and screeching brakes.

"*Idiota*!" Carlota screams. "Learn how to drive that thing, or we'll ban it from the Loft."

"What kind of car was that? I've never seen anything like it before."

"A Pagani Imola. Ridiculous car, and so much money. But Harold had a big investment payout this year. It won't last. Mark my words."

I'm about to ask whether she means the car or the investment windfall will be short lived, but she's already moved on to filling me in on the other neighbors.

Here is "Black Cap" Stan's house. He used to work in computers. He designed the program for the smart refrigerators that have caused so many problems for new residents.

Over there lives "Crazy" Carl, who you never want to run into on a hot, sunny day, though Carlota doesn't bother to mention why. Since every day here seems hot and sunny, crossing paths with "Crazy" Carl seems virtually inevitable.

And across the lake from me, on the other side of the circle, is Victor Collins's home. He's allegedly the most eligible bachelor in all of Egret's Loft, though no one has ever seen him out on a date. He prefers his own company, an attitude Carlota can't make sense of.

"There are five other neighborhoods just like this one," Carlota tells me when we get to the end of our circle. "But you might be feeling a bit overwhelmed, yes?"

"A little," I admit, trying to keep my new neighbors' names straight in my head.

"*Claro*! Let us go to the Golf Club. Do you play?"

"Does miniature golf, when the kids were little, count?"

She chuckles. "Not to worry. You will learn. We have a very good golf pro. He once played with Tiger Woods. You will like him."

A host of golf cart greetings interrupt the sightseeing as we make the short journey to the clubhouse.

"There is Dom now. *Hola*, Dom! We have a new recruit for you!"

A man in his early sixties, wearing shorts that are a little too short, walks toward the cart. He has thick, dark hair and an even thicker mustache. He looks a lot like that TV show actor, Tom Selleck.

"New blood is always welcome around here." He takes my hand and kisses it. "The name's Dom. Dom Skellig."

"I'm sorry, did you say Tom Selleck?"

His laugh sounds rehearsed. "Would you believe I get that all the time? Must be the mustache. I wonder if anyone ever confuses him with me."

Before I can ask why they would, Carlota jumps in. "We stole Dom away from the PGA Tour. Made him an offer he couldn't refuse. Isn't that right, Dom?"

"Sure is. Best decision of my life." He smiles.

I think he's lying.

"Why do you have rubber gloves, Dom?" Carlota asks. "Don't you have a lesson with Linda soon?"

"Yeah, she has the last lesson of the day. But, if you'll excuse me, I need to clean up a little accident on the driving range before she arrives."

"An accident?" The words are out before I can stop them.

"A bird. An egret, actually. It flew in front of Sam right after he hit a ball. Bad timing, poor thing."

Carlota's face falls, and she begins walking toward the driving range. I follow her.

Amidst the bright greens of the grassy knoll and deep blues of the man-made lake lies an unmoving mass of white feathers, black legs, yellow beak, and red blood.

A solitary tear rolls down Carlota's cheek.

In hindsight, maybe I should have seen the majestic bird's violent death as a sign.

CHAPTER THREE

"Mom? Mom, are you asleep?"

"Not anymore," I tell Eliza, rolling over in bed to check the clock. "But it's alright, dear. I'm retired. What else do I have to do at 7:30 on a Tuesday morning?"

"Sorry. Look, I have to get back to work in a minute. I just wanted to call and give you a heads up. The woman who lives next door to you is dead. She may have been murdered."

I learned a long time ago not to ask Eliza how she knows things. She can't even tell me where she works. She just knows things and I roll with it.

"Murdered? Here?"

"I don't have all the details yet, but the death was reported as suspicious."

Suddenly awake, I walk to the window in the study, which has the best view of the driveway. There's Jimmy's golf cart with the red cross, parked in Carlota's driveway.

"Carlota? But…but she gave me a tour yesterday and was going to teach me how to play bocce ball."

"It's not hard. Just throw balls and try to get them as close as possible to the pallino."

"The pallino?"

"Yeah, it's a smaller ball that gets thrown first. But you're missing the point here, Mom! I'm telling you your neighbor may have been murdered, and you're asking me how to play bocce ball!"

She's right. Poor Carlota. Though I'd only just met her, she seemed very pleasant. Not to mention, it's difficult to imagine anyone being killed in a place as domesticated as Egret's Loft.

"Do they know who killed her? Or why?"

"Not yet, but given who her son is, you can see why we'd be interested."

I don't even know who "we" is, but something else she said got my attention. "Her son?"

"He's a candidate to become the next President of Colombia. He's running on an anti-corruption platform and plans to take on FARC dissident groups that never disarmed after the peace accord. Didn't Ritchie tell you?"

I have no idea what she's on about, so I only respond to her question. "Ritchie didn't even tell me he'd spoken to Carlota."

I can practically hear her eyes rolling over the phone. "Of course, he didn't. He's such a weirdo. Anyway, I don't have any reason to think you're in danger. The girls and I were planning to drive over on Saturday, but I can be there tonight if you want."

"I'm sure that's not necessary. It was probably just some kind of accident. Nothing for you to worry about."

"I don't know, Mom, I just—"

"You know this is a retirement community, right? Ritchie said I'm not allowed to say we're all old here, but let's face it. We're all old. I'll be seventy in a few months! Are you going to offer to come over every time someone has a heart attack or falls over in the shower?"

"Of course not. But—"

"But nothing. I'm your mother, and I'm telling you to stay put. If I need anything, I'll let you know. Alright?"

"Alright. Well, I better get back to work. Call me any time. And Mom?"

"Yes, dear?"

"Be careful."

The phone line goes dead.

I'm sure she's already dialing Ritchie. They'll spend the next ten minutes or so blaming each other for moving me next door to a possible murder victim.

It wouldn't be the worst thing in the world for them to feel a little guilt about my current predicament. After all, they're the ones who arranged and paid for me to be here. And all mothers know the most powerful tool you can wield against your children is guilt. Works so much better than raising your voice. That only makes them defensive.

An ambulance pulls up on the curb between our houses. The siren is off. Murdered or not, Carlota's already dead.

I look down at my chunky-knit winter robe. At some point, I'll have to get a new one. Cotton or silk. Something more suited to the climate. Either way, I can't go outside dressed like this.

By the time I've put on a linen dress, a silk wrap, and enough blush to make sure the coroner doesn't try to load me into his van next to Carlota, a small crowd of residents has gathered in the street.

Directly across from me, a woman, who must be eighty-five if she's a day, is standing in the window. Her hair, which looks almost lavender, is short and curly. But her glasses are the first thing I notice. They look like giant saucers on her thin face.

That must be Phyllis.

She sees me looking and fades back into the shadows. Not wanting to appear rude for staring, I give a little wave as she makes her retreat. She doesn't wave back but I can see the lights in the kitchen flash on and off.

My focus shifts back to the activity next door.

Crime scene tape is going up between the palm trees on either side of Carlota's driveway.

A distinguished-looking man with salt and pepper hair stands on the business end of the police cordon. He's talking with his hands and pointing at the crime scene tape, then his heart. Probably trying to tell the police that, if they create too big of a spectacle, they might want to think about having more ambulances on hand.

On the other side of Carlota's house, the black widow she'd identified as Helen strokes a small furry dog clutched in her arms. There's a sweatband on her forehead and Lycra clinging to every curve. The dog won't stop barking. I want to say Helen looks concerned, but the skin on her face is so taut it's really hard to tell.

It's easier to tell what Raging Roy is thinking. Walking up behind Helen to see what all the commotion is about, he's clearly checking out her assets.

Closer to me, a very large woman wearing a brightly colored caftan waves a fan back and forth in front of her face. Tears of sweat run from her forehead, across her cheeks, and disappear into the folds around her neck.

Walking up to her, I ask what's going on. Nobody likes a know-it-all, and I don't want to make a bad first impression.

"Carlota is dead," she says with a thick Latin accent.

I wait for her to say more, but she doesn't.

"It's so shocking. I only just moved in yesterday. My name is Madeline, by the way. Carlota was my neighbor."

Without taking her eyes off Carlota's front door she says, "I know."

"I'm sorry, I didn't catch your name." I smile, to thaw the ice.

She looks at me, confusion on her face. "How could you? I didn't say it."

Then she turns back to stare at the man walking toward me. It's the same man who'd been speaking with the cops only minutes earlier.

"You must be Madeline. Under the circumstances, it seems odd to welcome you to Egret's Loft, but you are very welcome here nonetheless. My name is Victor Collins. I live on the other side of the lake."

"Pleasure to meet you, Victor. It is a shame we have to meet this way, isn't it? Do you know what happened?"

He glances over at the large woman with the fan. She's watching us intently.

"Nothing at the moment, I'm afraid," he says. "But the police do want to speak with all of Carlota's neighbors. Routine, I assure you."

16

Without realizing it, he's just alerted me to the fact that it wasn't an accident.

Carlota *was* murdered.

"Oh, I know it's routine. They can ask me whatever they like. That's no trouble at all."

"Great." He waves to a tall, bald man with a badge on his hip. "How about now?"

"Now?"

"Afraid so." Victor gives me a sympathetic smile.

His teeth are white and very straight. They look like his real teeth, but then they can work wonders with dentures these days, can't they?

"Of course. Shall we chat inside?" I ask, realizing I have once again forgotten my hat. Come to think of it, I still have the one Carlota loaned me. It's a bit late to give it back now.

"Perfect," Victor says, as the bald policeman begins walking in our direction. "If you'd like, the police have allowed me to be present. I used to be an attorney."

"That would be fine. Thank you."

Victor takes my elbow and begins walking me toward my own front door.

"Selena," my companion acknowledges the woman with the fan.

That's Selena? But Carlota said she always wore black. Maybe it's a coincidence she's chosen today to start wearing colors.

My late husband Clint didn't believe in coincidences.

Come to think of it, neither do I.

CHAPTER FOUR

"You have a very beautiful home, Ms. Delarouse," the bald detective says, taking big gulps of the air-conditioning.

"I'm afraid I can't take any of the credit for that. The sales team sent me photos of artwork and asked me to rank them in order of how much I liked them. They chose everything based on that. It was like this when I moved in yesterday."

"Seriously?" He says, looking around. "They decorated the whole place for you?"

"It's one of the perks. Each property is curated to the particular tastes of the residents." Victor joins the conversation, turning to me. "I recognize this package. You're an upmarket Monet."

"I always did have a soft spot for the impressionists."

"I'm more of a mid-range Picasso or Braque man myself. But this is nice too."

The policeman clears his throat. Probably trying to remind us that he's still in the room.

"What a terrible hostess I am." I'm surprised to find myself blushing. "Would you like some water after being out in that heat? It'll have to be from the tap, I'm afraid. The fridge and I aren't quite operating on the same intelligence level just yet."

The detective frowns but chooses not to pursue that particular line of questioning. "Water would be great, thank you."

Once we're all seated in the living room with full tumblers of tepid water the detective opens a little black notebook and gently begins his interrogation. "My name is Detective Pete Fletcher."

"Pete Fletcher? I was just reading a book on my iPad by a man with the same name! It was a mystery. What was it called? *A Sunny Day to Die*. Yes, that's it."

"Was it any good?" He asks.

"I enjoyed it very much. A good beach read." Though I can't remember the last time I went to a beach. There must be one close to Calusa. Clint always loved the beach.

"Probably just a coincidence. You know, having the same name," the detective says, but the smile on his face leads me to suspect there's more to the story.

I'll have to see if there's an author photo in the online book. I miss dust jackets. One of the many things I miss about proper books. But then arthritis can put a damper on holding anything for long periods of time.

"This is all very informal," Detective Fletcher continues. "I just have a few routine questions to help me get a better idea of what might have happened."

"Oh, I know the drill, detective," I assure him. "My husband investigated homicides for over thirty years in Washington, DC."

"Your husband?" Victor asks, eyebrows raised.

"Yes. Clint. That was his name. He died six months ago." I keep my voice steady, but regret bringing him into the conversation. It's still too raw.

"That's awful," Victor sympathizes. "My wife died four years ago. Feels like yesterday."

I nod. Rest in peace, my love.

"I'm sorry for your loss. I promise this won't take long, and there shouldn't be any surprises," the detective reassures me.

"Fire away. With your questions, I mean."

"Right. So, your name is Madeline Delarouse, and you moved into Egret's Loft yesterday?"

"That's correct."

"Did you have any interactions with the victim?"

"The victim? So she was murdered?"

"I can't reveal any information about an ongoing investigation," he says. "Did you meet her or communicate with her in any way?"

But Victor has taken my bait. "Technically, she could be a victim even if it was an accident. Couldn't she?"

I shake my head. "Legally speaking, 'victim' refers to someone who suffered harm as a result of the commission of a crime. So, it sounds like the detective is trying not to tell us what he already told us. She was murdered."

Detective Fletcher jumps in. "Hang on a second. I never said she was murdered."

"No, you didn't," I agree. "Not outright. But based on your wording, I think it's safe to assume that she was."

Victor isn't buying it. "You're correct about the legal definition, but this is an informal police chat. The detective isn't a lawyer, are you?"

"No, but—"

"You see! So, he might not be aware that, under the law, a victim of an accident is less of a victim than one who suffered as the result of a crime." Victor turns to the detective. "How did you say she died again?"

"I didn't." Detective Fletcher tries to reestablish his authority. "And if you don't mind…"

But I haven't finished. "What if she had a stroke? Would you still call her a victim? Or would you only call her that if she, say, got hit in the head by a falling coconut?"

"I didn't say she was hit in the head," the detective tries, once more, to take charge.

"Aha! So, she was hit in the head!" I exclaim triumphantly.

"Now why would you assume that?" Victor wants to know.

"Because he didn't say she didn't have a stroke. Simple really!"

"Astounding! I never would have thought about it like that." Victor smiles. "That's very clever. Is she right, Detective?"

Detective Fletcher seems desperate to rein in this conversation. "If it will get us back on track, I don't suppose there's any harm in telling you that, yes, the vic…the *deceased*…died from blunt force trauma. Now, back to my original question. Did you have any dealings with your new neighbor?"

"Blunt force trauma can result from a fall," Victor says.

I frown. "That would have to have been a pretty steep fall. Unless she hit something with very sharp edges. What package did she have, do you know?"

"She was upmarket Van Gogh if memory serves. Not a lot of sharp edges there."

"No, the expressionists wouldn't have, would they?" I agree.

"Were you ever inside Ms. Hernandez's house?" Detective Fletcher demands, voice slightly raised.

I turn, having almost forgotten he's still in the room. "I'm sorry. Inside, you say? No, I wasn't in the house. But she did let me pick a hat off the wall in her garage."

"Why did she give you a hat?"

The poor detective seems confused. He really needs to keep up.

"Melanoma of course! My dermatologist says it can be deadly! Especially with my fair skin."

Victor nods.

Detective Fletcher shakes his head. "No, no, no. I understand why you would want a hat. What I don't understand is why she gave you one!"

"So I wouldn't get burned when she took me on a tour with her golf cart."

"She took you on a tour? So, you spent time with her?"

"Yes, about an hour. Just around the neighborhood and over to the Golf Club. It was very pleasant, really. I was beginning to like her."

"She was very likable," Victor agrees.

"How was she acting? Did she seem normal?" Detective Fletcher asks.

"I'd only just met her," I remind him. "I have no idea what normal was like for her. Though she did seem rather sad about Sam's golfing accident."

"Who's Sam? What kind of accident was he in?"

"I've never met Sam. I just heard his name when they were talking about the dead bird."

"Dead bird? What does that have to do with Sam being injured?"

"No, no. Sam wasn't injured. He's the one who killed the bird!"

Victor has been watching the detective and I like we're playing a particularly fierce tennis match, but this last bit gets his attention.

"That was Sam?" Victor asks. "Poor guy, he probably feels awful."

"You know what?" The detective interrupts. "Forget Sam. Forget the bird. How sad did it make the vic…deceased?"

"It looked like it hit her pretty hard," I admit. "No pun intended. But I'm confused about the direction of this interrogation. Are you trying to ask me if I thought she was suicidal? People don't generally kill themselves by bashing in their own heads."

"I didn't say her head was bashed in."

"Was her head bashed in?"

"Yeah." The detective shakes his head. "Alright, fine. Did she say anything about any of the other residents? Did she seem worried about anything?"

"Spot on, Madeline! She was murdered!" Victor beams.

"Whoa! Again, I never said she was murdered!" Frustration is etched on the detective's face.

"You didn't have to," I tell him.

Victor nods in agreement.

"Not true. It could have been an accident," Detective Fletcher argues. "She might have been upset about an argument with another resident, got distracted, and had an accident. It happens."

"But we've already established she didn't have any sharp edges," I argue.

"And I saw the crime scene techs taking her golf clubs into evidence," Victor announces. "Was she hit with a golf club?"

"That definitely wouldn't be an accident," I say. "I mean, how do you hit yourself in the head with a golf club? Is that even possible?"

"I wouldn't think so," Victor agrees. "Detective, are you trying to say she fell and landed on a golf club in just such a way that it made a hole in her skull?"

The detective throws his notebook on the floor. "*Ugh*! You want to know what happened? Fine. I'll tell you! Someone hit her in the head with a 9 iron so hard it's still sticking out of her head! The techs had to cut off the handle just to get her into a body bag! Are you happy? Now, will you please tell me if she said anything about anyone wanting to hurt her?"

The only noises in the room after the detective stops speaking are the sound of his own labored breathing and the refrigerator informing us, "It's now 9 o'clock."

"Well." I'm the first human to speak. "That's a mental image I won't be unseeing anytime soon."

CHAPTER FIVE

"You really must try the arugula and pistachio pesto quiche."

"I appreciate the suggestion," I tell Victor, "but garlic in the morning gives me heartburn."

After my police interview, Victor invited me for a late breakfast at the Golf Club. In all the morning's excitement, we realized neither of us had remembered to eat.

There was a brief delay getting to the restaurant as he gave me a tutorial on my new golf cart. Apparently, every house here comes with its own. Nothing to it, really. As long as you remember to unplug it from the wall before taking it for a spin.

Which reminds me, I need to call maintenance about getting a replacement cord.

"Everything on the menu here is wonderful. You won't be disappointed," Victor assures me. "Ah, here comes our waiter."

He orders the quiche, which I have promised to try. A little bite won't kill you, he says.

I get the cranberry crumb cake with almonds and oats.

Both of our dishes are quite a mouthful to say. Like some kind of memory game. If you can remember all the words when ordering your entrée, you get to eat it. A clinical trial for the antidote to Alzheimer's.

"Are you too warm? Too cold?" Victor asks.

"I'm perfectly comfortable, thank you."

He wants to talk about Carlota's murder, I can see it in his eyes. But, at the same time, he doesn't want to talk about it. I can tell that too. Eventually, he'll make up his mind.

Turns out, he doesn't have to.

"Can you believe it? Carlota, killed with her own golf club?" This comes from a stunning woman with dark skin and gray hair that has a shock of white in the front. She pulls up a chair and joins us at the table.

Victor shakes his head. "Come now, Gina. Believe nothing of what you hear and only half of what you see."

"As much as it kills me to go along with this proverb thing you've got going, I have to ask. Should you believe the things you see *and* hear?"

Is she saying she witnessed Carlota's murder?

"Excuse me?" I ask.

"Oh, don't excuse yourself, hun. You can stay right where you are. This concerns you, too, you know. That was some bait and switch you used on that cop this morning. He thought he was doing the questioning, but he didn't stand a chance against you. Am I right?" She laughs, a big booming sound that warms your chest as it ricochets off the walls. I'm surprised at the size of her voice, which seems out of proportion to her petite frame.

How could she possibly know about that chat? I look at Victor. He puts his head in his hand.

"Gina, you didn't," he says.

"Darn tootin', I did! And none of this holier than thou business! This is the most exciting thing that's happened here since Jinny tried to go for a spin in the golf cart without George and very nearly ran over herself. I had to see *and* hear for myself!"

"I'm sorry. I'm confused," I interject. "What did you see and hear that you shouldn't have seen or heard?"

"You, hun. Talking to that police detective."

She says "talk," but it sounds more like "tawk" with her thick New York accent.

"How could you have possibly known about that conversation?"

Victor, seeing my discomfort, jumps in. "The security guards were being inundated with calls from relatives wanting wellness checks on residents. If someone didn't answer their phone right away, their kids would get nervous."

Gina huffs. "As if we couldn't possibly have anything better to do than sit by the phone all day, waiting for our kids to call. Right?"

"Anyway—" Victor takes back control of the conversation. "—the board decided to put cameras on the back patios of every house in Egret's Loft. Only the security guards have access, and they're only supposed to use them for *legitimate* wellness checks."

I'm still confused. "But if the camera is outside the house, how can anyone hear what's happening inside?"

"Oh, there are speakers inside. The sound goes both ways. Again, only the *guards* are supposed to be able to access that." Victor glares at Gina. She glares right back.

"I don't mean to be difficult, but is that even legal?" I have to ask.

"There's a disclosure in the contract you signed before moving in," Victor says.

"I don't remember seeing anything about that."

"It's in the fine print."

"You mean the really tiny bit that I couldn't even read before I needed readers?"

"Exactly."

"Again, I'm not trying to be difficult, but what can the cameras see?" I ask, pulling together the edges of the silk wrap draped across my shoulders.

"Are you worried that someone is going to take nudey photos of you?" Gina asks. "Not for nothing, I'm sure there's a niche market for that somewhere. But we're not involved in any of that nonsense here at Egret's Loft."

"Gina!" Victor exclaims.

"What?"

"Back to the question," he says in a way that broaches no argument, "each house has one camera, facing into the main rooms. It can't see you in the bedroom or any of the…more private rooms. And it has come in useful. Just last month, we saw that Ruth had taken a tumble and couldn't get up. We sent the medic over and a crisis was averted."

A thought occurs to me. "Do the cameras record?"

"What kind of perverts do you think we are?" Gina wants to know.

"No, nothing like that. I was just wondering. If the cameras do record, is there a chance we'd be able to see who killed Carlota?"

There's a moment of silence as we all look at each other, then Victor shakes his head.

"The cameras do store video for twenty-four hours, but Carlota didn't have one. She was the only board member who didn't agree to having them installed in the first place. I remember the conversation from a meeting."

Gina whistles. "I like the way you think though. I'm Eugenia. But everyone calls me Gina."

"My name is Madeline. It's nice to meet you, Gina. Do you mind me asking, how you were able to watch my camera if only the security guards have access?"

"My husband helped build this place. I know people." She winks.

"So—" I try to put this latest information into context, "— your husband and Carlota were partners?"

"In a way, I guess so. Yeah. He owned the property development company. She came up with a lot of the capital."

"Everything seems to have turned out well. I mean, the place seems to be thriving. No trouble with the financials?" I ask.

Gina stares for a second and then bursts out laughing. "Look at you. Asking questions. Looking for a motive. Egret's Loft has its very own Miss Marbles."

"I think you mean Marple?"

"The active elder white lady that was always solving crimes?"

"That's the one."

"Huh. I always thought it was Marbles. But that's not the point. Are you going to try and figure out who killed Carlota? The police seem clueless. You'd probably do a better job. Your husband having been a cop and all."

Some detectives, not wanting to expose their families to the horror of their jobs, never talk about their cases outside of work.

Not Clint. He used to tell me and the kids all about his cases over dinner. We'd sit there for hours speculating about who may have killed his latest victim and why. That was how I learned my kids were brilliant. I'd like to think we'd helped collar a couple of criminals over the years.

"Oh, I don't know. I guess it could be kind of fun."

"Yeah, it would," Gina says excitedly.

"No! No, it wouldn't," Victor protests. "This is a job for the police. It could be dangerous. You two need to stay well out of it. Promise me."

"You know what? I think he might be right, hun," Gina says. "We should just leave this to Detective Fetchner."

"Fletcher," I correct her.

"That's the one."

"It's agreed?" Victor wants to make sure. "You're going to leave crime solving to the professionals?"

"Yes, I think that's probably for the best."

"Yeah, alright," Gina grudgingly concedes.

Our food arrives, looking almost too good to eat. Victor bows his head and digs into his quiche.

Across the table, Gina and I come to an unspoken understanding.

We're going to solve this murder.

CHAPTER SIX

"The ball has to be facing up. This isn't bowling, hun."

"I have to throw it underhanded?" I ask. "I thought you told me to roll it to get it close to the other ball."

"Yes, you throw it up and then, when it lands, it rolls."

"I don't think I'm going to be any good at this," I fret. "But what the heck, here goes!"

Gina had suggested she teach me how to play bocce ball. It was part of a plan to shake off Victor so we could talk about the murder.

I throw the ball and, to both of our surprise, it lands within inches of the pallino.

"Will you look at that!" Gina whistles. "You're a natural."

I try not to blush. "Beginner's luck, I'm sure. How many balls do I get?"

"Four, hun. You get four. But cool your jets, it's my turn now."

Gina throws. Her ball hits the pallino, launching it away from my ball.

"You can do that? Move the pallino, I mean?"

Gina grins widely. "You sure can. All the balls are up for grabs."

Speaking of, I wonder how Victor is coming along with Helen. She'd called him saying the police wanted to question her, and she would feel so much more comfortable with him around. Gina said that, if Helen had her way, Victor would be husband number eight.

It would probably be rude to ask how all the others died.

"Your turn," Gina says. "Now that you've got the hang of the game, let's get down to more important business. How are we going to solve this murder? What would Clive have done?"

"You mean Clint?" Before today, I haven't said his name, out loud, in months. It's like rediscovering a favorite sweater, only to be disappointed when you realize it no longer fits.

"That's the one." Gina's voice slices through my thoughts.

Steadying myself, I throw my ball. It knocks Gina's out of bounds. "*Clint* would have started by trying to narrow down the list of suspects. Who had motive and opportunity? That kind of thing."

"Sounds like a good place to start." She pulls her arm back to throw.

"Agreed. Let's start with you," I say. "Did you have any reason to want Carlota dead?"

Her ball goes wide. "Why you little cheat!" Gina sizes me up. "You think you can win by distracting me. Well, I get to go again, because I'm furthest from the ball. No talking this time."

"I thought talking was the whole reason we were out here."

"Not anymore, hun."

She throws her ball, and it lands inches from the pallino. It's my turn again.

I pick up my third ball. "I'm not trying to distract you, but if we're going to work together to solve this, I need to know that you aren't the murderer. I have no desire to become an accomplice after the fact. My kids would be embarrassed. You understand."

"Yeah, kids are embarrassed far too easily these days, if you ask me. But if you're really worried about me being a killer, what's stopping me from killing you right now?"

"Too many witnesses. Plus, judging by your rather thick accent, I can tell you're from New York. Which means your bark is probably a lot worse than your bite."

She opens her mouth to object, but just then, my ball knocks hers outside the court lines. Three of her balls are now out of bounds.

"You did *not* just do that!" Gina sounds dumbfounded. "Here I am, thinking this is a friendly little game of bocce. Admit it, you're a ringer!"

"I look like someone else you know?"

"What?"

"A ringer. You know, like, you're a dead ringer for my friend so and so."

"No, no. Ringer like you're a fraud. Pretending to not know what you're doing. You've definitely played this before."

"I most certainly have not!"

"That sounds like a lie." Gina squints. "And if you're willing to lie about having played bocce, you're willing to lie about anything. Maybe you're the one who bumped off Carlota!"

"I barely knew the woman. Why would I have killed her?"

"Maybe someone paid you to do it. The monthly maintenance fees here aren't cheap!"

"Now that's just silly. Me, a contract killer? With my rheumatoid arthritis?" I hold up my heavily veined hands as proof.

"Yeah, okay. I'm moving a bit slower myself these days. Who's turn is it anyway?"

"It's yours."

Gina throws. Her ball is practically kissing the pallino when it lands. There's only one ball left, and I get to throw it. My ball lands wide. She wins.

Gina hoots and hollers. "That ended up being a close one. But experience prevailed in the end."

"It sure did," I say, wondering if she'll see right through me. "So where are you from in New York?"

"Born and raised in the Bronx. But eventually, Leon and me moved to the Upper East. We still spend our summers up there. Or try to."

"I went to the Guggenheim once. It was nice. I have the Monet package, by the way. What about you?"

"Kandinsky. Abstract suits me. But back to business. You say you didn't know Carlota and didn't kill her. I guess I'm going to have to take you at your word. I had no reason to kill her either. She made a lot of money for Leon and me. And I had no beef with her personally."

I extend my hand out to her. "I will choose to take your word on that as well."

She grabs my hand and gives it a firm shake. "Great, so we're solid, and we can get on with looking at real suspects?"

"Not quite so fast. What about Leon?"

"What about him?"

"He's your husband. You'd be loyal to him, even if he killed someone, right?"

"That depends on who he'd be killing."

"Gina, be serious!"

"I am. But Leon is no killer. He couldn't have done it anyway."

"Why's that?"

"He just had both his knees replaced. He can barely get himself off the toilet."

"That does sound like a pretty solid alibi."

"The next time I give him his pain meds, I'll make sure to let him know how lucky he is to have had the surgery."

"Please also tell him that I hope he feels better soon," I say. "It must be awful to be cooped up all day and in pain."

Gina's eyebrows lower. "You didn't lose on purpose. You know, at bocce. Did you?"

"Yes. Yes, I did."

She shakes her head in dismay. "I thought as much. I'm going to have to watch out for you, Mandy."

"It's Madeline, actually."

"Same difference. Alright, so now we've ruled ourselves out as suspects. What next?"

"Now, we need to find out who would have had a reason to want Carlota dead. What do you know about Selena?"

"The name doesn't ring any bells."

"Larger Hispanic woman. Usually wears black."

"Oh, her! I thought her name was Selma. I've seen her around enough alright. Hard to miss her. Between her size and those loud outfits she used to wear."

"What do you mean loud?" I ask.

"The most God-awful prints you ever saw in your life. All those fluorescent colors. Ask me, there ain't no reason to have neon anywhere on your body. Unless you're a hunter."

"Or a crossing guard, maybe."

"Fine. Them too. But that's it."

"Agreed. But Carlota told me Selena only wears black. Always black."

"That's only been for the past year or so. Started around last Thanksgiving, I want to say. No one knows why. And no one bothered to ask. She doesn't talk much, that one."

So, it hadn't been just me. "I saw her this morning, and she was wearing a brightly colored caftan. Do you think that means something?"

"Who do I look like? The color police? Maybe she just hasn't been to the dry cleaner in a while and all her dark clothes are dirty."

"I suppose." I'll have to shelve that line of inquiry until we know more.

"Is that all you got?" She asks. "Someone changing the color of their clothes?"

"Hardly," I assure her. "Come on. We're going for a ride in my golf cart."

"But we've only just played the first round of bocce!"

"Let's put the game on ice for the moment. Speaking of, I know exactly who we're going to question first."

CHAPTER SEVEN

"I'm so sorry, but can you explain that to me again?" I plead. "How can I get the free recipes? You say I can do it all on my phone?"

"Black Cap" Stan Polotski doesn't even try to hide his frustration. Turns out, the reason he's called "Black Cap" Stan is because he really does wear a black knit cap on his head.

"Like I've been saying, yeah. But you gotta download the Egret's Loft Fridge Friend app first," he says, very slowly.

"I think I just did that. But it's not showing up. Where did it go? Did I do it wrong?"

"It's probably on another page," Gina chimes in. "Did you try looking on the other pages?"

"Other pages? You mean on the Google?"

"No, not on Google. On your phone."

"But my phone uses the Google. Is the app not on the Google?"

Stan holds his hand out in my direction. "For fudge's sake, let me do it."

I happily surrender my phone.

Imagine that! Stan told me my fridge can be programmed to give me recipes based on what I have in my refrigerator. Apparently, there's a little camera that sees everything I have and can prepare meal plans based on that. I can't wait to tell Ritchie.

Once I understand how it all works, of course.

I notice Gina giving me the side-eye. She probably wants to get on with why we came here in the first place. Of course, she does. Her fridge is probably already programmed for meal planning.

"It was such a shock about Carlota being killed," I say, winking at Gina. "Did you know her very well?"

"More than most, less than some," he says without looking up from my device. "Any dietary restrictions?"

"Well, my cardiologist said I need to cut down on my salt intake. And, truth be told, I've never been partial to asparagus."

"No problemo," Stan assures me. "If it's not in your fridge, it's not on the menu."

"I read somewhere that there are people who are genetically predisposed to hate vegetables," Gina adds. "Isn't that interesting? I think I might be one of them."

"Oh, I like most vegetables," I tell her. "But not the bitter ones. I don't like bitter things."

"What time do you usually have dinner?" Stan wants to know.

"Does it matter?"

"Not to me. But I can program the fridge to alert you when to start cooking, based on when you generally eat," he explains. "I can also synch it so that your oven preheats, cooks, and shuts itself off based on the meal you're making."

"Will wonders never cease! Seven. I generally like to eat around seven."

"So late?" Gina wonders. "Doesn't that give you reflux?"

"No. Not if I stay up to watch the ten o'clock news."

It's dark in Stan's house. All the blinds are closed, and the overheads are dimmed. There is a beacon of light in the study coming from all the monitors he has arranged around the room.

It's hard to tell, but I think he probably got the M.C. Escher package.

"Almost there," Stan says.

"So, you wrote the program that does all of this stuff with the refrigerator?" I ask.

"Yeah," he says. "A little coding side project. There were a million inputs; that part was pretty sick. But the algorithm itself was smooth sailing."

I just nod. I have absolutely no idea what he's talking about. "Did you make the refrigerator too? How did you get the little TVs in there?"

He looks at me like he's trying to find the scars from my lobotomy. "Seriously?" He asks. "No, I didn't make the fridge." He hands me back my phone. "I also linked it to your Egret's Loft activity schedule. You'll get little reminders to eat some munchies before you go out golfing or sailing or whatever you do for kicks."

"These are in all the houses now, yeah?" Gina asks. "When we moved in, it was just a perk for board members, like Leon."

"Oh, yes, every house is hooked up with my software now."

"Amazing! How did that happen?" I ask.

"The board wanted the tech, so they bought the software and contracted me to maintain it." He shrugs. "It's a nice little earner. And it gives me a little break from spending too much time online with my Fortnite homies, you dig?"

The way he's talking, you'd think he was in his late teens, maybe early twenties. But the hair growing out of his ears is long enough that he should probably think about combing it.

He does have nice eyes though. It's never nice to only point out a person's flaws.

"Have you had many problems with the software?" I ask.

His nice eyes narrow. "What's that supposed to mean?"

"It's just that I had some trouble when I first used the fridge. Operator error, I'm sure," I quickly add. "But Carlota indicated that I wasn't the only one. Have you had many complaints?"

"What did she say? What were her exact words?"

"I don't remember her exact words." I suddenly feel very warm. "But she said something about needing to put a stop to your project."

Stan's face pinkens, and he slams his fist into the wall. Well, more of a tap, really. But the intention was there. You have to be careful with bones that have a lot of life experience.

"What?" He fumes. "Everybody loves Fridge Friend! Ask around! I can't believe she was slagging it behind my back!"

"No, no. She wasn't, what did you call it, slagging?" I assure him, though I'll need to look up the word in the dictionary later. "She just said she knew Victor wanted to help you, but the fridge was a menace, and it could have killed me."

Gina looks at me like I've suddenly lost my mind.

"A menace?" Stan demands. "A menace? Fudge that! See now, Victor, he gets it. He's my bro. Carlota, though, she's always causing problems."

"What kind of problems?" I ask.

"Oh! Get this. I was late once on my maintenance fees. Only by a few days. A few days! She petitioned the board to kick me out of Egret's Loft! Drama queen! Only happy if she is causing trouble, that one."

"*Was*, you mean," Gina corrects.

"Was what?"

"Past tense of is. She's dead now, after all," Gina says. "Speaking of, where were you when she was killed?"

He's breathing heavily. I want to ask if he needs some medication, but that might be impolite.

"Thank you so much for helping me set up my refrigerator. We should probably be on our way," I say, taking Gina's arm and marching her toward the door.

Stan doesn't offer to see us out.

As soon as we're on the other side of the door, Gina rounds on me. "Now why on Earth would you do that? I was just about to prove he had no alibi!"

"Shhh, not here," I whisper, practically dragging her back to the golf cart. She resists like a stubborn old dog.

Once we're driving away, I ask Gina, "Have the police told you the time of death yet?"

She doesn't speak, but some of her anger seems to melt away.

"They haven't told me either, which you know, since you illegally eavesdropped on my conversation with the detective.

So, when Stan asked you what time she was killed, what exactly were you planning to tell him?"

"Well, it had to happen sometime between Monday night and Tuesday morning. It's not like we have *no* idea when it happened!"

"And what were you doing during that time frame?"

"Leon and me were sleeping. We don't party like we used to."

"That's what he would have said too! It's what anyone our age would say! And we need to know more about Stan. He said he was late paying his condo fees one month. Do you know why?"

"No, but I can ask Leon."

"I just think we should find out more before we start making accusations." That, and I don't want him to get mad and turn my refrigerator against me.

Gina stares at me with something like appreciation. "You know what, hun? I think I might have underestimated you. What's next?"

As she asks the question, we pass by my house on the way to drop her at hers. There's an SUV parked in my driveway.

"You're close with the security guards, yes?" I ask.

"Yeah, sure. Why?"

"We need to know who was on the property when Carlota died. Any visitors or workers. That kind of thing. Do you think you can get a list of all the people who were here from your guard friend?"

"I'll get on it right away. What are you going to do?"

I clear my throat. "I have a little personal business to attend to."

I recognized the car parked in my driveway. My house is probably already being torn apart.

The blue-eyed assassins have arrived.

CHAPTER EIGHT

"I know they're here. Where did you hide them?" Her ocean blue eyes stare into mine. I flinch first.

The house is in shambles. Sofa cushions litter the floor, cabinets stand open, and the refrigerator's digital British voice keeps repeating, "Please, shut the door."

"There's nothing here," I try to convince her. "I don't have what you're looking for."

Despite the air-conditioning, sweat begins to form at my hairline, and I wonder if I'll get out of this alive.

"Don't worry, Mom. I've got some right here," Eliza says, pushing the fridge door closed with her hip.

She hands me a carton of Reese's Peanut Butter Cups, and I'm finally able to breathe again. I open the box and hand one of the packets to Tory.

"Here you go, angel. Try not to get the chocolate everywhere."

"Thank you, Grandma!" Tory's perfect little teeth are all now happily on display.

"Me too! Me too!" Emmy calls out. She always wants what her big sister has.

Eliza glares at her younger daughter. "What do you say, Emmy?"

"*Plllease.*"

"Alright! You, too, sweetheart," I say. "But only if Grandma gets a hug and a kiss first."

Both girls gleefully wrap their arms around my legs and then run off to sit at the table to savor their treats.

I love my granddaughters. They are lovely and sweet and always smiling. Still, I can't shake the feeling they would slit my throat in my sleep if I held out on their Reese's.

"I told you that you didn't have to come today," I say to Eliza now that we're alone in the kitchen. "I don't have anything ready for you. Are you hungry? Would you like something to eat?"

"What do you have?"

"Let's see!" I pull up the Fridge Friend app, and she selects a recipe based on the ingredients I have. An easy tuna casserole that she thinks the girls will eat too. I quickly assemble the ingredients and stick the casserole dish in the already preheated oven.

Whatever magic Stan performed on my phone seems to have worked.

"So, dear. You haven't told me why you're here now, even though we agreed you'd come on Saturday. But I think I can probably guess why."

"Can't I just be spontaneous and change my mind?" Eliza asks.

"You could. But that's not why you're here, is it?"

She sighs. "Alright, look. I just wanted to pop by to check on you. Carlota's death has now officially been ruled a homicide."

"Yes, dear. I already know that. The police have been over to speak to me."

"Detective Fletcher?" She asks. I nod, knowing better than to ask how she knows his name. "Did he ask you where you were between 10 p.m. and midnight?"

"Is that when it happened?"

"Yes."

"No. Detective Fletcher didn't ask me where I was. He just wanted to know if she seemed normal."

"Why would he ask you that? You didn't even know the woman!"

"That's what I told him, dear. But I did find out how she was killed. A golf club to the back of the head! Can you imagine it?"

"I don't have to. I've seen the photos. And before you ask, Mom, the answer is no. I can't show them to you."

"That hardly seems fair. Your father and I never held out on showing you and your brother the crime scene photos. But you can at least be honest with me about why you're here, can't you?"

"Ritchie and I were just worried, that's all."

She's withholding information. I'm her mother. I know these things. But you don't get to my age without having at least one ace up your sleeve. Guilt.

"I'll be fine. It wasn't my choice to be here, granted. You and Ritchie decided this would be the best place for me after your father died. You couldn't have possibly known that, right after I moved in, a woman would be killed next door. How could you? But don't worry about me, I'll make the best of it."

Eliza rolls her big blue eyes. "Ugh. Alright Mom, but you can't say anything to anyone. Promise?"

Something suddenly occurs to me. "Yes, I promise. But we should probably take this out onto the patio." I lean in and whisper, "The walls have ears."

"I'm sorry, the walls have what?" She asks, mildly incredulous.

I point to my ears and then put a finger in front of my pursed lips. She just stares.

"Girls," I call to Tory and Emmy. "Would you like to go swimming?"

Squeals of delight echo from the other room. In the time it takes me and Eliza to walk out to the living room, the girls have already stripped off their clothes and are standing in swimsuits.

"I should have known you'd come prepared," I say to Eliza.

She shrugs her shoulders. "We live in Miami. The girls always have their bathing suits on under their clothes. Saves us a lot of money on underwear, actually."

Eliza pulls some water wings out of her bag, and the girls race out onto my back patio. Under the screened-in canopy, there's a small swimming pool. The shallow end is only two feet deep. "Great for grandkids and active elders," the brochure had advertised.

Beyond the back patio, ducks squawk from the man-made lake.

As the girls splash around, I search the ceiling for the hidden camera. I think I spot it, angled toward the house. If we avoid sitting at the patio table, we might be out of range.

"Mom, are you alright?" Eliza asks, looking concerned.

"Yes, dear."

"What were you looking for?"

"Oh, nothing. Just the hidden camera."

"Hidden camera?"

"You can never be too careful, dear. You, of all people, should know that."

She pulls out one of the patio chairs, preparing to sit at the table.

"No!" I cry, my voice a little sharper than I intended. "Let's sit over here. Away from the house a little."

"Are you sure you're okay, Mom? You're acting weird. Did you forget your medicine? Or maybe take too much?"

"I'm fine. You and Ritchie just need to get better at reading the fine print."

"What fine print?"

"Nothing, dear. Now, we can speak freely. What was it you were going to tell me that I'm not allowed to repeat to anyone?"

Eliza examines my face for several long seconds and then sighs. "Remember how I told you that Carlota's son, Juan Carlo, was in the running to become Colombia's next president?"

"Of course, I do, dear. My joints aren't what they used to be, but there's nothing wrong with my memory."

"Right. Well, he used to be the country's attorney general. Really made a name for himself taking on the Mexican cartels that were teaming up with FARC to sell Colombian cocaine. He put away some very powerful people. People you wouldn't want to mess around with, if you know what I mean."

"What does that have to do with Carlota being killed?"

"Maybe nothing. The thing is, we don't know. Not yet."

"But surely anybody could find that out by looking on the Google."

"It's just Google, Mom. Not 'the' Google. And yes, they could."

"So why did I have to promise not to tell anyone?"

"I'm getting to that part," she says. "Juan Carlo was almost assassinated a few weeks ago. We were able to keep it under wraps, but he has a massive target on his back. With his stance against the FARC, it's in our interest to keep him alive."

I shake my head. "Your father and I never did like the way you were messing around with the politics of foreign countries."

"Yeah, Mom. You're right. I'm the one calling all the shots." She rolls her eyes, a nasty habit she's had since she was in diapers.

"No," I say. "But you're helping whoever is, right?"

"Not the point. We think, when someone couldn't get to Juan Carlo, they may have gone for his mother instead. Understand?"

"No."

"No?"

"You expect me to believe that a hitman for a drug cartel couldn't find a better weapon than a golf club? I'm sorry. I don't buy it."

"Oh, I assume you have a better theory?"

"In fact, I might."

"Such as?"

"I don't want to say too much until I have more information," I tell her. "But something's not right with Fridge Friend or the colored caftan."

"Are we still talking about the murder, or is this some new musical, like *Joseph and the Amazing Technicolor Dreamcoat*?"

"No, no! Carlota wanted to put a stop to Stan's Fridge Friend, and Selena always wore black, but today she had on a colored caftan. Get it?"

"Should I?"

"I don't know. You're right. Maybe it's nothing. But Gina and I will figure it out, one way or the other."

"Who's Gina?"

"My sidekick. She probably wouldn't like me calling her that, though. Don't tell her, will you? Nobody ever wants to be the sidekick. And for good reason. Everyone knows Adam West, but how many people have heard of Burt Ward?"

"You mean the guy who played Robin?" Eliza asks.

"You don't count. You know everything. Anyway, Gina and I are investigating. We already interviewed our first suspect this morning!"

"Mom, you can't do that! You have to let the cops handle this!"

"But your father said I was invaluable in solving some of his cases. I think I might be able to help."

"This isn't Dad's case. He's not around anymore!"

Tory and Emmy squeal with delight. Their mother and I sit in silence. It feels like a vise has tightened around my heart.

"I'm sorry." Eliza rests her hand over mine. "I didn't mean that the way it sounded. It's just, you could get in real trouble for getting involved. Not to mention, it could be dangerous."

"I'm sure you're right, dear. I'll try to stay out of it."

"You should just be enjoying this place. There's golf and bocce ball and Aqua Zumba. Why don't you relax and try to have some fun?"

"Are you trying to tell me there's more to life than murder?"

"Should I have to?"

"I suppose not."

"Exactly! Which reminds me, don't you have a golf lesson starting soon? I checked your schedule when I first came in.

Ritchie said he'd booked up your calendar for the first week, so you'd have plenty of things to do."

"I have a golf lesson? Now?" In all the morning's excitement, I'd completely forgotten that I had activities planned for the afternoon. "I guess I'd better change into something more suitable. Do you need anything while I'm gone?"

"We'll just have some of the casserole. Speaking of, do you smell something burning?"

We both stand up in time for the smoke alarm to start sounding inside.

CHAPTER NINE

"I'm so sorry," I apologize for arriving late to my first golf lesson. "I had a little crisis with a casserole."

"Not a problem." Dom Skellig smiles, the ends of his mustache tilting skyward. His Hawaiian shirt is jauntily unbuttoned revealing a carpet of chest hair. "You don't mind having a bit of company, do you?"

"Company?"

Standing about a hundred feet away, under a roof providing shade from the early evening sun, I see Helen tilting forward at the hips, club in hand, practicing her swing on the driving range.

"Helen's been working on her approach and asked if she could have a little coaching."

"No, I don't mind."

But suddenly, I feel horribly underdressed in the navy Adidas golf dress and white sneakers Ritchie had picked out for me.

Helen stands next to her Louis Vuitton golf bag, dressed in a gold lamé-collared tank top, white skort, and giraffe-printed golf shoes with gold trim. Even her clubs have gold in them.

"Your son told me this was your first time playing," Dom says, "so I took the liberty of bringing a set of clubs for you to try out. Come on, let's get you all set up!"

"Alright." I try to sound excited.

I follow behind Dom, his micro shorts leaving little to the imagination.

"Normally, we would have a chat beforehand." He talks as we walk. "Just to establish your goals and what you want to accomplish with your lessons. But let's just get right to hitting some balls today. Sound good?"

"Sure. I don't really have any goals, anyway. I just thought it might be fun."

"That's a great attitude, Madeline. When I started learning, I never would have believed I'd be playing next to Tiger Woods on a PGA course. It's all about having fun."

Dom walks over to a medium-sized Titleist bag sitting in the grass and begins rifling through the golf clubs sticking out of the top. I glance down the range at Helen, expecting her to look over and give some acknowledgment of my presence. She does not.

"Here we are!" Tom pulls one of the clubs high into the air, out of the bag. "Let's start you off with this. It's called a driver. It's easy to recognize because it has the biggest head and longest handle of all the clubs. It also hits the farthest. Why don't you swing it around a little, get a feel for the weight and balance of it!"

Helen is only a few feet away now. I do my best to mimic her stance, then start swinging the club back and forth.

"Great job," Dom tells me. "Loosen up those shoulders and just let it swing. I'll be right back with you."

Dom walks up behind Helen and puts his arms around her until they're both holding the handle of her club. He wiggles his impossibly short shorts against Helen's backside.

"What the…?" Helen says, moving quickly away. "I mean…oh my, sugar! Normally, a man will at least buy me dinner first."

Dom backs away, his hands in the air. "No, no. I was just trying to help you with your stance. But I'd be more than happy to take you to dinner, if you'd be into that."

I try not to listen but can't help myself. If they wanted privacy, they should have stood further away.

"Well, bless your heart. That's so kind. But I don't think that's such a good idea. You're my teacher. We need to try to keep this professional…for now," she drawls, tracing the outline of his jaw with her forefinger. "Alright, sugar?"

Dom looks crestfallen, but quickly shakes it off. "Anything you say. But you can get more speed off the ball if you spread your legs just a little bit wider."

"If I spread my legs any wider, sugar, I'll be doing the splits."

They both laugh. I'm about to throw up.

Since no one is paying any attention to me, I decide to try hitting a ball instead of just shaving the grass with my club.

"Fore!" I call out.

I think Kevin Costner did the same in an old golf movie where he was trying to win over Rene Russo. I'd asked Clint what it meant, and he didn't know either. So, we looked up why golfers do it. Turns out, nobody knows "fore" sure.

Clint got a kick out of that joke.

"That was a nice first drive there, Madeline," Dom says. "Be careful not to chip it on the side of the club, though. You want to hit it in the center of the head, so it flies straight."

I take another swing and watch the ball soar through the air before landing in the lake with a soft plop.

"Better! Now you want to tilt forward just a little bit more, move your feet apart, and use your hips to power your swing. Watch me, I'll show you."

I'm grateful he doesn't try to straddle me, like he did Helen. But he definitely needs to learn how to keep it in his pants. When he moves his hips, I can see a part of his babymakers pushing out of his shorts.

"See how it's done?"

I nod, even though I honestly didn't notice much about his swing.

"Do you want me to show you again?"

"*No*! That won't be necessary. I think I got the gist of it."

Something behind me catches Dom's attention. "If you ladies will excuse me, I'll be right back. Keep practicing."

After he's been gone a few minutes, I turn to see where he went. I find him in a seemingly pleasant conversation with a very tall woman. She has short, dark gray hair and round glasses. She looks to be my age or, dare I say, a little older.

"Well, that didn't take long, now, did it?" Helen says, as she tees up another ball.

"I'm sorry? What didn't take long?"

"Astrid," Helen replies after she takes her swing. "Ain't seen her around in a month of Sundays."

I think that means a long time. "Does she live in Egret's Loft too?"

"Goodness me, no. She's not even supposed to be here now. Though I guess all that changed. When Carlota died."

"She and Carlota didn't get along?" I ask, telling myself I'm just making conversation. I did promise Eliza I would try to leave things alone, after all.

She laughs. "Does a stray cat take to a hunting hound? Naw, those two couldn't be in the same room without going for each other's throats."

"Any idea why they disliked each other so much?"

"One doesn't like to gossip, sugar. All I know for sure is, they used to be best friends. Were planning to open this place together. Next thing, Astrid has her own development."

"Her own development?"

"Shady Palms. Just outside Calusa. A vertical living community for seniors," she says, wiggling her behind as she prepares to swing. "Carlota was madder than a wet hen when it opened."

"So, they were competitive with each other?"

She laughs again. A dainty kind of sound. "Aren't all women, sugar?"

Dom is still talking to Astrid, so I just keep teeing up balls and taking swings. I hit five balls in quick succession and feel like I might be getting better already.

"I heard you had the police detective knocking at your door today," Helen eventually says.

"Detective Fletcher? Yes, he came by to ask some questions. I just moved here, so I didn't know anything. But he was just doing his job."

"Victor was there with you?" She sounds casual, but her body looks tense.

"Yes, he offered to be there during the interview. Said he used to be an attorney."

"And you took him to breakfast afterward?" She asks, preparing to swing.

"Actually, he invited me."

Her ball goes far left.

"Did he now? Well, isn't he just the consummate gentleman? He asked me to be his partner in the scramble this season. He and I will be seeing a lot of each other. Between you and me, I think he has a bit of a soft spot for me."

"What's a scramble?"

She looks askance at me, probably wondering why that was the part of her soliloquy that interested me most. "Kind of a league championship, but you get assigned to play with other couples randomly."

"So, it's a couples' thing?"

"Yes." She flashes me her most dazzling smile. The tight skin around her eyes doesn't budge. "That's not to say you couldn't play with friends. But no one really does."

"Is that so?"

"Of course, with your face and figure, I'm sure you'd have no trouble finding an *available* partner. There are plenty of single men here that wouldn't be too picky."

"How lucky for me," I say, turning in time to see Astrid getting into a silver Mercedes roadster.

Dom rejoins us. "How is everything coming along, ladies? Who wants to show me what they've got?"

Helen looks at me, deferring.

"Right. I guess it's me then. I've never played before, so please go easy on me."

Dom grins. He seems happier than before. "Just give it your best shot. Everyone has to start somewhere."

I assume the stance, pull the club over my right shoulder, and swing with all my strength. Too late, I realize I undercut the tee and hit the ball with the top of the club. The ball shoots upward, slams against the roof, and ricochets down, straight at Helen.

She collapses on the ground grabbing the left side of her chest.

"Aieeeee!!!" She shrieks. "My breast! She broke my breast!"

"Oh, my goodness. I'm so sorry," I say. "Are you alright?"

"Are you crazy? No, I'm not alright!" Helen screams.

"Ice, we're going to need some ice." Dom is trying to act cool, but he's practically shaking with excitement. "But first, why don't you take your top off so we can see the extent of the damage?"

"Have you gone soft in the head, Dom? Get me a doctor. I need a doctor."

"I can call the doctor," I offer, wanting to help.

"You silly cow! Haven't you done enough already?" She screeches. If she weren't flat out on the AstroTurf, I might be nervous.

"I really *am* sorry! It was an accident. I don't know how it happened!" I say, genuinely remorseful but also shamefully amused.

"You did that on purpose, you…you stupid hillbilly! I *will* get you back for this!"

Dom grabs my arm and pulls me away. "Try not to feel too bad. This does happen from time to time. You get on home. I'll look after Helen."

I wonder if he's sending me off for my own sake or because he wants to take another stab at sneaking a peek at Helen's gravity-defying chest.

Either way, leaving would probably be for the best.

"Again, I am so sorry."

Helen doesn't move, but her histrionics chase me all the way back to my golf cart. I drive away, wanting nothing more than to get home and take a nap. It's been the longest day I can remember having in a while.

Eliza's car is gone, but there's a woman in a pink tracksuit standing in my driveway, holding a large basket with a bow on top.

Murder, it would seem, is not an excuse for missing a chance to welcome the new neighbor.

CHAPTER TEN

"Hiya, neighbor! It's such a pleasure to meet you!"

The petite woman, dressed in head-to-toe pink, corners me before I can even disembark from my golf cart. Even her dyed blond hair has a pinkish tint.

"I'm Jinny Myrtle. George is my husband. George Myrtle. He's at home with the sciatica at the moment, or he would have come to say hello himself. It's had him out flat for the past few weeks, even though I keep telling him the only thing for it is exercise. Men never listen, though, do they? But he should be right as rain soon. We both wanted to come over and give you a little something to welcome you to Egret's Loft. Since he couldn't come, you're stuck with just me. Anyway, here you go!"

She hands me a basket full of diabetic sweets, low-sodium crackers, and fat-free cheese.

"This is so thoughtful, Jinny. Thank you. It's nice to meet you as well. I'm Madeline."

"That's such a pretty name. A pretty name for a pretty lady, eh? You must tell me what moisturizer you use, because you don't look like you belong here! I simply won't believe you're a day over fifty-nine! No, I won't. I tried to come by earlier," she continues, "but you seem to have been out for most of the day. Only just moved in and already your dance card is full, eh? That's the way you've got to do it. Stay busy. I tell George the same all the time. Use it or lose it, I always say."

My arms, weary from an active day of bocce ball and golf, feel suddenly heavy under the weight of my welcome basket. "Would you like to come inside for some coffee or tea?" I offer, balancing the basket on my hip, while typing in the code to get in the front door.

Ritchie's birthday. He set it up himself.

There are no keys in Egret's Loft.

"Coffee would be absolutely lovely. I always take mine as a double-double. Do you know what that means? A little expression from home. I thought it was a normal thing until we started coming here and everyone thought it was the darndest thing. A double-double. It means double cream, double sugar, of course. But not that many people know that here, eh?"

"I certainly didn't. But it makes sense. And where is home?"

Stepping inside, I see the house has been immaculately put back together after the girls tore it asunder earlier. The burning smell is gone, replaced by the scent of fresh laundry. And there's a bouquet of fresh flowers on the dining room table.

"Oh, George and I were born and raised just outside The Peg. Oh, there I go again. If you're not from Canada, you probably have no earthly idea what I'm talking aboot. It's short for Winnipeg. Have you ever been to visit? If not, you really must. It's a beauty in the summer. Winter is nice, but too cold for my taste these days. It does a number on George too. He gets SAD, you see. Not sad, sad. When he first told me I thought he had depression or something. But no, it's a real thing. Seasonal Affective Disorder. See, SAD. Even though he's not. Sad, I mean. It just makes him anxious aboot leaving the house."

In the time Jinny has been talking, I've put water in the coffee maker, pulled the milk out of the fridge, located the sugar in the pantry, and read a note Eliza left for me saying she had to get back to Miami, but she would call me later to check in.

"And how long have you been living in Egret's Loft?" I ask, searching for the coffee filters.

"Oh, we don't actually live here. Not year round, anyway. We're snowbirds. Get it? We spread our wings and flock south for the sun. Clever, eh? But to your question, we've been coming here for the past five years. It's nice to get away, but by the end of winter, George and I are always longing for home. Not that it doesn't feel like home here. It does and it doesn't, since we're not from here. But the people are nice."

My recently departed neighbor might disagree. Odds are, one of those "nice people" may have killed her.

"I'm so sorry about what happened to Carlota," I say. "Did you know her well?"

A look of horror smooths out the laugh lines on her face.

I hand her a steaming mug.

"It's just the most tragic thing, eh? I mean, at our age, you never know how much longer you have, but you just expect it to run its natural course, don't you? You never think aboot being murdered. Of course, I didn't want to bring it up first thing, with you just moving in and all. But it's been all anyone can talk aboot. Did you hear how she died? Hit in the head with her own golf club. Though you never know how much of what people say you can trust. Still, the thought of it! Don't think I haven't thought aboot starting to wear a helmet, but George said that would be overreacting. He's right, of course. It's probably just a one-off, right? I mean, it's not like someone is going to go around killing people with sporting equipment for fun, eh?"

Jinny takes her first sip of coffee. I hope it hasn't gone cold.

"I certainly hope not! Though I guess that depends on who killed her. And why."

"You're right aboot that. Yes, you most certainly are. Until the police know who killed her, I'll be sleeping with one eye peeled, I will. You, too, probably, eh? Just moving in and having your neighbor beaten to death! Why it doesn't bear thinking aboot. Except to think that you hope it wasn't a random thing. Then any of us could be at risk. Which is a horrible thing to say, for Carlota, I mean. Since she's the one who was murdered. But you have to hope someone had a reason to want her dead, don't you?"

My lip has been resting on the rim of my cup, but I've been afraid to take a sip, worried I might spit some of it out. Jinny certainty speaks her mind, almost callously, if truth be told. But it's also strangely refreshing. You know what's on her mind because she seems to say everything that goes through her head.

Which does make me wonder…

"Do you know anyone here that would have wanted her dead?" I ask.

"No, I'm sure I don't. Well, I guess it's possible, maybe. It's hard to tell. People say so many things they don't mean these days, don't you know? I mean, just the other day, I was playing croquet with Gina, and she was upset because she was losing. And you know what she did? She told me to shut my trap. I need to learn when to stop talking, she said. Now, Gina and I go way back, and New Yorkers aren't known for being polite, don't you know. She never did apologize, come to think of it, but I know she didn't mean it. She was just upset about losing. So you see, people sometimes say things they don't mean when they're feeling a bit out of sorts."

"Uh huh," is all I can think to say.

"For example, just last week I was out at the River Club— that's the one out by the river, not the main clubhouse where you go for golf. This one has a pool. It's very fancy, and they have concerts there in the evenings sometimes. I was out enjoying the pool after Aqua Zumba and what didn't I overhear but a fight between Carlota and Helen. Now, a lot of women don't take to Helen so much, but she's never tried to make a move on my George, so I have no issues with her, no I don't."

I know I promised Eliza I wouldn't try to investigate the case, but what harm can come from indulging my curiosity just a little?

"You mentioned the two had a fight? What was that about?"

"Oh right, yes, the fight. Now, I couldn't hear what Carlota was saying, but she looked very serious. Like she meant business and wasn't going to take any malarkey. She'd been a good friend of Donald, you see, so she was pretty broken up about that. And she'd never really been friendly with Helen before, don't you know. I even heard the term gold digger bandied about, but you didn't hear that from me. Carota would have never said anything negative about anyone to me, of course. If you have a problem with someone, she would say, go straight to the source. Talk *to* people, not *about* them. That was Carlota alright."

Dare I ask? "Who is Donald?"

"Oh, dear me, of course. You wouldn't have met Donald. He was Helen's husband. Died last year. Kidney failure, I want to say. Very sad. Helen took to wearing big sunglasses all the time. Didn't want people to see her eyes all red and bloodshot from crying, more than likely. She even had them on when I'd pop round with casseroles. People who are grieving never have the energy for cooking, don't you know. So, I would just take some food over now and again. She even bagged up all poor Donald's things and asked George to get rid of them. Couldn't bear to look at them, she said."

"And Helen? Could you hear what she was saying?"

Jinny raises an eyebrow. "What Helen was saying when?"

"During the fight with Carlota."

"Oh, silly me. Of course. I'd gone off on one, eh? Now, I couldn't hear much. They were on the other side of the pool, you see. But I did hear Helen say something like 'You wouldn't dare.' Which, by looking at Carlota's face, you could see that, yes, she very well would dare. But then Helen said, 'If you try to stop me or do anything to meddle in my business, I'll kill you.' That might not be exactly what she said, but close enough, I would think. And that's what I was talking aboot earlier. Helen would never kill Carlota. Obviously, right? But they were fighting, and she said something she really didn't mean. Happens to the best of us. Why, just the other day—"

"I'm sorry to interrupt, Jinny. But I'm curious, what did Carlota say? After Helen threatened her?"

"Oh, I wouldn't call it a threat. I don't want to start any rumors, don't you know. And Carlota didn't take it very seriously either. She just laughed, and they both walked away.

Nothing to it really. Just two lady moose locking antlers. These things tend to blow themselves out, eh? I mean, there are times I get so frustrated with George I want to deliberately forget to iron his underwear. But then, cooler heads prevail, and you know you've been getting yourself all bothered for nothing."

My phone begins to ring. The refrigerator announces that it's Eliza calling, though she pronounces it more like Alyssa. The voice is programmed to sound British, yet it doesn't recognize the name of the female lead in *My Fair Lady*?

"I don't mean to be rude," I say, "But I need to take this. It's my daughter calling."

"Oh! Isn't that just the thing? Your daughter is calling you! George and me have six children and fifteen grandchildren. Can you believe it? Twelve girls and nine boys, between them. They prefer to text though. They're busy people, can't make time for the phone, don't you know. Now, they'd be right here if there was an emergency. But calling out of the blue? Why, it'd be a cold day in H-E double hockey sticks before that would ever happen with our lot."

She laughs.

The phone has stopped ringing. I missed the call.

"I think she's just worried about what happened. I should ring her back, so she doesn't worry. You know kids." I smile, despite my growing fatigue. "Thank you so much for the welcome basket, Jinny. It was very kind."

"You're welcome from me and George. I know he'll be dying to meet you. But don't let him talk your ear off. He tends to go on and on if you let him, don't you know. You'll be lucky to get a word in edgewise, you will! Maybe you can come around for dinner when George is feeling a bit better. I've got a poutine recipe…it's been in the family for generations…that will knock your socks off! What do you say, eh?"

I've been leading Jinny toward the front door as she's been talking. I'm holding it open now, my hand on her elbow, gently guiding her through.

"That would be lovely. Again, thank you, and George, so much. I'll be seeing you again soon. Bye now."

When the door is finally closed, I lean against it and take a deep breath.

The busy day has taken its toll on me. I think I can feel my ankles beginning to swell.

I text Eliza to ask if I can call her back tomorrow, then consider reheating what's left of the slightly charred tuna casserole I made earlier. Deciding it's too much of a bother, I collapse on the sofa with Jinny's fat-free cheese and low-sodium crackers.

As I drift off to sleep, I see Helen's angry face promising that she'll get me back.

CHAPTER ELEVEN

I'm sound asleep on the sofa when I hear it.

A metallic creaking coming from the screen door on the back patio.

My eyes fly open, but it makes no difference. The only light in the room, a nightlight preprogrammed into the fridge, barely puts a dent in the darkness.

It must still be nighttime. No one has any business being here at this hour. Instinct makes me reach for Clint. He had a talent for flattening any bumps in the night. But, of course, he's not here.

Did Carlota hear her assailant before she had her head smashed in? I wonder. Was she asleep when she was killed?

Another sound from outside, like rubber-soled shoes shuffling on tile.

Reaching out my hand, I search for my phone. Did Ritchie put in the number for the security guards? What name would we have saved it under?

Then I realize it doesn't matter. The phone is still in my purse on the kitchen counter, where I left it last night. Half a room away. If there is someone on my patio, they might see me crossing the room.

Tap, tap.

It's coming from the sliding glass door. There's definitely someone there. And they're trying to break into my house!

I try to think, knowing that time is running out. If I don't grasp the element of surprise, I might be the next resident of Egret's Loft with a golf club in my skull.

Clint, darling, what would you have done?

The handle on the sliding glass door begins to rattle and I act without thinking.

In one motion, or probably several, because my reflexes aren't what they once were, I grab a vase off the coffee table and rise to my feet, trying my hardest to snarl.

"Agh!" I hear on the other side of the glass, then shuffling feet, then a splash. I caught the intruder in the swimming pool.

"I've got you, now," I say, throwing on the porch lights to face my attacker.

Gina's head surfaces above the water line.

"What the heck, Mandy?" She sputters.

I'm so distraught, I don't even correct her. "Gina! I'm so sorry," I say after unlocking and opening the sliding glass door. "I thought you were trying to break in! What are you doing here in the middle of the night?"

"Middle of the night?" She chafes. "It's twenty to seven. What are you still doing asleep?"

"Some people do sleep until after the sun comes up," I say, handing her a towel. "Here, take this to dry off while I make us some coffee. Would you like a double-double?"

"A double what? No, I don't like to eat in the morning. Just the coffee."

The coffee maker is sputtering out a fresh pot of Starbucks House Blend when she walks in from the patio, drier, but no less annoyed.

"You know I could have hit my head on something," she complains. "You gave me such a fright. I think my heart actually stopped for a minute there."

"As I said, I'm very sorry. But what did you expect, creeping around in someone's backyard in the dark?"

"Creeping? Who said I was creeping? I was really worried about you. I tried coming by last night, and there was no answer. Then, this morning, I was walking on the lake path and saw all your lights were still out. One woman has already died here, hun. I was just checking to make sure you weren't number two! And this is the thanks I get?"

"Well, thank you for worrying, Gina. But I'm fine. I'd had a long day and fell asleep. Here's your coffee."

"Can I have milk and sugar?" She asks. "Two of each?"

I can't resist. "You mean a double-double?"

"I don't know what that is, but I already told you I don't eat in the mornings."

"Never mind," I say, opening the fridge and taking out the milk. The bottle feels warm, and I can't feel cold air from the vents. "Oh no, I think something is wrong with the fridge. It's not cold."

"You can call maintenance to look at it. But I could have told you not to bother with that Fridge Finder app thingy."

"You mean Fridge Friend?"

"That's the one. Nothing but problems."

I open the milk carton and smell its contents. "It smells alright, but what do you think?"

"Why not? I'm one cigarette away from a stroke and two donuts away from needing dialysis. Food poisoning isn't at the top of my list of health concerns."

I pour milk in both of our coffees and spoon some Splenda into hers. "Were you able to ask Leon about why Stan was late paying his maintenance fees?"

Gina shakes her head. "I asked him, but it was no use. Leon said the man's business was the man's business and that none of it was *his* business. He gets like that sometimes, especially when money is involved. We'll have to find out from someone else."

"Maybe Jinny knows something? She came by last night. Seems more than happy to chat."

"If only she were so happy to shut up. But, yeah, you may be right. One thing Leon did tell me, Carlota was putting a lot of pressure on the board to use different smart fridge software. Which would have taken a lot of money out of Stan's pocket."

"That is interesting. We need to know how badly he needs that money. Oh!" I exclaim. "Jinny did have an interesting story about Helen last night. According to her, Helen and Carlota got into a fight last week. And, get this, Helen threatened to kill Carlota!"

"Really? What for?"

"I don't know. Not yet. Something about Helen not wanting Carlota messing in her affairs."

"Well, there would have been plenty of those."

"Affairs? Maybe she said business. I don't want to give the wrong impression!"

"Oh no, hun," Gina enunciates the words carefully, then takes a sip of her coffee, "you've got the right impression there. She'd slip a little blue pill in any man's drink for a bit more spending money. Although, she may have to cool her heels on that front for a little while."

"What do you mean?" I ask.

"She had to go to the hospital last night. One of her implants exploded. Something about taking a stray golf ball to the chest." Gina's eyes dart up to meet mine. "You wouldn't know anything about that now, would you?"

I choke on my coffee. She laughs.

"If I didn't know it was an accident, I would hug you."

"It really *was* an accident," I assure her.

"Don't worry, hun. Operation Inflation will save the day." She winks one of her warm brown eyes. "But I wonder what the fight was about. Carlota was always real nice to Helen in front of me."

"Jinny thought it had something to do with Donald. Maybe they were in a love triangle and Carlota couldn't let it go?"

"I don't know. Donald was eighty-five years old. If he was getting busy with two women, it would have been his heart, not his kidneys, that failed."

"Either way, we now have two suspects. And we need to find out more about Selena. Something is bothering me about her colored caftan."

"You and that darn caftan thing again," Gina says, shaking her head.

A text message interrupts us. It's Eliza.

Hi Mom! You remember your promise about not trying to solve the case?

"Darn it," I say out loud. I should have known better than to tell Eliza about the camera and speakers.

"What's wrong?" Gina asks.

"Nothing. Just my lovely daughter trying to babysit me. You know what? The sun is about to come up. Why don't we finish this conversation out on the patio?"

My phone buzzes. Another text from Eliza.

Don't you dare!

"Sure, yeah," Gina agrees, standing and walking back through the sliding glass doors.

"I'm just going to leave my phone in here," I say out loud. "So we're not interrupted."

"You know, you really shouldn't leave your back door open like that," Gina warns as we take our seats in the early morning sun. "Just last month, an alligator crawled out of the river and walked right into Marjorie Higginbottom's kitchen!"

"No!"

"Oh yes! Luckily, she dropped chicken on the floor, which she was fixing to defrost. That distracted the gator long enough for Marjorie to get to her walker and out the front door."

"I didn't realize there were gators here!"

"This is Florida, hun. It's a swamp. Which means gators."

"Well, that's mildly terrifying." I shiver despite the heat.

"It's worse on the river side of the street. You're much better off with your patio facing the lake. Just keep your screen door closed for snakes and your house doors closed for gators. You'll be safe."

"From animals, maybe. But looking into this case could be dangerous. I mean, if we did get close to solving it, wouldn't that make us targets?"

As much as Eliza's overprotectiveness bothers me, I know she has good reason.

Murder was a family affair when the kids were growing up. But Clint was big and strong, and we all knew he would always protect us.

He can't do that anymore. Am I strong enough to do this on my own?

"So—" Gina squinches her eyes, "—are you saying, when I get the list this afternoon of all the people who were in Egret's Loft when Carlota died, you'd have no interest in seeing it?"

I had checked my itinerary for the day before falling asleep last night. At 9 a.m. I have pickleball, followed by a watercolor class at 11 a.m. After that comes lunch, book club, and then *Dance, Dance Revolution* (ballads) on something called the Wii. Whatever that is.

Plenty of activities for a very full life.

I smile. One more couldn't hurt, now, could it?

CHAPTER TWELVE

"Madeline, hello!" Victor waves me over. There's a handsome middle-aged man with dark hair and a strong chin standing beside him.

They seemed deep in conversation when I first spotted them as I drove into the parking lot for my pickleball class, but they're all smiles as I dismount my golf cart and walk over to them.

"I'd love for you to meet my son, Lucas."

"Well, aren't you just a young Sean Connery?" I blurt.

Victor's eyes sparkle. "I've told him the same thing. *Dr. No*. Spitting image!"

I squint one eye, skeptically. "I was thinking *Thunderball*, myself."

"Really, was there that much of a difference? They were only a few years apart."

"Oh no, Sean Connery looked exactly the same. But I know the reason that particular film popped into your mind. Ursula Andress and her little white bikini."

Victor chuckles. "Hmmm…you know, I think you might be onto something."

Lucas groans playfully. "I think it's time for me to leave."

"No, can't you stay a little longer?" Victor asks.

"Sorry, Dad. I need to hit the road. The plane is waiting. I have an appointment in Manhattan at three, and the memorial service for Jeremy in the evening."

Victor turns to me. "Lucas's business partner. He died last week. Car accident. Terrible business."

"How awful, I'm sorry for your loss," I sympathize.

"It's been tough." Lucas lowers his head briefly. "But Madeline, it was delightful meeting you. I trust you'll give some consolation to my aggrieved father in my absence?"

"I'll do my best." I wink at Lucas. He winks back.

"Bye, Dad. I'll see you again real soon."

Lucas waves and walks quickly to a rented red convertible. The engine roars to life and Lucas drives out of the parking lot and onto one of the complex's main roads. Just then, I see the fancy Italian car Carlota had called a panini, I think. No, that can't be right. But I'm clueless with cars. Harold must be behind the wheel again, because it's going way too fast. And it's closing the distance with Lucas's rental.

"That crazy fool is going to hit Lucas!" Victor's body tenses.

Lucas's car picks up speed. The panini or pigali, or whatever it's called, starts to gain momentum, but then there's a horrible grinding of gears, and the fancy car comes to a stop. A short man with a full head of hair, a nose like a beak, and wearing large-framed glasses, struggles out of the driver's seat. From this distance, it looks like he has no neck, like his head is almost resting right on his shoulders. He kicks the tires, then stumbles backward in apparent pain.

Victor lets out a deep breath. "Sorry, that made me nervous."

"I completely understand," I assure him. "Carlota and I saw Harold out driving the day I moved in. He'll get into an accident, driving like that."

"You've met Harold?" Victor asks.

"No, I'm only acquainted with him by way of seeing his car. It was nice meeting your son, though. You must be very proud."

"He's an investment manager. If you don't have a private jet and a summer home in the Hamptons, no one'll trust you with their money." His attempt at humor doesn't mask his obvious unease.

"Shame he had to leave so early. But then kids always have somewhere else they need to be, don't they?" I commiserate. "I'd be lucky to get mine to stay for more than a few hours!"

"Don't I know it. Lucas just arrived the other day for a little impromptu visit. And he had to work all day yesterday. He was on the phone until all hours. But I suppose I should be happy he dropped in at all."

"I'm sure he'll be back soon," I say, trying to lighten Victor's mood. "And until then, there seem to be plenty of distractions here at Egrets Loft to fill the days!"

"True, true." Victor still seems preoccupied, but then he looks at me and smiles. "I take it you're signed up for the nine o'clock pickleball class?"

"My son, Ritchie, signed me up. But can I let you in on a little secret? I have no idea what pickleball even is!"

Victor laughs, loosening the tension in his shoulders. "Can you play tennis?"

"I can't move around the court like I used to, but I do alright."

"Then you'll be just fine," he assures me. "It's basically the same thing, except the serve is different and the ball isn't as bouncy."

"So why is it named after a vegetable?"

He frowns. "I thought cucumbers were fruits."

"Technically, I think they're both. But does that matter? In naming the game, I mean."

"No, no. I think that was a dog."

"A dog named the game?"

"No, I believe the game was named after a dog. A dog named Pickles." Victor tilts his head. "Though, when I say it out loud, that doesn't seem to make much sense either."

We make our way to the courts where several other active elders stand chatting.

It's only 8:30. We've all arrived early. I was worried I'd have trouble finding the place. As for the others, I suppose with all the wellness checks around here, arriving ahead of schedule could be seen as proof of life. If you're late, people might start to think you're dead.

"Do we play in teams?" I ask, noticing that most of the other players are paired off. "Oh no, I'd hate for someone to get saddled with me as a partner!"

"We do play in teams. So, saddle up." He laughs. "Trust me, though, you'll appreciate having a partner when you don't have to cover the whole court by yourself."

"Where is your partner?" I ask, feeling my cheeks growing warmer.

He hesitates, the tension in his shoulders returning. "Carlota and I used to play together."

"Oh, Victor. I'm sorry."

"She was a great partner." His lips curve into a smile, but his eyes look haunted. "She'll be missed."

"Have you heard anything more from Detective Fletcher?"

"Last I heard, he was still interviewing people and waiting for the autopsy results to come in. We haven't had a homicide in Calusa since—" he whistles, "—who can even remember? It's been so long."

"Is this the detective's first time working a homicide?"

"As far as I can make out, yeah." He stops, turns his head, and looks at me suspiciously. "You're not getting any ideas about him needing help from a former detective's widow, are you?"

"I wouldn't dream of it." I give him an exaggerated wink. "But no, my daughter has already told me to stay well out of it. You can't help being a little curious though, right? To think someone right here in Egret's Loft might have killed her!"

"Try not to think about it for now. We're out here to have fun! How would you like to partner up for pickleball?"

"Are you sure? You're probably setting yourself up for failure," I warn.

"Ah, I won so often because of Carlota, I could probably do with a little humility," he teases. "I should probably wait to see how you handle yourself, but are you already paired up for the scramble? I find myself suddenly short of a golfing partner as well."

A surprised yelp, like the sound a puppy makes when its tail has been stepped on, escapes my lips. I manage to turn it into an unconvincing cough.

"You don't say?" I finally manage to reply.

"Are you alright? Do you need some water?" Victor asks.

"I'm alright. Just got a bug in my mouth or something. What happened to your partner?" I think of Helen, in the hospital with a ruptured implant. A rupture I caused.

"Heart palpitations, I'm afraid. The doctor prescribed her bed rest for the next few weeks."

So that's what Helen is telling people. At least her pride will spare me all the sideways looks on the golf course. She'd be livid if she knew Victor was asking me to be his new partner.

"I'd love to be your scrambles partner," I blurt out.

He grins. "Excellent. Maybe we can start practicing tomorrow morning. If you have room for me in your busy schedule."

"I'll consult my secretary and get back to you."

The instructor arrives, and we're all assigned opposing pairs. We make our way out to the courts.

I keep thinking of how mad Helen will be when she finds out Victor and I are scrambling together. How long will it take her to find out? I hope not long. She threatened Carlota at the pool and promised to get back at me on the driving range.

If she is mad enough to kill, Victor might just be the incentive I need to make her try.

Eliza is going to be so mad at me when she finds out.

CHAPTER THIRTEEN

"Stroke gently. Very, very gently."

Gina giggles like a teenager as Serenity Karma leans over my shoulder, giving me pointers on the best way to paint flower petals.

"Think of the canvas as your lover's body," Serenity instructs, her closeness and the scent of patchouli nearly choking me. "The paintbrush is the feather you're dragging over his skin. Tease out your flower."

"Not for nothing, Summer," Gina butts in, "but she has grown kids. I think her flower was teased out a long time ago."

"My name is not Summer!" An agitated Serenity rounds on Gina. "And perhaps you should focus on your own artwork. What is that? A horse?"

"No, it's a golf cart."

Serenity stares at it for a moment, says, "huh," and then walks away to give feedback to other artists.

"A golf cart reminds you of Carlota?" I can't help but ask.

In honor of our slain neighbor, Serenity assigned all five students in her 11 a.m. watercolor class to paint something that reminded us of Carlota.

"Yeah," Gina replies. "She was always driving it around everywhere."

"Doesn't everyone around here drive golf carts?"

"Hers had purple seats. I just haven't gotten to that bit yet. What kind of flower are you 'teasing out' anyway?"

"A hibiscus. She had them planted all around her house."

"Really? I never noticed. Ah well, art's not really my thing. I just checked your activities schedule and knew you'd be here."

If she deliberately sought me out, she must have some news. "Have you gotten the list from the security guard already?"

She shakes her head. "Not yet. But I did get some more info on our fridge guy."

The door to the clubhouse solarium opens, and Selena barrels through. Her frosted blond hair hangs to her shoulders in loose curls. A caftan hugs her ample curves, this one a zigzag pattern of pinks, reds, and oranges.

She stands by the door for several seconds before announcing the obvious. "I'm late."

Serenity glides over to the class's new arrival in a whirl of long, white hair and flowing fabric. We watch as Selena sits down in front of an empty canvas on the other side of the room and receives her instructions.

"Another colorful outfit," I whisper to Gina.

"You really need to let that go," Gina replies out of the side of her mouth. "But I wouldn't have expected to see her here. She never takes any of the classes."

"So…several of her habits have changed since Carlota died. You don't find that curious?"

"Not really. Maybe she just got tired of dark colors and being bored. Do you want to hear about Sam or not?"

"Sam?"

"The fridge guy."

My paint brush pauses mid-stroke. "You mean Stan? You really do struggle with names."

"What's in a name anyway? Like Shakespeare said, they still smell the same."

"I don't even know what to say to that…"

"Good, because I've been trying to get you to shut up and listen for the past ten minutes!"

"I'm listening!"

Our nearest neighbor gives us a look bordering on disgust.

"What are you looking at?" Gina demands. But lowers her voice after the other art student averts her gaze. "Turns out, it wasn't a fluke that Sam was having trouble paying his maintenance fees."

This time, I don't even try to correct her. "So, he was struggling financially? Did someone on the board tell you that?"

"Naw, I cornered his cleaning lady."

"He can afford a cleaning lady?"

"Uh yeah," Gina looks at me oddly. "It's part of the maintenance fee, hun. We all have cleaning ladies."

"I don't have a cleaning lady!"

"You do!"

"No, I don't. I would have said hello!" Or if she does exist, would she have even come by to clean yet? I've only lived in the house for two days.

"Trust me, you do have a cleaning lady!" The volume of Gina's voice has been going up, and the other four art students are looking at us like it's time to mute.

"Why don't I put on some nice relaxing music so we can all focus better on our art," Serenity says, shooting us a look that's anything but serene.

"Is Serenity a resident here? Or does she just teach?" I wonder as the sound of Tibetan music bowls fills the room.

"She lives here, and she teaches. Had some show on TV years ago about painting. Apparently, she made a lot of money in the '70s, selling a series of psychedelic nudes. But as I was saying—" Gina circles back to her earlier point, "—you do have a cleaning lady. You just haven't seen her. They only come in when you're out doing activities."

That *would* explain why the house was immaculate when Eliza and the girls left yesterday. I should have known my daughter didn't clean. Once, when the kids were teenagers, the fire alarm had gone off at the house. After taking one look in Eliza's bedroom, the fireman had ordered us all out of the house. All the closets and drawers had been rifled through, he said, so we must have been burgled.

He obviously didn't have a teenage daughter.

"Oh wow, I have a cleaning lady! What's her name?" Then I remember who I'm asking. "Never mind. I'll find out. I'd like to leave her a thank you note!"

"She'd probably appreciate cash a lot more, but we're getting sidetracked again. I was talking about Sam!"

"Right, you were. What did his cleaning lady tell you?"

Gina leans toward me, her voice lowered. "She overheard him on the phone with his financial advisor—"

"I thought the cleaning ladies only came when we were out," I interrupt her. "How did she hear Stan's call?"

"*Because*—" Gina seems annoyed to explain, "—Stan never leaves his house. She's got to clean at some point! Anyway, back to the call. Apparently, he was screaming about putting all his money in something called cryptocurrency and that it had to still be there somewhere."

"I know you'll be upset with me for interrupting again, but I get confused about cryptocurrency. Is that what the drug dealers use as money on—oh, what do you call it?—the shadow net or dark web? I can't remember. Anyway, there was a show about it on Netflix that Clint and I watched about a year back! Ritchie recommended it."

"Oh, it's money?" Gina asks. "I thought it was a place to store valuables. You know, like a safety deposit box. What does this money look like?"

"I've never actually seen any in person. But, on the show, it looked like the casino chips they use in Las Vegas."

"Interesting. Well, apparently, that's where Sam put all his money. Only now, I guess he can't find his little chips."

"Did he check the sofa? I was always finding Clint's loose change under the cushions."

"His cleaning lady said he sounded frantic, so I'm guessing he did a thorough search of the house. She said she hadn't found anything either, and she probably would have looked there, right?"

"It seems like a logical place to start. But how much money are we talking about? I mean, if it was his life savings, that would be a lot of chips. Or maybe not, I guess it depends on the denomination."

"What does religion have to do with anything?" Gina wants to know.

"No, no. Not that kind of denomination. The face value of the money kind of denomination."

"Oh. Right. Anyway, he was apparently bankrupt. Then he got the contract with Egret's Loft for his refrigerator app. No more money problems."

"Unless," I point out, "Carlota got her way and that cash cow stopped giving milk."

"That's the weirdest analogy I've ever heard, but I guess so. Yeah."

"Brushes down, everyone!" Serenity calls out. "Except you, Selena. You were a bit late, so we'll come to you last. The rest of you, it's time to start the show and tell, before the meditation and a short remembrance celebration. Let's begin with you, Gina."

Halfhearted claps accompany the reveal of Gina's golf cart painting. My flower gets only a slightly warmer reception. One of our classmates drew a Colombian flag, and another tried to draw an egret, but is told her bird is actually a heron.

"Nice work, everyone," Serenity says. "Remember, we're here to practice. We're not here to be perfect. Yeah? And this class is all about remembering Carlota. That's what matters. Selena, are you ready to show us your work?"

Selena looks up, the folds in her neck shifting shape. "Yes."

She turns her canvas around so everyone can see. We all take a collective gasp.

"You said something to remind us of Carlota, yes?" Selena asks.

She's drawn a golf club. And it's dripping blood.

CHAPTER FOURTEEN

The first thing I notice when I walk into the house is that it smells clean. The maid must have come around. The second thing that occurs to me is the sensation that someone else is in the house. I am skipping one of the activities on my schedule, so maybe she's still here!

"Hello?" I call out. "Hello?"

"No need to shout, Mom. I'm right here," Eliza says, her slim body perched on a ladder leaning against my kitchen cabinet.

"Eliza? What are you doing here? I thought you were the cleaning lady!"

"No, she took off about half an hour ago. She was here for ages. I thought she was never going to leave. But what are you doing back so early? Aren't you supposed to be in a dance class?"

"Dance class, my foot! My arms are sore, my ankles are swollen, and all I want to do is sit down. With the amount of physical activities Ritchie booked me in for this week, I think he may be trying to kill me!"

"It would give him the perfect alibi," Eliza responds, still fiddling with something above the cupboards.

"Yes, it would. Does she seem nice?" I ask. "The cleaning lady. Did you happen to catch her name?"

"No idea. I didn't want her to see me here, so I waited in the car until she wrapped up. Which means we don't have much time left."

"Much time for what?" I look around, trying to remember where I hid the peanut butter cups. "And where are the girls? You didn't leave them in the car, I hope."

"No, they're back in Miami. At the house with Tom."

Phew. "I thought Tom was out of town for work all month. Did he get back early?"

Eliza sighs, tosses her long blond hair over her shoulder, and climbs down the ladder. "Mom, as much as I'd love to answer your litany of questions, we don't have much time before the cops get here."

"Why are the cops coming here? I already talked to that detective yesterday! And what were you doing up there by the cabinets? Is the roof leaking?"

"Mom! I just said, enough with the questions! I'm trying to get this system set up quickly, so I can watch your police interview without anyone knowing I'm here."

Eliza darts into my bedroom and returns a moment later with some kind of joystick. She moves the stick, and there's a slight murmur of mechanical gears grinding.

"You're setting up a camera?" It's more of an accusation. "What about the one on the patio?"

"Too far away. And the speakers in the wall sound tinny. I needed better quality."

My voice drops to "scolding mother" level. "You better be planning to take that down afterward, young lady! You do enough spying as it is, and I'm still your mother."

"Fine, I'll take it down." She stops moving long enough to roll her big blue-green eyes. "And I'm not spying on *you*, I just really need to hear what this new guy has to say. By the way, I need you to make sure they're in the seats facing the front door. Okay?"

"New guy? Did they take Detective Fletcher off the case? Not that I would blame them. He seems like a nice enough man, but he's horribly out of his depth."

"No, he's still in charge. Will probably even try turning it into a bestseller when someone else solves the case too. Anyway, given who Carlota was…or more importantly, who her son is, the Colombians sent one of their guys. All caught up now?"

"I wondered if that was him! I read one of his books!"

"Mom, focus. They'll be here any minute."

"But what do they want to ask me about?" My eyes open wider. "Do you think they know Gina and I are trying to find out who killed Carlota?"

Eliza finally stops moving and turns to glare at me. "You promised to stop all that."

She has me there. "Don't you need to finish setting up, dear? Like you said, they could be here any minute."

There's a knock at the front door.

"Buy me two minutes, then let them in," Eliza whispers and disappears into my bedroom.

"Who is it?" I ask.

"This is Detective Fletcher. Please open the door."

I walk slowly to the peephole. "Can you please hold up your badge so I can see it?"

"Oh, for the love of…I was just here yesterday," Detective Fletcher laments. "Surely you remember me!"

"A woman was just killed next door," I remind him. "You can't be too careful."

"Yes, I know! I'm the one investigating her death, that's why I'm here! That's why I was here yesterday." He pulls out his badge and holds it aloft. "Now will you please open the door?"

I would, but it hasn't been two minutes yet.

"There's someone else out there," I stall. "Who is that with you?"

An olive-skinned man dressed in a green military uniform stands beside Detective Fletcher. With a brimmed cap, dark sunglasses, and a mustache the size of a small rat, his face remains largely anonymous. The temperature outside is topping ninety degrees, but he's not even breaking a sweat.

"Come on, Mrs. Delarouse. He's with me, and I'm a detective. You think he'd be dumb enough to do anything to you? Right in front of me?"

Through the peephole, I watch Detective Fletcher toss a smile at the other man, while making a circular motion with his finger next to his ear. The other man remains stoic.

"I can see you, you know," I call out.

Detective Fletcher has the good sense to look ashamed as he drops his hand to his side. Sweat runs in a stream off his bald head. I do feel bad. It's obvious he's trying to impress the other man. But Eliza needed some time, which should be just about up.

My hand reaches for the door handle as the other man begins to speak.

"Sorry to disturb you, Mrs. Delarouse. My name is Coronel Arturo Sánchez. I am with the National Police of Colombia. Would you be so kind as to open your door…"

I swing open the door.

"...so that we might have a word?" He finishes.

"Please come in," I tell the Coronel, blushing slightly. I've always been a sucker for good manners. Detective Fletcher's face is bright red. To him I say, "You really should consider wearing a stronger sunblock."

I offer refreshments, and we all sit down, with the men facing the door as Eliza requested.

"I just have a few more questions for you, Mrs. Delarouse," Detective Fletcher begins.

Coronel Sánchez sits silent. His sunglasses are still on; I can see myself reflected in them. I wish I'd had a chance to fix my hair.

"You can ask whatever you like, detective, but I won't have any better answers. As I said yesterday, I've only just moved in."

"Yes, Carlota was killed on the same night you moved in. You say you'd never met her before?"

"Before I moved in? No, never."

"Had you ever heard of her or her son?" He asks.

"No, I had not. A son, you say?" I play dumb, not wanting to let on that I've received covert intelligence from Eliza. "How is he holding up, poor dear? That had to have been a shock."

"I'll ask the questions, thank you." The detective's attempt at dominance borders on petulance. "Where were you on Monday between ten o'clock and midnight?"

"I'd just traveled and moved into a new house. I'm not as young as I used to be. By eight o'clock, I was in bed for the night. Please forgive me," I continue, "I'm not trying to tell you how to do your job, but I don't understand why you're asking me about my whereabouts. Other people here had real motives to kill Carlota. I didn't even know her! What are you really hoping to get from me?"

"What motives?" Detective Fletcher practically pounces. "What do you know? Who have you been talking to?"

"I really couldn't say. It's just gossip, you know. People do like to talk, don't they? How seriously can you take any of it at the end of the day?"

"What was the gossip about?" He asks, leaning forward in his chair.

"I don't feel right about spreading rumors, detective. Not to mention, nothing I tell you would be admissible. It would all be hearsay. That is, until I had more proof as to why certain people would have wanted her dead. Oh! Is that what you're hoping I can help you with? Possible suspects?"

"I don't need your help." Detective Fletcher smiles with clenched teeth. "I just want to know where you were and what you've heard."

"Well, I've already told you where I was. And if I hear anything more, anything I can prove, I promise to give you a call! Does that sound alright, detective?"

Detective Fletcher starts sputtering.

Coronel Sánchez rests a hand on the detective's arm. "*Por favor*, Detective Fletcher. Might I be allowed to ask the lady a question?" When there is no objection, Coronel Sánchez pulls a photo out of his jacket pocket. "Have you ever seen this woman?"

He hands me a photo of a beautiful brunette, probably mid-forties, dressed all in white. Her figure is a quintessential hourglass—small waist, big bust, curvy hips. The image looks fuzzy, like it was taken from far away or was in someone's wallet for a long time.

"I'm sorry. I don't recognize her," I tell him. "She's certainly not anyone I've seen around here. But, then again, I haven't met a lot of the staff yet."

"*Disculpeme*, I did not explain myself well. This photo is nearly thirty years old, but it is the only one we have. Perhaps this—" he hands me another photo, "—would be of more assistance."

I can see Detective Fletcher trying to look over the edge of the paper. It seems like this is a new line of questioning to him, as well, poor thing. He always seems so left out.

The new image looks more like a painting. Clint had brought something like it home once. It had to do with a cold case he was working on. He needed to know what someone would have looked like years later. He'd used some kind of age-progression software.

This must be what Coronel Sánchez's mystery woman is supposed to look like now.

"I think I do know who this is." I look up at Coronel Sánchez. "And you're probably going to be interested in her artwork."

CHAPTER FIFTEEN

"I come bearing gifts," Gina says, handing me a ribbon-tied bouquet of golf clubs.

"Oh, Gina, you shouldn't have!"

Not least because a golf club had just been used to kill my neighbor.

"Good, because I didn't. They were leaning up against your door when I arrived."

"They were? But who could they be from?" I wonder. "Do you think it's a threat?"

"Are you going to make me stand out here while you try to figure it out? There's a card. If you invite me in, you can read it."

"I'm sorry! Please come in." I take the clubs and usher her inside.

Before closing the door, I wave across the street at my neighbor, Phyllis. The sun has set, and there are no lights on in her house, but I wave anyway. The lights in her kitchen flash on and off.

"Good Lord, it's hot out there," Gina says, standing next to an AC vent. "Even for this time of night. Do you have anything cold to drink?"

"Only tap water, I'm afraid. The fridge is still on the fritz. I haven't had a chance to call maintenance."

The minute Detective Fletcher and Coronel Sánchez departed, Eliza had burst out of my bedroom demanding any information I had on Selena. Which didn't take long, considering I didn't even know her last name and could count on my hands the number of words we'd exchanged.

I'd tried to explain the oddity surrounding Selena's clothing colors, but Eliza said she didn't have time for fashion critiques.

Eliza was barely out the door when Gina came knocking.

"Never mind." Gina pulls some papers and a bottle of wine out of her purse. "Good thing I planned ahead. Do you have any glasses for this?"

"Of course!" I set down the golf clubs and grab two wine goblets out of the cabinet. "Is that the list from your security guard source?"

"Sure is! But first, let's see who gave you those." She points to the clubs.

I hesitate. "Do you think I should put on gloves before opening the card? In case there are fingerprints."

"If someone was really trying to threaten you, do you think they would have tied a yellow bow around them? Red, maybe. Not yellow."

"I suppose you're right. And they can always exclude my prints later if they have to."

The card is nestled in between a driver, a putter, and a wedge. I only know their names because whoever left them also, very kindly, labelled each club with a label maker. I gently pull the card out and examine the envelope's contents.

"So," Gina asks, "is it someone telling you you're next?"

I blush. "No. They're a present from Victor. He asked me to be his scramble partner. Apparently, Dom told him I didn't have any of my own clubs."

Gina lets out a low whistle. "Holly's not going to like that!"

"You mean Helen?"

"That's the one. Do you know how much she had to fork over bribing the committee to pair her up with Victor?"

"She said he asked her to be his partner!"

Gina snorts loudly. "Victor's never asked a woman to be anything to him. All the Egret's Loft widows wanted to try him on after his wife died a few years back. No dice. He just wasn't interested. Until now, anyway."

My face feels like it's on fire. "I'm sure he's just being friendly."

"Yeah, sure. Men always spend hundreds of dollars on golf clubs for a woman they just met because they're hoping she wants to be *friends*."

The look she's giving me tells me it's time to change the subject. "You'll never guess what happened right before you arrived!"

She smiles and winks. "Alright, I'll bite."

As she pours the wine, I fill her in on the visit from Detective Fletcher and Coronel Sánchez.

"Why would that Colombian officer be interested in an old photo of a much thinner Selma?" Gina asks.

"Selena. He wouldn't say, but it has to mean something, right?"

"I doubt he would have come all this way to track down an old girlfriend. I wonder what it could be. Maybe she's living here under a fake name! Or…or maybe she's wanted for murder in Colombia!"

"Before we get Interpol on the line, should we at least see if she was on the property when Carlota was killed? May I take a look at that list?"

Gina sighs and hands me the papers. "Sure can, for all the good it'll do you."

"What do you mean?" I ask, scanning quickly. There she is. Selena Fuentes.

"My guy would only give me a list of all the people who were here for the forty-eight hours around her murder—twenty-four hours before and twenty-four hours after. He said the police didn't ask for it, and it'd take too long to narrow it down by hour just because I was being nosy."

"Detective Fletcher didn't ask for a list?" I shake my head. "This case will never be solved if we don't help that poor man out."

My phone alerts me that I have a text. It's from Eliza. *Seriously, Mom? Are you trying to get yourself killed?*

She'd raced out in such a hurry, I forgot to make sure she took the camera down. Clearly, she didn't forget that she left it behind.

There's only one way to handle this. I turn off my phone.

"I looked over the list before I came over," Gina says, refilling her glass. "Everyone on our street was here and a couple kids—including your own. Nothing out of the ordinary. But there was one name on there that caught me by surprise." She points to the name Astrid Roosevelt.

"The owner of Shady Palms?"

Gina nods, raising her eyebrows. "I'm impressed you know about her. You may just have what it takes to solve this, after all! Back to what I was sayin'. She wasn't supposed to be on the property. Standing order from Carlota. Those two hated each other!"

"I heard they used to be friends. Do you know what happened?"

"All I know is, Astrid's father was some kind of diplomat, so they went to school together in Colombia. Friends their entire lives, until suddenly they weren't. Carlota brought Leon on board to replace Astrid after they had their falling out. Do you think we should tell that detective that she was here?"

I take a moment to think. "You say this list covers the twenty-four hours after Carlota was murdered?"

"Yeah. Why?"

"Because I saw Astrid on Tuesday evening. She was talking to Dom out at the golf club. That would explain why she's on the list."

"What was she talking to him about?" Gina wants to know. So do I.

"They were too far away. I couldn't hear anything. Did Dom get along with Carlota?"

"No idea. I don't play golf. But you're thinking maybe they could be conspiring together or something?"

"I don't know. We'll just have to—"

The rest of my sentence gets swallowed by the roar of an engine and screeching tires. A dog starts yapping from out in the street. Brakes squeal. The barking stops. Then moments later, a woman wails.

Gina and I rush out the front door.

"*Mitsy!*"

Helen stands in the street. She's wearing sweats, doesn't have any makeup on, and her hair looks matted. She's grimacing as she tries, unsuccessfully, to pick up her Pomeranian. Her doctor probably warned her not to lift anything after getting the replacement implant. She doesn't seem to be in any mood for the reminder.

Mitsy stands in the road, completely unharmed, but completely unmoving. Like she's gone into shock. The absence of barking feels eerie and unnatural.

"Harold!" A red-faced Helen screams at the car that has long since driven out of sight. "I'm going to get you for this!"

I take a deep breath.

At least I'm not at the top of her hit list…for the moment.

CHAPTER SIXTEEN

"Put the ball by your left heel, just like that," Victor coaches me. "Now walk backward until the club and your legs form a triangle with the ground. Now swing."

Rotating my torso, I hold the club high and slice it down toward the ground. The ball sweeps into the air and lands with a satisfying plop in the water near a floating marker that reads 150 yards.

"How was that?" I ask, squinting into the early morning sun.

"You're a natural!" Victor smiles.

I smile back. "Or I have a good teacher."

"Let's keep that between you and me. I wouldn't want Dom thinking I'm after his job."

"Our little secret." I give him a quick wink. "Thank you again for the clubs. It really was too generous."

I don't mention that, when I first saw them sitting on my doorstep last night, I thought whoever sent them planned to kill me with them.

"Really? Generous? Huh," he says. "Well, let me assure you that my intentions were purely selfish. If you take to golf, I have an excuse to spend more time with you."

"Is that so? Well, in that case, I also need some proper shoes, oh, and one of those wheely bags to put my new clubs in."

"Your wish is my command."

My mouth drops open. "Oh no, Victor! I was only teasing! I'm perfectly capable of buying my own gear. You've done more than enough!"

He laughs. "I was wondering how far you'd be willing to take it. Not to be critical, but you folded disappointingly early."

"I'll try harder next time," I promise, teeing up another ball.

We both swing. His ball, naturally, sails yards past mine.

"So, you've been here for a full three days now. How are you liking Egret's Loft?" He asks. "Acknowledging, of course, that your new life here got off to a rather rough start."

"Yes, poor Carlota. She seemed lovely. But, in spite of everything, people have been very welcoming, and there's always something to do."

"And what is it that you like to spend your time doing? Aside from waking up early to come golfing with me, of course."

"Well, obviously that," I assure him. "But I'm enjoying trying new things. Pickleball and painting and all the other activities my son signed me up for. I've always been a bit of a homebody. Down here, on my own, I think Ritchie was worried I'd get bored. So, he packed my schedule full of every single activity he could find."

Victor chuckles. "It's funny, really. When they were kids, we did exactly the same to them. Packing their day so full of activities they had no energy left by the time they got home. I mean, you love your kids when they're little, but it's so much easier to love them when you can almost pretend they're not there."

"You're terrible! Your son, Lucas, seems like such a nice boy!"

"Trust me, he has his moments. He's made me proud, and he's broken my heart. But I'd do anything for him. The only problem is, he knows it."

I smile. "Don't they all?"

The driving range is beginning to fill up with other golfers, all anxious to get some practice in before the midday heat tires them out faster than their grandkids ever could. White balls with Egret's Loft logos slice through the cloudless blue of the Florida sky, like shooting stars. The only white things flying through the air this time of year back home in DC are snowflakes. I guess life here isn't so bad.

"What else is on your agenda for the day?" Victor asks. "What kind of things does your son think you'd enjoy doing?"

"I have some kind of Scrabble game later today at the River Club, but other than that, I really couldn't say. The refrigerator isn't being very cooperative."

"Ah, you only have the digital version of your schedule?"

I nod. "Ritchie must have set it up that way. The schedule used to be on the screen of the fridge, but the whole system seems to have shut down."

"Do you need some help with any of the settings? They can be a bit tricky at first. I'm happy to come around and take a look."

"Thank you for offering, but the maintenance guy— Howard?—is trying to fix it right now. Poor guy. He seemed so frustrated. Says he's sick and tired of having to fix fridges every five minutes."

"Oh, I'm sure Howard's just exaggerating."

"Really? I told him I was leaving to meet you, and he said he was just over at your place last week. Something about your ice maker shooting ice cubes across the room…"

"Oh, that. That was nothing. Operator error, I'm ashamed to admit."

Victor places another ball on a tee and prepares his swing.

Operator error doesn't line up with what Howard told me. He said the motion sensors on the ice maker went haywire. Sensors that Fridge Friend is supposed to regulate to make sure there's always ice available on warm days.

Old age and dehydration are never a good mix.

Why would Victor hide that? He must be trying to cover for something, but whether it's the technology or the man behind it, I can't say for sure.

When I first met Carlota, she said Victor was trying to help Stan. Does Victor know that Stan lost all his little cryptocurrency chips? Does he know that, without Fridge Friend, Stan would probably be bankrupt? Is that why he's not saying he could have been hit by flying blocks of ice shooting like machine gun fire out of his refrigerator? Or is he simply trying to defend a friend?

"Stan helped me set up the app on my phone the other day." I start laying the bait. "I was excited that my appliances could suggest new recipes for me! Though I did have some issues with the oven. My casserole burned. I should go back and ask him about that. Do you know him well?"

"He's an interesting guy, helped me fix my computer a few times. He kept trying to get me to upgrade from Windows 98, but I told him it works just fine." Victor pauses and seems to decide to add, "Just be careful around that one. You can't trust anything he says."

Okay, so not friends then.

"Oh. I thought you too might have been close. Carlota told me you're the one fighting to keep Fridge Friend at Egret's Loft. She said so many people were complaining about it that she wanted to cancel Stan's contract." I'm embellishing a little from the offhand comment Carlota made during our tour of the neighborhood, but it's worth it to see Victor's reaction.

He disappoints me, simply teeing up another ball. "Carlota really didn't like Stan. She used to say only children play with toys all day. And she *hated* that he smokes marijuana every now and again. No cartels in Egret's Loft. She actually said that once, at a board meeting. Then again, maybe she did have good cause to be concerned."

"About a cartel? Here? Seriously?"

"Absolutely." He leans in close. "If you ever need to score some blood thinners or ACE inhibitors, there's a certain street corner I could definitely recommend."

I laugh and slap his arm. "I thought we weren't supposed to joke about being ol…'active elders.' And you call yourself a member of the board."

He holds his hands up in surrender. "Come on, Madeline, even the people making the rules need to break them every now and again. It's how we know we're still alive."

"Maybe you should write a screenplay about it. I can just see the marquee now. Tonight only: *Rebel Without a Cane*."

"You better watch out, you beautiful *lady with advanced life experience*." He makes air quotes with his fingers. "I might have to make an example of you with the board."

"Please, kind sir. Don't do that!" My face is starting to hurt from smiling so much. "Honestly, it's so refreshing to know someone else finds it all ridiculous. I'm old. I don't mind people saying I'm old. I've earned it. Tell that to the board."

Victor's attention is pulled to something happening over my left shoulder.

"Speaking of the board," he says. "I'm going to have to leave you for now, I'm afraid. Emergency meeting. It was called last night."

As he moves to put away his clubs, I take a quick peek in the direction he'd been looking. A tall woman with circular glasses, wearing a business suit, is walking into the clubhouse.

Astrid Roosevelt.

"Isn't that the woman who owns Shady Palms?" I ask.

Victor looks up at me, then over to where Astrid had been. He returns to his golf bag. "Yes, she asked for the meeting."

"Really? What about?"

"She said she wanted to discuss the future of Egret's Loft."

"Why would she have any say in that?" I wonder.

"I'm about to find out. Maybe I can appease your curiosity on the subject over dinner? My house, eight o'clock?"

"Oh, I can't. Gina already invited me to dinner. Can I get a rain check?"

"Of course. Great job today. I think we're going to have a lot of fun playing together," Victor says, then quickly adds, "Golf, I mean. In case that sounded creepy."

"It did." I laugh.

"Well, hopefully, my creepiness won't put you off that dinner you've promised me. See you soon, Madeline."

As he walks away, I can't help but think Carlota's only been dead a few days and already the egrets are circling.

CHAPTER SEVENTEEN

"Why you geriatric Jezebel!"

There's a rental car in my driveway, and an angry woman pushing a baby carriage coming at me across the road when I arrive home from golf.

Out of the corner of my eye, I spot a flash of pink moving quickly down the sidewalk away from us. I sigh and climb out of my golf cart.

"Helen, how are you feeling?"

"Don't you go actin' like you care," she fumes. "I was born at night, but not *last* night. Did you think I wouldn't find out that you poached my scramble partner?"

Jinny must have told her, which is why she raced home so quickly after I showed up.

"I can see that you're upset, but please try to be reasonable." I keep my voice calm. "Victor asked me because you were…indisposed."

"Oh, sugar, don't even try and pretend that this is my first rodeo. You attacked me on purpose so you could get your Yankee claws into my man. I'm madder than a cat gettin' baptized!"

"Why would anyone try to baptize a cat?"

"That's not the point!"

"Oh, I'm sorry, there was one?"

"One what?"

"A point."

Helen sneers. "The point is, you wanted to get me out of the way so you could have Victor all to yourself. You're lower than a snake's belly in a wagon rut. And I'm just here to tell you, God don't like ugly."

"Helen, it was an accident, and I'm truly sorry. I know you think it was intentional, but that was my first time even hitting a golf ball! You saw me. Do you really think I have the skill to have engineered that shot on purpose?"

"Excuses don't amount to a hill of beans. I know what you did and, on account of it, my poor, sweet Mitsy might have been killed!"

She adjusts the baby carriage just enough so I can see Mitsy inside, resting happily on a cushion. I reach in to pet the little Pomeranian, and she licks my hand. Helen violently jerks the carriage away.

"What? You want to finish the job? Leave my Mitsy alone!" Helen screams.

"You can't think I'm responsible for Harold's driving, can you? I've been here less than a week, and I've seen him almost mow down another driver and your dog! It's a wonder he has his license."

I don't mention that the car he almost rammed into was being driven by Victor's son, Lucas. I'm hoping we've already moved on from the Victor portion of the conversation and don't want to antagonize her any further.

Never wrestle with a pig if you don't have to, Clint always used to tell the kids. You just get dirty, and the pig actually likes it.

"Well, if you hadn't hit me with that golf ball, then Mitsy wouldn't have been out in the road!" Helen screams. "She slipped out the door, and I couldn't pick her up! So, when you think about it, that was your fault too!"

Across the street, a curtain flutters at Phyllis's house. Behind me, I hear my own front door opening. Ritchie and his six-year-old son Curt stand there, looking confused about all the commotion. I didn't even know Ritchie was coming, but that explains the rental car in my driveway.

"Helen, I've said I'm sorry. It was an accident. I never meant to hurt you. Is there anything I can do to make it up to you?"

94

"Well, sugar—" she lowers her voice, "—if you've got half the good sense the Lord gave a billy goat, you'll tell Victor you can't be his partner after all. Tell him what you did. If you're really such a bad golfer, you wouldn't want to run the risk of hurting him, too, now, would you?"

"I'm confused. You want me to tell him I ruptured your implant?"

Her bottom lip drops open as she draws a quick breath. As her mouth closes, her eyebrows draw down. The pupils in her eyes turn to pinpricks.

"I know that common sense isn't a flower that grows in every garden, so let me give this to you plain-like. I'm not the kind of woman you wanna mess with."

With that, she turns the baby carriage, tosses her bleached blond curls over her shoulder, and storms back across the street to her own house, her low wedge sandals slapping the bottom of her feet the whole way.

I give a wave to Phyllis, turn around, and walk toward my front door, where my son and grandson are waiting for me.

"It's good to see you're making friends with the neighbors," Ritchie says before I even have time to give him a hug. "What was all that about?"

"Her breast, her golf partner, and her dog. Long story." I kneel slowly to get eye-level with my young grandson. "It's so nice to see you, Curt! Do you have a hug from your grandma?"

He cocks his buttery blond head. "That would be unwise. We've been on a plane all morning, and the person sitting next to me kept sneezing. Do you have some Purell I could use before we hug?"

"Never mind, you just come here!" I grab him and pull him into my arms. "I've missed you too much to be worried about germs."

"You should always worry about germs, especially at your age," he insists. "Due to a combination of cell aging and the impact of the senescent on proliferation and differentiation in response to antigenic stimulation, elderly people have a diminished ability to fight off infection."

My arms are still around Curt as I look up at Ritchie. "Did you teach him that?"

"Please, lady. You know I haven't had to teach him anything since he was three and taught *himself* to read."

"Well, it's a lovely surprise to have you here!" I say, ushering them into the house. "Eliza was just here yesterday. She didn't mention that you were planning to come!"

"Well, she thought it might be good to have someone down here with you for the time being. Just a precaution. And my surgery schedule was light this week, so one of the other doctors offered to cover for me."

"That's so nice, Ritchie, but I hate that you went to so much trouble. Why the concern all of a sudden? Has something happened?"

"We'll get to that in a minute. Eliza sent an overnight package. Rush delivery. You haven't gotten anything yet?"

"No. What did she send?"

"A surface to air missile and some anti-tank mines," he deadpans.

"What on Earth does she think I need those for? Carlota was killed with a golf club!"

"I'm just teasing you, lady. It's a home security system, but with all the bells and whistles. Which is why I'm here, to set it up. Curt wanted to come along to help. He's very handy with technology."

Speaking of, my fridge should be fixed by now. "Can I get either of you a cold drink or something to eat?"

Ritchie shakes his head. "We stopped at Chick-fil-A on the way over, but some water or iced tea would be nice. Curt, do you want water or iced tea?"

"Can I have a Yoo-hoo instead?"

"Sorry, buddy." Ritchie sends an exasperated look my direction. "We'll pick some up when we go to the store. Right now, your only choices are water or iced tea."

"Is the iced tea sweetened?" Curt asks.

"I think so, yes," I tell him. "Would you like some?"

"Only if it is sweetened with natural sugar, please," Curt replies. "I don't consume any products that contain aspartame."

I look at Ritchie. He shrugs his shoulders.

"And what is it that you have against aspartame?" I want to know.

"While its long-term effects are still being debated, the fact that prenatal exposure to aspartame increased cancer risk in rodent offspring is enough for me to say no thanks."

"Rodent offspring? You don't say?" I can't keep the smile off my face. "You're always teaching me such wonderful new things, Curt."

"You're welcome, Grandmother. To be safe, why don't I just stick with water, please. And I might want to go swimming later. Dad, can I go outside to test the free chlorine concentration and pH levels? You know I have very sensitive skin."

"Knock yourself out, buddy." Ritchie opens the sliding glass doors for Curt.

"I'll bring your water out to you in a minute!" I open the refrigerator to pull out the pitcher. "Well, that's not good."

Ritchie sneaks up behind me. "Would it be possible to get a little water with my ice?"

The entire pitcher, along with the rest of the contents of the refrigerator, is completely frozen.

"What in the world?" I lament. "Yesterday, it wasn't cold at all. Now it's too cold!"

"And you were hoping it would be *just* right, weren't you, Goldilocks?" Ritchie smiles.

"You think you're so funny, don't you?"

"Only because I am."

"And humble too. But really, I haven't even been here a week, and this refrigerator is driving me crazy. This Fridge Friend app is no friend of mine, I can assure you."

"Fridge Friend? I thought it was just a regular smart fridge."

"No, it's Stan's handiwork, and the only reason he's still here at Egret's Loft, it would seem."

"You seem to know a lot about Stan. You're assimilating quickly, I see." He beams, proud of how well I'm settling in. "How about we get Curt to take a look? At the fridge, not Stan. My boy loves tinkering. He won't touch footballs, and he refuses to wear shorts, but he does love tech."

"He's perfect the way he is," I say. "Do you think he would be alright with tap water?"

"Sure. Just whatever you do, don't *tell* him it's tap water."

"Right, now do you want to tell me what you're really doing here and why I need a home security system?"

He looks out at Curt on the back patio and turns back to me. "Have you ever heard the name Jesus Castillo?"

"Is he that Latin pop singer?"

"Not quite. You've really never heard the name before? What about Alvaro Castillo?"

"Are they related?"

Ritchie sighs. "You're clearly not doing anything with that Netflix subscription we gave you for Christmas. There's a documentary you should watch. It's probably easiest to start with that."

"A documentary? About what?"

"One of your neighbors isn't who they claim to be."

CHAPTER EIGHTEEN

"The sadistic killing of his rival, still believed to be one of the most brutal murders in the history of Colombia, created a citadel of fear around Alvaro's cocaine-trafficking empire.

"Capitalizing on his image as the Solitario Guerrero, or Lone Warrior, Alvaro created a vast network of informants and enforcers—all unknown to each other. Fiercely secretive, none ever penetrated Alvaro's inner circle.

"Even the identity of his wife was a closely guarded secret. Only one photo, taken in the 1980s, exists today of the woman widely believed to be the mother of his son and successor, Jesus Castillo."

Richie pauses the show on a shot of the same photo Coronel Sánchez showed me yesterday.

"You alright there, lady?" Richie asks. "You're looking a little green."

"This show is very explicit! You don't think Curt heard any of that?"

Ritchie waves his hand dismissively. "Naw, he's too busy trying to fix the code on your smart fridge. Watch this. Hey, Curt, do you want a Yoo-hoo?"

Cross legged on the floor in the kitchen, Curt doesn't even look up. He's too absorbed with his iPad, which stands upright in its child protective case—the kind that has arms and legs and is covered in foam. It's connected, via a series of wires, to the refrigerator.

"See. Even genius kids never listen," Ritchie says.

"Well, that's a relief. I'm going to have nightmares after watching that!"

"I can prescribe you some sleeping pills if you want. Though, if I were you, with Alvaro Castillo's wife living down the street, I'd seriously consider sleeping with one eye open."

"But all the stuff in the show happened over forty years ago. What happened to Alvaro? Surely, he's in prison or dead by now. Your father always used to say that drug dealers have short shelf lives."

Ritchie leans back in dismay. "I can't tell you! What if you want to watch the rest of the documentary? I don't want to spoil the ending!"

"I've seen enough, thank you very much."

"There's also a series on Amazon Prime! Benicio del Toro plays Alvaro. We could start watching it tonight!"

"Or you could do as your mother asks and just tell me what happens. If you're worried enough to come all the way here to install home security, how can you be sure I'll live long enough to watch the whole series?"

"It's only four episodes…"

"Ritchie!"

"Alright." Ritchie laughs. "But don't be surprised if you catch me up late tonight binge watching it. I got sidetracked now. Where were we?"

"You were about to tell me what happened to Alvaro Castillo."

"Oh, right. So, yeah, Dad was on the money about short shelf lives. Alvaro was gunned down by a rival cartel in the mid-'90s."

"If he's been dead for years, why is Coronel Sánchez asking about this picture now?" I point to the television and the old photo of Selena.

"Were you not listening to the documentary? Gosh, lady, you're just as bad as my son." He rolls his eyes dramatically.

I want to glare at him, but it's hard enough just trying to keep from laughing. "The son?" I guess. "Alvaro and Selena had a son."

"Ding, ding, ding! Jesus Castillo. Not a nice guy, except probably to his mother. Have you ever noticed that all these drug dealers are closet mama's boys?"

"No. I'll have to take your word for it." I glare at him to get back to the point.

"Anyway," Ritchie continues, "eventually, Jesus took back his father's empire. Ran it for years, but was put away a few years back. Charged with money laundering."

"Was Carlota's son the prosecutor on the case?" I ask, remembering that Eliza had mentioned he'd been the attorney general.

"Two for two, lady! I told Eliza you weren't going senile yet."

I ignore this last bit. The kids have been good-naturedly playing me against each other for far too long for it to still have an impact.

"So—" I try to move back on topic, "—Carlota's son was the person responsible for putting Selena's son behind bars. Selena Castillo must have been furious, but she probably couldn't say anything because it would have blown her cover as Selena Fuentes."

"All true. And that's not even the worst part."

"There's more?" I ask.

He nods. "Jesus died in prison last year."

"Oh, poor Selena. She must have been devastated."

Ritchie leans toward me. "Um, before you start feeling too bad, let's not forget her son was a psychopath who sold drugs to children and probably wasn't very nice to animals."

"I know," I agree. "But he was still her son. A mother always loves her child, even if she knows they've done bad things."

"Good point. After all, you still love Eliza," he says with a wink.

"Your sister hasn't done bad things. And even if she had, I'm sure it would have been for a good reason."

"Whatever you say, lady."

Neither of us know what it is, exactly, that Eliza really does for a living. Her résumé says she works for the Internal Revenue Service, but how would an IRS agent know that my neighbor was killed even before the police did? Dilemmas like that keep us guessing.

"Anyway," Ritchie continues, "call us crazy, but we were a bit worried, knowing that the wife of one vicious drug dealer, who's *also* the mother of another vicious drug dealer, lives down the street from *our* mother, whose neighbor was just killed."

"You don't seriously think I'm in any danger, do you? I mean, I've barely spoken to the woman, and I haven't done anything to any of her family members. Plus, if you're so concerned about the potential for violence, why did you bring your six-year-old son?"

"Please, lady." Ritchie's eyebrows raise in disbelief. "You remember me trying to set up the PlayStation at home. Do you honestly think I can figure out how to install the home security software without Curt?"

I nod. "Fair point. Do you happen to know when her son died last year?"

Ritchie pulls out his phone and does a quick search. "End of November. Why?"

"Aha! I was right! There *was* a reason Selena was wearing all black! Do you think it's a coincidence that she started wearing colors again the morning Carlota was found dead?"

His brow furrows. "What are you on about?"

I sigh. Nobody else gets it.

"Suffice it to say, I think Selena was definitely harboring resentment toward Carlota." Whether or not she was prepared to kill her out of revenge is less clear. "But the police must already be onto Selena, if that Colombian officer showed me her picture."

"If they know who she really is, I think it's safe to assume she's at the top of their suspect list," Ritchie agrees.

"Alright, so what should we do?" I ask.

"Umm, nothing."

"But we don't know for sure that she did do it, right? I mean, there are other suspects. Stan was about to lose his livelihood because of Carlota, and someone overheard Helen threatening to kill her. Your father always used to say, don't get so caught up in one clue you forget to look at the whole picture."

"It was Dad's job, not yours. Why can't you just enjoy your retirement?"

I want to tell Ritchie that not a day goes by when I don't miss his father. That, by doing something Clint loved, something that he loved talking about with us, it makes me feel a little less lonely. That, in some way, it feels like Clint is still here with me.

But Ritchie is my son. As his mother, I don't want my hurt to hurt him. So, I say nothing.

"What activities did I schedule for you today anyway?" Ritchie continues his train of thought. "Don't you have strip bingo or synchronized swimming or something?"

"You really had no idea what you were signing me up for, did you?" I ask.

"Not a clue! But everything sounded fun at the time!"

"Well, I think there's a Scrabble tournament this afternoon. Before I knew you'd be here, I was planning to go to that."

"Excellent! You should go!"

Curt walks in from the kitchen, dragging the arm of his iPad case. "I have successfully unfriended your fridge, and it seems to be working properly. The code was a nightmare to correct, but I was able to add in some upgrades, so the recipe and oven connection options are back online. Dad, can I have a Yoo-hoo now?"

Ritchie looks at his son. "I have an even better idea! How would you like to go play Scrabble with your grandma and some of her new friends?"

He considers the offer. "I suppose, given their advanced years, they might be able to introduce me to some new vocabulary words. And you know I love anagram challenges. I accept."

"That's wonderful! Maybe we can team up against some of the other players," I suggest.

"No, thank you." Curt shakes his head. "Team sports aren't for me. Do you think they'll have Purell there to sterilize the pieces or should I take my own?"

"I'll put some in my purse, just in case," I assure him as I pack up my things to leave. "And if you're a really good speller, I might even let you drive the golf cart back home!"

Curt looks confused. "Why would I want to drive, if you're willing to do it for me?"

"Oh, no reason. I just thought you might like the challenge. That's all."

Enthusiasm replaces the confusion on his little face. "Oh, yes, please! Can I drive the golf cart, Grandmother?"

"Let's see how things go, shall we?"

With a wave to Ritchie, Curt and I walk out into the sunshine, excitement humming through both of us.

As much as all the evidence seems to point to Selena as the killer, I'm not convinced she's the only one who had a motive to kill my neighbor.

Carlota was the Scrabble champion of Egret's Loft. She told me so herself. Maybe it's not such a bad idea to check out how fierce the competition was.

CHAPTER NINETEEN

"Oh dear, how old did you say your grandson is?" Jinny asks, a pair of pink-framed reading glasses perched on the edge of her dainty nose as she looks at a sign-in sheet.

"He's only six, but he's very smart for his age, and is perfectly capable of playing against anyone here," I assure her.

"This puts me in a bit of a pickle. Usually, only residents are allowed to play in the tournaments, though we have had some children come along on occasion to make their parents happy. Why, a few months ago, Victor's son was here, chatting away and playing. He had such a good Scrabble word. I think it was 'portfolio' which he built off another word 'port,' but he landed on the triple word score, so it served him quite well, don't you know. I think he was paired up with Marjorie Higginbottom. Or maybe it was Harold Small. I can't remember off the top of my head, but I'm sure George has it written down somewhere. George?"

Her husband looks up from the book he's reading, a biography of Wayne Gretzky. He's apparently recovered from his sciatica enough to come and help Jinny administer the Scrabble tournament. He's a tall man, bald on top but the white hair on the back of his head wraps around his face in a neatly trimmed beard and mustache.

"Do you remember who Victor's son played against? You remember he was here. Such a nice boy, always dressed so smartly, and pretty easy on the eyes to boot. Not unlike his father, if you ask me. But then, I'm a very happily married woman and only have eyes for my man right here. What's that George? You think he's a bit flash? Well, I don't think so…"

Curt and I look over at George as Jinny continues to talk. He hasn't said a word, just nods his head at whatever his wife says. Curt slides his hand into mine and stays quiet.

"How about if Curt just plays on a team with me?" I ask when Jinny comes up for air.

"Well, I don't want to be a keener, but I sure don't know about that. It doesn't matter to me so much, but sometimes people can get very particular aboot the rules. I mean, there'd be two of you then playing against just one other person, and it might cause a kerfuffle…"

"But, as you pointed out, he is only six years old. Surely nobody would get that upset." I smile inside, knowing Curt could beat the pants off any person in the room. Including me.

"Well, he is precious, I just want to pinch his cheeks and feed him a beavertail, eh? What's that George? Oh, no. Don't worry, Madeline, it's not a real beaver tail! We Canucks don't go around chopping off animals' tails and feeding them to children. That wouldn't be so nice. It's a special dessert, like a donut, but it's shaped like the tail of a beaver. My grandkids just love them, can't get enough! Except Jackson, but he never did have much of a sweet tooth."

"Hey, Jinny! What's a guy gotta do to get signed up to play?" A booming male voice behind me asks.

Turning around, all I can see is Roy Everhard's shirt, a dark blue Hawaiian deal with light blue palm fronds and white flowers. I have to tilt my head back to see his face. His impossibly white teeth smile down at me.

"We meet at last," he says, taking my hand, the one not currently being used by Curt, and kissing it. "I've been hoping to bump into you at some point."

The way he says "bump" almost makes me cringe.

"Well, now, Roy, you're going to have to wait your turn," Jinny interrupts. "We're just trying to figure out what to do about Madeline and her little grandson. He wants to play, but putting the two of them on a team would be unfair to whoever they play against, eh? And he can't play on his own, because he's far too young to be a resident, and, technically, only residents are allowed to play. Though we did make an exception for Victor's son, didn't we, George?"

"Yes, dear," George says.

Hearing his voice for the first time startles me. I'd begun to think he couldn't speak.

"How about this? Why don't they both square off against me?" Roy offers. "I think I'm man enough to take on both of them at once."

"Are you sure?" I feel Curt's hand start to sweat. "We don't want to cause any problems."

Jinny opens her mouth to speak, but Roy cuts her off.

"It's all settled," he announces. "Mark it on the sheet that Raging Roy Everhard is facing off against Madeline and…sorry, son, I didn't catch your name."

Curt, his hand still gripping mine, squares his shoulders. "My name is Curt, but as we have no biological connection, I would appreciate it if you'd refrain from calling me your son."

Roy stares briefly at Curt before throwing his head back and howling with laughter. Other players, setting up their game boards around the room, stop and stare.

"Your boy's got spunk," Roy tells me. "I like that."

"Well, if you're sure you're alright with this, Roy, I don't suppose there's any harm, eh?" Jinny cuts in, noticing that a line has assembled behind us. "It might be kind of fun to have a youngster playing. You never know what they're going to say! There are words my grandchildren use that I've never even heard of before, don't you know. Why, just a few months ago, my grandson, Paul, who's just about old enough to drive, called his father a 'manther.' Now, I have no idea what that means, but our son got very offended and told Paul to go to his room. George and I didn't know what was going on, did we George?"

"No, dear," George replies on cue.

"Put us down at table five, Jinny," Roy says, sliding his hand onto the small of my back. "That's my lucky table."

The pressure from Roy's hand on my back propels me forward, toward a small table by the window, with two chairs, a dictionary, and a Scrabble board already laid out.

"Now, I don't want you feeling in any way intimidated." Roy smiles.

"Why would I?" I ask.

"True, I don't know anything about you. It's just that most people don't get too many brushes with celebrities. I didn't want you thinking I was any different from any other man. Just because I won a couple of Super Bowls and used to party with Joe Montana, doesn't mean I'm not just like any other ordinary guy."

"Who is Joe from Montana?" Curt wants to know.

"No, son...I mean, *Curt*. Joe Montana. That's his last name. Quarterback. Played for the 49ers."

"You just said a whole lot of words that mean nothing to me." Curt shakes his head. "Are those sports references?"

"Of course, they are! Doesn't your daddy let you watch football?"

"Actually, neither of my daddies have any interest in sports."

Roy coughs to cover a choke. "Neither of your daddies? You're adopted then?"

I open my mouth to put Roy in his place, but Curt beats me to it.

"No, nothing like that. My daddy, Richard, and the sister of my other daddy, Craig, made me in a test tube. Which makes me a product of science, like a superhero."

I give Curt's hand a squeeze.

"Well, how about I go wrangle another chair for our little superhero?" Roy chuckles and pats me on the behind before walking off to find a seat for Curt.

"His teeth look too big for his mouth," Curt says after Roy has walked away. "Do you think he suffers from macrodontia?"

"I don't think so, sweetie. I think he just has bad veneers."

Curt looks up at me. "You mean he did that on purpose?"

108

"I'm afraid so. But he's coming back, let's keep that between us, okay?"

"Okay."

"Alrighty then," Roy says, setting down a folding chair. "Here's a seat for our little superhero. Shall we get down to business? Go ahead and pick a tile out of the bag. The letter closest to the start of the alphabet goes first." Roy rubs his hands together in anticipation.

I reach into a cheap velvet bag and pull out an "A." The smile on Roy's face falters slightly. He puts his hand in the bag and pulls out a "Z."

"Gosh darn it!"

"If you'd like to go first, we really don't mind," I tell him.

"No, no. That was a fair catch, and the rules are the rules. Kickoff time!"

We all draw our pieces, and in the center of the board, Curt spells out the word "quick."

"That's twenty points for the word, and since the starting tile is a double word score, we get forty points total," Curt narrates as he writes down the score on a piece of paper.

Roy's mouth hangs open.

"How old did you say your little MVP here was?" He asks.

"He just turned six. But he's very bright for his age," I brag.

Though Curt allows me to make a few suggestions, the game predominantly becomes a force of wills between Curt and Roy. Curt, because he really enjoys the mental challenge. Roy, because he can't bear the thought of losing to a first grader.

Time ticks away and, with the tile bag empty, it's still anyone's game.

Roy has begun to sweat. Curt wants to know if we can get an ice cream afterward.

"I'm in the lead now," Roy muses.

"Only by five points," Curt reminds him.

"Well, you only have four tiles left. I have five…hmmm."

Seemingly worried that we might be able to score on the bottom row with two triple word scores up for grabs, Roy lays out his tiles in dramatic fashion.

T-H-E-N. With the 'H' on a double letter score.

It doesn't do much for his score, but then the points aren't really the point.

"Ten." Roy wags his finger at the paper for Curt to write it down. "And I've blocked you from getting any last-minute touchdowns."

I look at our remaining tiles. Two "As," an "S," and an "I." It's going to be impossible to break Roy's fifteen-point lead with a bunch of one-point words.

"Very clever," Curt says, stroking his little chin. "Unfortunately, it wasn't clever enough."

Curt uses the last of our tiles to spell out the word "asthenia." The first tile is on one triple word score, as is the last.

"That's nine points for the word, times nine for the two triple word scores, which brings us to a total of eighty-one points. Plus, the value of your one remaining tile, which is…" Curt looks up to Roy for the value of the last tile on his rack.

"I think you're making that word up," Roy sneers. "It was a good try. But I'm not falling for that, son."

Since Curt is more than capable of fighting his own intellectual battles, I simply pick up the dictionary.

"First of all, I asked you to refrain from insinuating that you and I come from the same genetic source," Curt lectures. "Second, asthenia is a word. Merriam-Webster defines it as the 'lack or loss of strength' or 'debility.' Feel free to look it up."

Before Roy has a chance to take a swing at my grandson, I hand him the dictionary, my finger pointed to the word and the verbatim definition Curt just delivered. Roy tilts his head back to see the word more clearly, and then we watch as his face turns the color of a boiled lobster.

"Why you! This is cheating! You're both dirty, stinking cheats!"

110

Roy starts screaming as he leaps up from his chair and launches the Scrabble board into the air. Tiles scatter around us. One lands in the water glass of the woman at the table next to us.

"I demand a redo," Roy shouts. "They played two-on-one. They had an advantage! Referee? I need a referee over here."

I turn to Curt. "What do you say we get you some ice cream?"

"Yes, please. He's being a very sore loser. It's embarrassing."

Roy seems to have overheard Curt, because he starts screaming some more. George Myrtle has to come over and restrain the former football star, while Curt and I slip out of the clubhouse game room.

As we walk out into the heat and sunshine, listening to the crack of clubs on golf balls from the driving range, I can't help but wonder if Roy took it just as badly when Carlotta beat him out, repeatedly, for Scrabble champion of Egret's Loft.

And what he might have been willing to do to win.

CHAPTER TWENTY

"I'm not surprised. Rob isn't the kind of guy who takes defeat well."

"You mean Roy?"

"Are you sure about that?" Gina scratches her forehead.

"Yes. It's Roy. 'Raging Roy' Everhard. You can check the Google," I tell her.

"Are you sure it's not just 'Google'?"

"Oh shoot, you're right. My daughter said the same thing. But you should have been there! I've never seen anything like it in my life! He was so…so angry!"

"Did you read anything about him?"

I shake my head. "That felt too much like spying on my neighbor!"

"You're more comfortable gossiping?" Gina asks.

"I suppose that's more the natural order of things, right?"

We're sitting on the back porch of Gina's house drinking mint juleps. It's nice to relax after a busy day of golf and board games, but my head is already feeling a little fuzzy and I've only had a few sips.

Ritchie and Curt are with Leon in the garage. Gina said I could bring them over for dinner, as well, seeing as how they were in town. We hadn't been in the house longer than five minutes when Leon mentioned his model train set. Curt insisted on inspecting it immediately.

"So," I prompt her, "what can you tell me?"

"Back in the day, Rob was the golden boy. Star quarterback of his high school football team, full scholarship to the University of Texas and, from there, straight into the pros. He played more Super Bowls than Terry Bradshaw."

"So, he had a good run. That doesn't explain why he's such a sore loser now. I mean, you can't play professional sports forever. Too hard on the knees."

"And the hands. Arthritis is a killer."

I nod my head in agreement.

"But back to Rob—"

"Roy."

"That's the one. Anyway, everyone was telling him it was time to pack it in. But instead of retiring, he signed on with some team in the Midwest. Even got them to the Super Bowl for the first time ever."

"So, he proved all his critics wrong." I'm still confused. "How does that explain why he yelled at a six-year-old for beating him at Scrabble?"

"I haven't finished yet, hun. Have some patience!"

"A New Yorker is telling *me* to have patience?" I smile.

"Do as I say, not as I do." She smiles back and raises her glass. "Anyhow, it's the day of the big game. Rob's doctors told him his knee was about to go, that he needed to have surgery right away. But he played anyway and gave the other team a real run for their money. The game was tied with two minutes left in the game. Rob caught the ball within ten yards of the end zone. The other team had no one to stop him, so he ran. But less than five feet from a game-winning touchdown, his knee gave out. He crumpled on the field like one of those inflatable advertising puppets after someone cut the air off."

"Oh no, he must have felt awful. Did his team win?"

"Nope. The other team won by two points. He lost the Super Bowl, and he never lived it down. I think that's the reason he really hates to lose. I mean, *really* hates it. My three-year-old granddaughter doesn't have tantrums as bad as his."

As I take a sip of my mint julep, I think about what it all means. "Carlota was the resident Scrabble champion, so she must have beaten him at some point. Do you think that would have made him mad enough to kill her?"

"Anything is possible, I suppose," Gina concedes. "But I'd put my money on Selma. Especially after what you said about her son dying in the big house."

"You mean Selena. It's true. She had motive. Plus, neither her husband nor her son seemed to be too troubled about committing murder. And let's not forget her colored caftans!"

"You and those dang caftans!"

"Well, it makes sense *now*, doesn't it? She started wearing black after her son died. She's been here awhile, right? What do you know about her?"

Gina takes a sip of her drink and contemplates. "Not much. She moved in four years ago. Paid for her place *in cash*. But no one has any clue where the money came from or what she did before she moved here. Honestly, everyone was too afraid to ask."

"Doesn't she have any friends here?" I ask.

"Friends? Hardly. She barely says a word to anyone."

"Carlota mentioned that Selena talked to her gardeners. Maybe they know something?"

"Do you speak Spanish?"

"No, why?"

"Then good luck having a conversation with the gardeners. They only speak Spanish. Which, come to think of it, might be why Selena talked to them so much."

"Maybe," I add, getting excited, "she doesn't say much to other people because her English isn't very good!"

"Great! Does that help us figure out whether she killed Carlota?"

"No," I admit. "It just seems like a lot of this is conjecture. We're assuming she's the woman in the photo, but we don't know for sure. I mean, it might not even be her!"

"We still have some other suspects. Who else could it be?"

"Well," I consider. "According to Jinny, Helen threatened Carlota right before she died. And it sounds like Carlota would have made life pretty tough for Stan if she canceled his Fridge Friend contract. So, there are two other possibilities."

"Not to mention Astrid Roosevelt," Gina adds. "Oh, did I tell you what Leon told me about her?"

"No, you most certainly did not! What did he say?"

"He said Carlota found out that Astrid asked our golf pro to design a course for Shady Palms!"

"Wait, you're saying that Astrid was trying to steal Dom Skellig away from Egret's Loft to design a golf course for Shady Palms? And Carlota found out about it?"

Gina stares straight at me. "That is literally what I just said."

"Sorry, I just wanted to make sure I was clear," I tell her. "Between my medication and the strength of your cocktails, things are starting to get a little muddy."

"We'll get some food into you in a minute. I just want to wrap this up before we join the others," Gina whispers in a voice that's definitely not a whisper. "Leon doesn't want me involved in any of this."

"My kids are the same. Ritchie will be very upset if he hears us chatting about suspects. He just wants me here playing bocce ball and doing water aerobics."

"*Pff*, as if that's all we're good for," she huffs. "We should add Astrid and Dom to the list, then?"

"I guess that depends on what Carlota did when she found out. Did Leon say how she reacted to the news?"

"He said she was livid! Wanted to fire Dom on the spot. As for Astrid, let's say legal options were discussed. And some not so legal ones."

"Then, yes, I agree, we should add their names to the list! Which brings us to five."

"What should we do next?" Gina asks. "Should we confront them, one at a time?"

"What I need to do next is eat something." I feel my head swimming. "How much bourbon did you put in these juleps anyway?"

"Enough."

"Yeah, enough to get me tipsy! That's for sure."

"Alright, you big lightweight. Let's round up the boys and get some food on the table."

Before either of us have time to stand up, Gina reaches her hand across the patio table and puts her hand on top of mine. "No talk about any of this at dinner, right? Leon just had that surgery; I don't want him stressing about anything else."

"Mum's the word." I raise my forefinger to my lips. Or try to. It lands on the tip of my nose.

"Right." Gina turns her head and assesses me out the sides of her eyes. "One more thing before we head in, did you know Holly's raising holy heck with the board about Harvey nearly running over her dog with his car?"

"You mean Helen and Harold! It doesn't surprise me. She looked pretty mad when we saw her in the street afterward. I would *not* want to be Harold right now."

"Evidently, neither does he. No one's seen him around since it happened."

I want to say Harold is worried for nothing, that Helen will calm down, and everything will be fine. But there's no denying the woman has a temper.

Not to mention, according to our calculations, she has a one in five chance of being a murderer.

116

CHAPTER TWENTY-ONE

Sleeping, I have learned, is a luxury of the young.

The older you get, the more you find yourself waking up in the middle of the night. You need to use the toilet. Your hip hurts from sleeping on your side. Sometimes, you wake up just to reassure yourself you're still alive.

This morning, it's none of those things that pulls me, reluctantly, from my bed. This morning, I wake to the scent of something burning. Something that smells like nuts, with a hint of caramel—like coffee.

Wandering out into the kitchen, I see the coffee maker has been hard at work as I slept.

My phone, which I left on the counter last night, buzzes.

Good morning, Grandmother. Your coffee is ready.

I look around for Curt, half expecting him to jump out from behind the counter to surprise me with his unexpected thoughtfulness. But I could swear I hear him, still snoring in the small guest bedroom.

"Do I smell coffee?" Ritchie says, rubbing his eyes as he emerges from the larger guest room next to the master.

"You do. Your son made it."

Ritchie looks confused. "Is he awake? You don't usually see that kid before noon when he doesn't have school."

I show Ritchie the text message and he laughs.

"He must have programmed your coffee maker when he was fixing the fridge. My boy loves to show off."

"Do you want some?"

"Yes, please," he says as his phone alerts him that he has a new message. "I have a bunch of work emails to respond to.

Questions about whether certain brain tumors are operable. How did you sleep?"

"Not that well, actually," I admit. "I kept hearing noises. I'd swear there was a car drag racing up and down the street."

"Either it happened, or we had the same shared fantasy, because I heard it too."

"Really?"

"No."

"What?"

"Yes, I really heard it! Why else would I have said I did?"

"Oh." I glare at him. "I'd forgotten how charming your sarcasm can be."

"That's me. All charm." He smiles. "So, are you going to pour me some coffee now or do you want to wait until it gets cold?"

"I'm not sure I can handle this much charm at eight o'clock in the morning."

Coffee poured, I hand Ritchie a mug and keep one for myself. Ritchie's phone chirps again. While he goes through his messages, I sip quietly and look out the window at another sunny winter day in Florida.

"You're very quiet," Ritchie says, glancing up from his iPhone.

"You always tell me you hate being interrupted while you're working," I remind him. "And I'm just thinking about that car last night. It sounded a bit like Harold's panini."

"He drives a sandwich?"

"Oh no, that's not it. Carlota told me what kind of car it was, but I can't remember. It's some fancy Italian thing. The motor on it is really loud."

"You mean the engine?" Ritchie asks. "Or is it an electric car?"

"I don't know. I just know it's loud and he drives fast. Where was he going so late last night?"

"Why do you care? Was he breaking some kind of Egret's Loft curfew? Do all residents have to be tucked up in bed by ten o'clock?"

"Of course not! Though, to be fair, most are. No, it was just something Gina said. No one's seen Harold since he almost ran over Helen's dog. But then he's driving around in the middle of the night?"

"I'm sure it's nothing to concern yourself with." Ritchie shrugs. "The only thing you need to be worried about is what exciting activities you have scheduled for today! What's the plan?"

I walk back into the kitchen to look at the schedule on the fridge door. Ritchie's phone buzzes again.

"Well, if you have work, and Curt will be sleeping for a while, I might go down to the driving range and do some more practicing for the scramble. I have a lesson scheduled to start in an hour. Maybe we could all do lunch later?"

"That sounds great. I can get some of my work done in the meantime," he says.

As I rejoin him in the living room, he gets another text message.

"Do you always get so many messages?" I ask. "It seems pretty early to be getting so many."

"Oh no, these aren't texts. Well, they are, but not the kind you're thinking of."

"I see," I tell him.

"Do you really?"

"Not at all."

"Ha! Nice one. It's part of the security system. See that little camera on the island between the kitchen and the living room?"

My eyes follow the direction his finger is pointed. I spot what looks like a one-eyed robot. It reminds me of one of the cartoons Tory and Emmy like to watch.

"Yeah, I see it. But why is it sending messages to your phone?"

"It's motion-activated. Every time someone walks through the room, I get a text with a link to watch the video. Curt and I set it up last night, while you were getting ready to go to Gina's for dinner! Isn't it great?"

"Oh no! You need to take that down immediately!"

"Relax, lady. You'll get used to it!"

"What I won't get used to is my children spying on me! Eliza's already watching me from that camera on top of the cupboard. I don't need you getting a text every time I walk across the room. This is ridiculous! I'm still your mother!"

"And we want you to continue being our mother. Which means you need to stay alive! We'll take them down, I promise. As soon as this is all over," he assures me.

"All of what is over? Nothing has happened to me. Just my neighbor!"

"Yeah, but from what I hear, you can't keep your nose out of it. We just want to make sure you're safe until the police take Selena Castillo into custody."

My mouth opens, prepared to argue that Selena might not be the killer. But if I do that, my kids will know how involved I am and might set up even more cameras in the house. Instead, I ask, "Did you speak to Eliza last night? Has she heard anything about when the police plan to charge Selena?"

"Yeah, I called her after you went to bed. Apparently, that cop from Colombia took Carlota's body back to Bogotá. Now, he's trying to get confirmation that Selena is the woman in the photo. Without proof of who she is, they've got nothing."

I nod. "True. If they took her in for questioning now, they'd only be tipping their hand. She'd be out and covering her tracks while they tried to build the case."

"See, lady. You *did* learn something from all those shop talk dinners with Dad!"

"For your information, your father was talking about his cases with me long before you were born. And he always said I was a great help to him."

120

"Yeah, yeah. I'm sure you were." He waves me off. "Don't you need to start getting ready for golf practice?"

"I guess I should."

I walk past the camera to get to my bedroom and hear Ritchie's phone buzzing again. When I pause to glare at him, he just chuckles.

But I'll be having the last laugh. Ritchie has been trying to push me out the door to get me to do activities. Little does he know, he's shoving me right back into the middle of things.

My golf lesson is with Dom. And he's just been added to the list of possible suspects!

CHAPTER TWENTY-TWO

I could tell something was wrong by the length of Dom Skellig's shorts.

Walking up to the driving range for my golf lesson, I spot Dom wearing shorts almost down to his knees and a loose-fitting polo shirt. A baseball cap covers his hair, and his eyes are obscured by sunglasses. The only parts of him I can see are his shins, his forearms, and his mustache.

"Good morning, Madeline! Are you ready to practice your swing?" He asks in a voice laced with a desperate kind of happiness.

"I suppose so." His forced merriment only heightens my nerves. "After our last lesson, I was wondering if you would even allow me on the driving range. It really was an accident, despite what Helen might think."

"Oh, you don't have to worry about that," Dom assures me. "Everyone clips the ball wrong once in a while. In fact, I even saw Tiger Woods do it once when we were on the PGA Tour."

"Tiger Woods ruptured a woman's implant?"

"Heck no! Nothing like that!" He catches himself when he sees the look on my face. "I mean, his ball just went into the rough."

"So, you haven't actually seen anyone injure another person with a bad swing?"

Dom suddenly looks nervous. "Well, no. Not exactly. But it was just an unlucky shot."

"Unlucky?"

"Really, it's our fault. The roof is a hazard. If it hadn't been there, your ball wouldn't have had anything to ricochet off." He's speaking so quickly, it's hard to catch all his words. "It's not your fault. I'll have it taken down. Please don't complain about me to the board!"

"Why on earth would I do a thing like that?" I ask him. "Are you alright, Dom? You seem a bit out of sorts today."

He stares across the turquoise waters of the lake. On the other side, a golf cart pulls up to the fifth hole, unloading golfers eager to tee up their next shots.

"I'm just a little on edge. I'll be fine. Shall we practice your stance?" His mouth turns up in a smile, but his mustache still seems sad.

"Okay," I say, deciding not to push him. "I was told to put the ball by my left foot, then take a few steps backward from it, like this." I demonstrate.

"Perfect! Only, why don't you take three large steps toward the lake and set up the shot again?"

I look down at the square mat of AstroTurf beneath my feet. "But isn't this where I'm supposed to hit from to accurately measure the distance of my shot?"

"It is. But we're not going for distance just yet. Let's just practice your form for now," he says, one hand on my back, gently pushing me out into the sunlight. "And until we take that roof down it's probably best to play it safe."

My cheeks flame as the warmth of the sun burns my scalp. "Oh dear," I exclaim. "I didn't bring my hat! I thought I'd be in the shade. Let me just pop home and grab one."

"No need you can borrow mine," Dom offers, removing his fading PGA Tour hat and holding it in my direction. The hair underneath looks unwashed and oily.

"I couldn't, really," I protest. "It'll only take me a few minutes to swing by the house."

"Don't be silly, just take the hat."

"Are you even wearing sunblock?"

"Never use the stuff. Tan looks good on me."

"Oh my! Your dermatologist might have something to say about that! Have you been checked for skin cancer?"

"Cancer doesn't run in my family. I'm fine," he says, now shaking the hat at me.

"Genetics aren't the only factor in—"

"Just take the hat!" Dom demands.

He's making a mistake not worrying about his skin. His face is already red, and he's only been in the sun for a few seconds. But I keep that to myself.

"Alright," he says once I've put on his hat. "You want to hit the ball right in the middle. If it goes to the right, that's called a slice. If it goes to the left, that's called a hook."

"And if it goes straight?" I ask.

"Let's call that a miracle," he says under his breath. "Alright, show me what you've got."

Already in position, with the ball several steps in front of my left foot I take a few practice swings with the driver. Right as I am pulling the club back to take my shot, the edge of the driver catches the ball and launches it backward. Holding my breath, I watch as the ball collides with the pole holding up the roof and sails sideways into Dom, clipping him in the ear as he's trying to duck.

"Dom! Are you alright?"

A scream forms on his face, but his throat seems to swallow it down. He sinks to his knees and puts his head in his hands.

Not again!

"I'm so sorry, Dom! Should I call a doctor?"

"No!" Dom looks up pleadingly. "Don't call anyone. It was just a little accident. Give me a minute. I'll be fine."

"Are you sure? I really think I should call someone!"

"Please don't. I really can't afford to draw any more attention to myself right now."

"What do you mean…more attention?"

He takes a deep breath, his hand still clasping his injured ear. "I might as well tell you. This might be our last lesson together anyway."

I kneel down beside him. "Don't give up on me, Dom! I can get better!"

"That's not what I mean. Half the board already wants to fire me."

"But why would they do that?"

"Because they think I betrayed Egret's Loft," he admits.

I hazard a guess. "By designing a golf course for Shady Palms?"

"How do you know that?" He moans. "Oh no! Does everyone know?"

I want to make him feel better. "Maybe not everyone…"

"It's been a lifelong dream of mine to design a golf course," he laments. "It's every pro golfer's dream, really, and mine was about to come true. All I had to do was design it behind the backs of the people paying my salary."

"Well, I think you know that wasn't very nice," I point out.

"There's no *nice* in golf!"

"But I don't understand," I say. "Astrid asked you to design her course, but how would you have been able to take credit for it if you were working here?"

"Astrid recruited me to work at Shady Palms once the course was built. It was part of the contract she drew up. No one was supposed to know until it was a done deal!"

"But Carlota found out somehow and threatened to fire you?" I ask.

"I don't know how she found out, but yes. As soon as she confronted me, I went to Astrid and asked if I could start working at Shady Palms right away. But she told me she didn't have the budget for a new golf pro until the course was finished."

"So, you gave up on the idea of designing a golf course and decided to stay here?"

Dom looks away. "Not exactly."

"What do you mean?"

"Carlota gave me a week to *think through my options,* as she said."

"When would the week have been up?"

"Today," he groans, still not looking at me.

"So, if Carlota hadn't been killed, you would have had to make a choice between your dream and your livelihood? Now that she's dead, you don't have to."

His mustache twitches, like a deer's tail when the deer knows it's being hunted. "Wait, you're not implying I had anything to do with her death, are you?"

"Did you?"

"No!" He practically shouts.

"Would you tell me if you did?"

"But I didn't!"

"That's what murderers always say before they know they're caught."

"I'm not a murderer! I'm not going to get caught!"

"Are you saying you're not a murderer, or you don't plan on getting caught?"

Dom puts his head in his hands. "My head hurts."

"Yes, I am very sorry about that. Are you sure I can't call you a doctor?"

"No. I have more lessons after yours, and I can't cancel them. Not now," he laments.

"Your plan is to keep working here as long as you can? What about the golf course at Shady Palms?"

"That's over." He sighs deeply.

"Why? There's no one standing in your way anymore."

"Astrid called me this morning and told me the deal was off. She's looking to take over Carlota's shares in Egret's Loft and said she didn't want to work with a backstabber."

It strikes me as beyond hypocritical that the woman who backstabbed Carlota by trying to steal away her golf pro, would then accuse the pro she lured away of being a backstabber. She has no right to be pointing any fingers at Dom. But, right now, I need to focus on how all these developments will impact him. "Just to make sure I'm clear, you will not be designing a golf course at Shady Palms and, if Astrid gets a majority share here, you won't have a job at Egret's Loft either?"

He nods.

126

I put my hand on his shoulder. "Poor thing, you *are* having a rough day."

"Nothing like this would ever happen to Tiger Woods," he says, clearly feeling sorry for himself.

Dom definitely had a motive for wanting Carlota dead, but if he did kill her, his plot completely backfired. Looking down at his shorts, which, for once, are loose enough to leave everything to the imagination, I can't help feeling sorry for the guy.

"How about we quit my lesson early so you have some time to compose yourself?" I offer.

"Actually, I prefer to work. Having time to think will only make things worse."

"If you're sure. I'll tee up for another swing."

He's suddenly on his feet. "Haven't we already established I'm having a rough day? No, we're moving your lesson off the driving range!"

"To where?"

He smiles, the first real one of the morning. "Why don't I teach you how to putt?"

CHAPTER TWENTY-THREE

"Grandmother, do you think there are alligators in the lake?"

Curt and I are strolling along the lake path behind my house. More of a large pond, really, it sits at the center of the circular street. Every street in Egret's Loft has one, complete with a water fountain in the center and about a dozen ornamental ducks all happily splashing away.

"I don't think you have anything to worry about, sweetie. This is a man-made lake; how would they even get in here?" I ask, refraining from mentioning the curious incident in Marjorie Higginbottom's kitchen.

"Easily enough. They're crocodilian reptiles known to inhabit tropical freshwater wetlands, like the rivers around Egret's Loft. While they normally haven't been inclined to kill humans, encroachments on their habitat have led to an increased frequency of attacks."

"Is that so, sweetie?"

In truth, I'm only half listening. The earlier conversation with Dom still dominates my thoughts. The key to finding killers, Clint taught me after he became the youngest detective ever in his squad, was finding out who stood to benefit the most from that person's death. Selena may have killed for revenge, Helen to keep a secret, and Stan to keep from going bankrupt, but Astrid seems to be the one poised to benefit most from Carlota's passing.

"Grandmother, are you listening to me?"

"Of course, I am, sweetie!" A little white lie.

"Well, you didn't react when I told you there have been 257 attacks on humans in Florida since 1948. Granted, only twenty-three of them were fatal, but given my prepubescent musculature, I don't think general statistics would be an accurate barometer of my survivability."

"Oh, sweetie, don't you worry. It's a big state and that's a long time. What is that? One person killed every four years?"

"Actually, every 3.26 years."

"I stand corrected," I tell him, trying not to smile. "What made you even think about any of this anyway?"

He shrugs. "Nothing in particular. I like to be prepared whenever I go somewhere new. It only makes sense to investigate potential dangers inherent in new environments."

"That's a rather pessimistic way of looking at new experiences, isn't it?" I ask.

"Not at all, I can be more optimistic about staying alive if I've adequately prepared for any potential threats," Curt assures me. "You're just lucky that the most recent case of malaria in the state was in 2012, otherwise you never would have gotten me down here!"

I ruffle the top of his head with my hand. "That is very lucky for me then!"

"Grandmother?"

"Yes, sweetie?"

"Why is that man washing his pants while he's still wearing them?"

I follow Curt's pointed index finger and spot Victor in his back garden. As Curt indicated, Victor has the garden hose on full blast aimed at his pants. His thighs are locked in a bracing position as the water molds the fabric to his skin.

"I'm sure there is some sort of logical explanation," I tell Curt. "Should we go ask?"

"No!" Panic flares in his eyes. "What if he has dementia? He could be unpredictable and dangerous!"

"Victor? No, he doesn't have dementia. We're perfectly safe with him, I promise." I take Curt's small hand in mine. "Maybe he had a little accident. Come on, let's go find out."

Victor doesn't notice us approaching until we're standing a few feet away.

"Victor, is everything alright?" I ask.

"Madeline, hello!" He looks up at us, then back down at his soggy trousers. "This is a bit embarrassing. You must be wondering why I'm showering outside with all my clothes on!"

"When I was younger, I used to wet my bed," Curt offers up. "Urinary incontinence is quite common in the young and the elderly. It's nothing to be embarrassed about."

"Curt!" I exclaim. "I know you didn't mean to be, but that was very rude!"

"Why?" He asks. "It's true."

Before I can admonish my grandson any further, Victor starts laughing. "What's your name, young man?"

"Curt James Delarouse, but you may call me Curt."

"It's a pleasure to meet you, Curt. You can call me Victor." He holds out his hand, which Curt declines to shake.

"Germs," I whisper.

Victor nods, still smiling. "I'm afraid you caught me in an unusual situation, Curt. You see I picked up some weed killer to try and get at the pesky bracken that's trying to strangle my late wife's prized roses. But I had some trouble with the childproof seal they put on the darn bottle and spilled some of it all over my pants."

"Were you experiencing mild skin irritation as a result?" Curt asks.

"As a matter of fact, I was," Victor confirms. "I also didn't want the stuff to ruin my pants. Since the hose was right there, I thought I'd take care of both problems at once."

Curt nods his approval. "That was wise, though it is recommended to use soap in addition to water when the dermis is exposed to products containing glyphosate."

"Aren't you a smart young man?" Victor sends a wink in my direction.

"Yes. I have an IQ of 185. My daddies had me tested."

"Is that so? I suppose someone as brilliant as you would have no trouble finding the chocolate bars on the second shelf in my pantry then, would you?"

"That hardly seems like a mental challenge when you just told me where to find them," Curt says.

I squeeze Curt's hand, not hard, but enough to make him glance up at me. "Sweetie, you're being offered candy. All you have to say is thank you. Now off with you! Go grab a chocolate bar. But only one," I call as he makes his way toward the patio door, "we're having lunch with your father soon."

"He seems rather precocious," Victor says once Curt is out of earshot.

"Yes, he is. He's also a very sweet boy, he just likes to show off what he knows. He doesn't mean any offense by it."

"None taken," he assures me.

My feet begin to sink into the wet soil, making me glance down. On the way, my eyes linger on Victor's pants, clinging to the curves of his lower body. He sees me and we both blush.

"So how was—"

"I should probably—"

We both speak at the same time, then stop when we realize we're interrupting each other.

"Please, go ahead," Victor says. "You were saying?"

"I was just going to ask how your meeting with Astrid went yesterday."

He sighs. "It was nothing we hadn't expected. Astrid has wanted to be on the board since she and Carlota had a falling out years back. Carlota's son will probably want to sell her shares, so it's good to have some capital on offer to buy him out. But the board would have to make a unanimous decision." He makes that sound like an unlikely outcome.

"Is there anyone on the board who wouldn't want Astrid to have a majority stake in Egret's Loft?"

Victor raises his hands, as if in surrender. "I don't like to gossip, but it's not much of a secret that certain members of the board don't particularly like Astrid."

"Really? Why not?"

"She's had a habit of trying to sabotage the competition, if you know what I mean."

"Like trying to steal Dom away to build a golf course at Shady Palms?" I ask.

"How do you know about that?"

I tilt my head and bat my eyelashes. "I have my ways."

"I'm quite sure you do. Perhaps you'd like to discuss them more over dinner tonight? Here at my place, six o'clock?"

I wanted to ask him more about Astrid, like if he thought she could have killed Carlota. But the moment has passed, and he's looking at me expectantly.

"I'd love to. Really. But my son and grandson are in town for a few days. They're probably expecting me to have dinner with them. Can I get a rain check?"

"Of course. If you change your mind, the invitation still stands. You're welcome to bring them along. My son hasn't done me the service of giving me a grandchild yet. I could use some practice in having a little one around."

Just then, Curt comes strolling out of the house to rejoin us. He smells like soap. He would have washed his hands before and after eating the chocolate.

"Curt, what do you say to Mr. Collins?"

"Thank you for the candy bar, Victor. That is what you said I should call you, correct?"

"Yep, but only for you. All the other boys your age have to call me Mr. Collins."

Before Curt can retort, the roar of screeching tires echoes from the street. Through the hedges, I can just make out the lines of Harold's fancy Italian car parked with its front tire perched on the sidewalk.

"Is that Harold?"

"Sounds like it," Victor says.

"I thought I heard him driving around last night, but no one has seen him since he almost ran over Helen's dog. Doesn't he live nearby?"

132

"Yeah. He's about five houses down on the other side of the street."

"What do you think he's doing here?" I ask.

"Probably visiting Stan next door," Victor guesses while trying to peel wet fabric away from his thighs. "They've been friends for years."

"Oh, I thought Stan's friends were mostly on the computer," I say, then realize how that sounded. "I didn't mean that in a bad way. He just seems to spend so much time on the internet!"

"There's nothing wrong in saying things that are true," Victor assures me. "Isn't that right, young man?"

Curt nods. "Truth is generally the least complicated option. And since we're advocating honesty, I'm hungry, and I want the two of you to stop talking so we can meet my daddy for lunch."

Caught somewhere between amusement and embarrassment, I look apologetically at Victor. His lips are shaking from the effort to hold in his laughter.

I hear Harold's car door slam shut out on the street.

"Alright, sweetie, we'll head back to the house now to pick up your father," I say, reclaiming Curt's hand. "Victor, thank you for your hospitality."

"My pleasure."

We're halfway home when I hear Harold's car roar to life and speed down the street and out of the complex.

CHAPTER TWENTY-FOUR

"Daddy, can we go now? We had a deal, and I upheld my end of the bargain," Curt begs from the back seat of Ritchie's rental car.

In exchange for not using the words *elderly*, *incontinent* or *dying* in front of anyone who approached us during lunch at the clubhouse, Ritchie had promised Curt they would go to the store and buy a case of Yoo-hoos.

"He was very well behaved," I argue on my grandson's behalf, even if it was awkward watching him sanitize himself after all the active elders wanted to shake his hand or pinch his cheeks.

"You're right, buddy. A deal is a deal," Ritchie reluctantly agrees. "Lady, do you want me to drop you off at the house first?"

He must have noticed that I was moving slower when we left the restaurant. It's been an active week, and my bones are starting to feel it. Even a fifteen-minute nap while they're at the store sounds like heaven.

"That would be great, but you can just drop me off at the corner here. There's no need to take me all the way to the door."

"Are you sure? It'll only take a second."

"No, this is fine. You guys go get your Yoo-hoos. Take your time, and I'll see you when you get back."

"Alright, lady. Watch the curb as you're getting out. See you soon!"

I shut the car door behind me, and they drive off.

After having so many visitors since I moved in, the silence soothes my aching brain.

When he was alive, Clint and I often sat together, saying nothing. We would read or daydream. Together, but separate. There was a certain comfortable companionship about it. After he died, everyone back home in DC wanted to talk. I think they were afraid I'd retreat into myself, that silence was somehow more pitiable when you were enjoying it alone. Maybe they were right.

To get to my house, I have to pass by Carlota's. The crime scene tape has long since been removed from her front door, and there's a stack of mail half sticking out of the letterbox. A riot of red hibiscus flowers lends a false sense of vibrancy to the house, like a tasteless joke.

Before turning into my driveway, I glance across the street and see Phyllis standing in her window. At least, I think I do. The image fades so quickly into the shadows I can't be certain it wasn't just a trick of the light.

Relieved to have a few minutes to myself, I walk up to my front door and gasp in horror.

White feathers have been strewn across the welcome mat. Yellow feet attached to thin black legs claw lifelessly at the wooden door and an orange beak rests on the driveway paving stones. Someone left a dead egret on my doorstep.

My heart beats faster in my chest. There's no blood or any other obvious sign of injury. Is someone trying to threaten me?

Stepping carefully around the poor creature, I enter the house and try to pull up the security footage from the cameras Ritchie and Curt installed. They put an app on my phone, so I can see what's happening on the cameras in real time, but I don't know how to access any stored video.

Pushing one button prompts the app to ask me if I want to delete all saved video. Hands trembling, I quickly hit "No" and exit the app.

Only minutes ago, I was praying Ritchie would take his time at the store. Now I want him back as soon as possible. I consider calling him before realizing that the security cameras might not be the only way to find out who left the dead bird. Phyllis was at her window. Maybe she saw something.

After leaving through the rollup garage door, to avoid further injuring the poor animal, I walk briskly across the street to knock on my neighbor's door. Seeing the curtains flutter ever so slightly, I start off with a gentle tap. When there's no response I tap again, this time calling out "hello" at the same time.

No answer.

"Phyllis? It's Madeline, from across the street. I really need to ask you something."

Becoming frustrated, I knock harder on the door, all to no avail.

"Madeline?" I whirl around, startled, when I hear the voice behind me. Jinny and George stare at me from their golf cart, paused in the road. "What are you doing?"

Frazzled, I try to compose myself before they look across the street and spot the carnage at my front door. "I wanted to drop by and introduce myself to Phyllis," I say, approaching their cart. "Have you seen her around by any chance?"

"Phyllis doesn't like visitors very much, don't you know. In fact, I haven't seen anyone come to visit her in the entire time we've been here. Why, when we first moved in, I thought it was the most curious thing that you would see her in the windows one moment and then she would…poof…disappear, and you might not catch sight of her for another week. Kind of like Harold, eh? After the incident with Helen's dog, no one has seen hide nor hair of him. Though I don't think that's the issue with Phyllis. I've never heard of her almost running over anyone's pets. Have you heard anything like that, George?"

"No, dear," George says, smiling pleasantly from the driver's seat.

"No, I haven't either, and you'd think we would know if something like that had happencd. I think Phyllis just likes being on her own, and there's no one can say a bad thing about wanting a little bit of peace at her age. Harold's the same age, of course. Maybe even a few years older, but he has a different reason for not wanting to socialize at the moment. Why, if he hadn't nearly run over Mitsy, he'd be playing cards with Stan down at the clubhouse or driving his car up and down the street. No, that's a whole different story altogether."

"You didn't happen to see anyone at my house in the past two hours or so, have you?" I ask. Jinny seems to have her finger on the faint pulse of the community. She might have heard or seen something.

"Now let me think about this for a minute, because sometimes I get my days confused a bit, don't you know. What's that, George? I have a perfect memory, you say? Well, you are just the sweetest thing. But there are times I do question. Like when I thought your second cousin's birthday was on the Monday, but it was really on the Sunday, and I missed it. But, as for today, I did see a handsome young man at your house earlier today. With that little grandson of yours from the Scrabble tournament. They went in there, but, come to think of it, you were there, too, so you probably don't need me to tell you who went into your house if you were there with them, now do you?"

Jinny laughs. George smiles on like he's loving life. I just want to get back into my house and call Ritchie to come back from the store.

"This sun is so strong, and I walked out the front door without a hat on again," I say, circling the golf cart and walking backward toward my house. My body should block their view of the dead bird.

"You can borrow mine if you want. I have dozens," Jinny offers. "One can never be too careful with melanoma, don't you know."

"That's what I always say! But I need to pop into the house anyway. You both enjoy your day!"

I'm backed up to the stoop and can feel the egret's beak tickling the back of my calf. If they wait until I'm in the house to drive away, we could be standing here a while. Luckily, George looks down at his watch then up at Jinny.

"What's that, George? We're going to be late? Oh, sorry, Madeline, we really must run, but we'll have to schedule that dinner sometime soon, eh?" Her voice fades away as George drives, five miles an hour, up the street and around the corner.

I let out a heavy sigh, lowering the garage door after using it to get back into the house. Pulling the cell phone out of my pocket, I scroll through my recent contacts for Ritchie's number. As I sink into the living room chair, I hear a noise from the other side of the room.

There's a thin, reed-like woman sitting on my sofa. She has tan knee-high stockings, one of which has slid down to her ankle. She's wearing a light blue polka dot dress that almost matches the color of her salon-ready hair. But the focal point of her appearance is the Jackie-O sized glasses with Coke bottle lenses that suffocate the rest of her face.

I scream.

"Would you quit that racket already? I'm eighty-eight years old. I couldn't hurt you if I wanted to."

"Phyllis?" I ask, my heart slowly regaining its normal rhythm.

"I ain't no whistling Dixie."

"But why are you in my house?"

"You nearly broke down my door to get into mine!"

"I was knocking! You think it's better to just break in?"

"Please, this place has been like Grand Central Station since you moved in. Why would one more visitor make any bit of difference?" She coughs, and I would swear smoke comes out of her lungs.

"I don't mean to be rude," I say, "and it is nice to finally meet you, but my other visitors were all invited. There is a difference."

"At my age, you don't waste your energy on trivial things like that."

"Trivial things like breaking and entering?"

138

"Look, do you want to know who left the bird or not?" She asks.

That gets my attention. "You saw who did it?"

"You think I walked all the way over here for my health?"

Now that she mentions it, how did she get over here? Jinny, George, and I were all in the street. One of us would have spotted her making her way to my house. I don't imagine she moves too quickly.

But, for the moment, the dead bird takes precedence.

"Who did it?" I ask.

"Roy Everhard. I saw his golf cart pull into your driveway about an hour ago. I think he had a card in his hand. Go check. See if he left a card."

I glance at the front door, then back at her.

"Do you plan on just sitting there and staring at me like an idiot?" She prompts.

With a sigh, I stand up and walk to the front door. Gently maneuvering the feathers, I search for a letter of some sort, but find nothing.

"There's nothing there," I say, walking back into the living room.

The sofa where she had been sitting is now empty.

"Phyllis?"

Phyllis is gone. But how did she leave the house without me seeing her?

I sink down onto the sofa. If it weren't still warm from her body, I might begin to think I'd imagined the whole thing.

CHAPTER TWENTY-FIVE

"You do realize I'm trying to solve a murder involving a person, not a wild animal?" Detective Fletcher asks petulantly.

Ritchie had called the police as soon as he returned with Curt's Yoo-hoos.

After he called Eliza, of course. Based on what I could hear of their conversation, I'm guessing there will be a whole family reunion in my house within the next few hours. If nothing else, moving in next door to someone who was murdered has meant I get a lot more time to spend with my children.

"Isn't it possible there's some kind of link between the two?" Ritchie asks in his most diplomatic, if slightly patronizing, way. "I mean, do you think it's a coincidence that a woman is killed, and her neighbor gets a dead bird tied to her door?"

"And you say Raging Roy Everhard left the bird at your house?" Detective Fletcher seems skeptical.

"Phyllis, the woman across the street, saw him on the property. Not to mention we have video from the home security system! It was definitely him!" I exclaim, perilously close to losing my patience.

We've already shown the detective video of Roy walking up to my door, carrying a live egret. Unfortunately, the bird's beak took out the camera Ritchie had installed in the doorbell, so there was nothing else on the video. We never saw Roy do anything to the bird, but he was clearly the one who brought it.

"What I don't understand is…why?" Detective Fletcher scratches his head. "Raging Roy had no reason to kill Carlota. He's a legend. I just don't think he's good for it."

"It sounds like you're a big fan." Ritchie smiles, trying to build rapport with the detective.

"Huge fan!" Detective Fletcher's face lights up. "I grew up watching him play. Shame about that last game, but in his third Super Bowl, he threw 495 yards, including an 81-yard touchdown pass!"

Ritchie and I look to each other for understanding, but neither of us has a clue what he's talking about.

"I'm sure it must feel like a real home run, meeting someone you respect—" I begin.

"You mean touchdown?" Detective Fletcher interrupts. "Home runs are in baseball."

"Does it matter? It's just a metaphor," I say.

"But you're mixing them. Your metaphors. It's confusing."

"Fine. I'm sure it's great to meet someone you admire," I speak slowly, "but I've heard that after that last Super Bowl, he became quite a sore loser. I even saw it myself with asthenia!"

"Who's Asthenia?" The detective asks, opening his notebook.

"It's not a person. It's a word. A Scrabble word. My grandson used it to win a game, and Roy nearly lost his mind, he was so angry."

"That's a word? It sounds made up." Detective Fletcher sneers.

"It is a word. It's not made up. And Roy nearly blew his top when he lost the game!"

Detective Fletcher clears his throat. "Alright. I'll accept that the thing you said is a real word. But how does Roy losing a game have anything to do with Carlota's death?"

I open my mouth to speak, but Ritchie cuts me off.

"Your skepticism is understandable about the murder," he says. "But we would like to know why Roy brought a bird to my mother's house. Perhaps we can all go over and just ask him a few questions about it?"

"I don't know…" Detective Fletcher hedges.

"I bet he has some really cool memorabilia in his house," Ritchie suggests. "Have you been inside to question him?"

Detective Fletcher tilts his head, considering. "No. We had no real reason to question him before, so we just took his statement outside Carlota's house."

"So, what do you think?" Ritchie urges.

"I suppose it wouldn't do any harm."

I have to turn my head, so the detective doesn't see the exasperation on my face. We're telling him Roy may have threatened me and probably violated several animal protection laws in the process, but Fletcher's only worried about offending his childhood hero.

"Great," Ritchie says, standing up. "Let's go."

Leaving Curt behind with an online practice Mensa admission test, Detective Fletcher, Ritchie, and I walk up the street past Selena's house. Gardeners mill around her front yard, drinking iced tea, their eyes on us as we pass Harold's house next door. Harold's windows are dark, and his driveway sits empty.

Just past Harold's house is Roy's. The man himself is in the driveway, loading clubs onto his golf cart.

"Hidey-ho there, neighbors!" Roy smiles brightly as we approach. The top of his head is shiny and red. "What can I do you for?"

Detective Fletcher takes the lead. "It's nothing to be alarmed about, Mr. Raging Roy, we're just here for a friendly chat about an incident involving a bird left on Mrs. Delarouse's doorstep."

Roy's smile grows wider. "Did you like it?"

My mouth drops open. "No, Mr. Everhard. I'm not overly fond of finding dead birds in front of my house!"

The smile falters. "What's that now?"

"The dead egret you left tied to my door! Were you trying to threaten me?" I demand. "Some kind of bizarre payback for my grandson kicking your behind in Scrabble?"

Detective Fletcher puts a hand on my shoulder. "I need you to calm down, ma'am. This is police business—"

Ritchie takes a step toward us. "Don't tell her to calm down. She has every right to be upset!"

The bickering is abruptly silenced by the sound of Roy's ear-piercing whistle.

"Now that I have your attention," Roy says, wiping the two fingers that had just been in his mouth on his pant leg, "what is all this monkey business about a dead bird?"

Ritchie is the first to speak. "We have surveillance video of you walking up to my mother's house with a bird. When she got home, that bird was dead, and we think you killed it to threaten her."

"Whoa there, son. You've got this all wrong."

"I am not your son," Ritchie spits out. "Please don't call me that."

"You have a little boy? About yay big?" Roy holds his hand roughly three feet off the ground. "Knows lots of grown-up words?"

"Yes, why?"

"No reason. Just I can see the resemblance. You've got yourself a good kid there." Roy winks at Ritchie, then turns to face me. "This is all some sort of misunderstanding. I felt bad about yelling at you and the little fella the other day. I thought I would do something nice to apologize."

"Your apology was a dead bird?" Even Detective Fletcher doesn't understand the logic.

"No, the bird was alive when I left it there! It was a rescue. I found it online and thought it could be like a pet. I'd read that egrets are meant to represent good fortune and prosperity. I was trying to do something nice."

"You thought I would want a bird as tall as my grandson for a pet?" I ask. "Is it even legal to own one?"

Detective Fletcher shrugs. "This is Florida, you can own pretty much anything."

"They're not endangered in any way," Ritchie whispers to me. "Curt says their conservation status is 'least concern.'"

I silence Ritchie with my hand on his shoulder. "How did the poor thing die? Because it was definitely dead when I found it!"

"The rescue people said it might not survive, but I thought they were just covering their butts," Roy defends himself. "It looked healthy enough to me. Which was kind of surprising after an alligator took a chunk out of its wing."

I walk directly in front of Roy and stare up at him. "That was a very thoughtless present, Roy. What if my grandson had stumbled on it before I got home?"

"Actually—" Roy scratches one side of his head, "—*that* little guy probably would have wanted to dissect it to see how it's innards worked."

"Fine. You're probably right," I have to admit. "The point is you showed terrible judgment and you are going to pay for a proper funeral for that beautiful bird. You owe it that much."

"Like with a coffin and everything?" He asks.

"Yes, Roy. And everything," I insist.

Ritchie again leans in, whispering, "Lady, I think we're losing sight of the bigger picture here."

"You know we can hear you, son?" Roy asks.

Ritchie stands up straight. "For the last time, I asked you *not* to call me that."

Roy chuckles. "Alright, alright. No need to get bent out of shape about it."

"Me? Getting bent out of shape?" Ritchie's face flames. "You yelled at my six-year-old son because he beat you in a game! You're the one with the anger management issues, *Roy*. Has that temper ever made you violent?"

"Excuse me?" Roy demands, standing up to his full height, which must be over six and a half feet.

Detective Fletcher chooses to rejoin the conversation. "It's silly really. Not even worth mentioning, if you think about it.

144

These two were just wondering if you might have lost your temper and killed Carlota."

"*What?*" Roy screams.

"I told them, no way would Raging Roy do that." Detective Fletcher does everything but get down on the ground to show his submission. "As a police detective, though, I have to investigate all leads, no matter how ridiculous. Which I just did. So, you're free to go Mr. Roy."

"He didn't even answer the question!" Ritchie argues.

"What question would that be?" Detective Fletcher asks.

"If he killed Carlota!"

Detective Fletcher steps in between Ritchie and Roy. "I think this is all a waste of time. Clearly, Roy didn't mean to kill your bird, and he had nothing to do with Carlota's death."

"Heck no, I didn't! I'd never waste a good golf club on Carlota," Roy fumes, his tone laced with animosity.

So, Roy did have something against Carlota, maybe something more than her beating him at games.

Detective Fletcher, predictably, ignores Roy's last comment.

"Well, Mrs. Delarouse, I think this has all been a big misunderstanding. Why don't you and your son go on home now."

Ritchie takes my arm, and we begin walking away. "Let's go home, lady. Sorry for my behavior back there. I can't believe I let that oaf get to me."

We're almost out of earshot when I hear Detective Fletcher ask Roy for his autograph.

CHAPTER TWENTY-SIX

"I've got to say, I'm with Mom on this one. She needs to solve this murder," Ritchie tells his younger sister.

"Does this place make people completely lose their minds?" Eliza demands. "Both of you, only here a few days, and all of a sudden, you're ready to take on the widow of a notorious drug dealer and an ex-quarterback six times your size?"

"I'm a lot younger and faster than him," Ritchie defends himself.

"Right, and I'm sure when he punches you with a fist the size of your head, that will come as a real comfort!"

My children have been bickering since Eliza arrived over an hour ago. For the most part, I've left them to it while I plied Tory and Emmy with Reese's Peanut Butter Cups and offered the wrappers to Curt so he could do a complete health assessment of the ingredients.

"Look," Ritchie implores, "you haven't seen this detective in action. He's a buffoon. We could all be dead before he figures out who killed Carlota!"

"Ummm, I *have* seen him in action. Have you forgotten I was here when Mom identified the wife of Alvaro Castillo?"

"Yeah? How's that coming along? Because it's been two days, and you still can't prove the woman who lives down the street is the woman in the photograph."

"These things take time," Eliza moans. "And don't you dare say '*it's not like it's brain surgery*!' Yes, we all know you're a brain surgeon! Get over yourself!"

"I hate to interrupt." I do anyway. "But it's after ten o'clock. Shouldn't the kids be going to bed?"

Curt looks up from his candy wrapper. "What? It's past my bedtime? Daddy, how could you let this happen? You know sleep plays a critical role in brain structure development!"

"You're right, buddy. I'm sorry." Ritchie sighs. "Why don't you run along and brush your teeth. I'll be in to tuck you in shortly."

Curt runs from the living room as Eliza searches under the table for her missing toddlers.

"Has anyone seen Tory and Emmy? Darn it! They can't have gone far!"

"Relax," I tell her. "They collected up all the pillows in the house and took them into my bedroom about fifteen minutes ago. They're probably sound asleep on the floor in their cushion fort by now."

Eliza peeks into my bedroom, nods, and takes a deep breath. "I swear, one day they really will run away, just to mess with my head. Then Tom would kill me. He worships the ground those little monsters walk on."

"You can't fool me," I tell her. "I know you love them just as much. How is Tom?"

"He's good. Said to give his best. If he wasn't out of town on an important job, he'd be here too. Speaking of guests and sleeping arrangements….is there somewhere else you can sleep, Mom? If I move the girls now, they'll never go back to sleep. And if you stay in there with them, they'll be climbing all over you come morning."

"Of course, dear! I'll take the bed I made up for you, and you can sleep in my room with the girls. How does that sound?"

"Perfect, thanks. Those girls are going to be the end of me," Eliza moans, sinking into an armchair.

"You should've had boys," Ritchie laughs. "Curt would never run away, too dangerous. And even if he did, he'd leave a complete map and detailed notes about where he would be and when."

"Yeah, but at least my girls will be teenagers before they start treating me like I'm an idiot," Eliza retorts. "Curt's six and he's already telling you how little you know."

"Enough, you two! Your kids are behaving better than you are right now," I scold them. "Ritchie, go put your son to bed. Eliza, move your things into my room. When that's done, we're going to have a civilized conversation about Carlota's murder and how we can go about solving it. Go!"

Half an hour later, we're all sitting at the kitchen table drinking coffee. It took all of us about ten minutes to figure out how to override Curt's programming on the coffee maker, but we eventually got it working.

"The way I see it," I begin, "we have six relatively good suspects—Selena Castillo, Stan the fridge magnate, Astrid the jilted co-owner, Helen the black widow, Raging Roy, and Golf-Pro Dom. Obviously, they all have very different motives. What are your thoughts, Eliza?"

As I listed them out, I wrote their names on Tory's fancy new Etch A Sketch. It comes with a special pen now! When the kids were little, all they had to work with were two very awkward knobs.

"What's with the black widow again?" Eliza asks.

"Oh, I was just calling her that because she's had seven husbands who all died. No one's ever investigated, so I suppose it's all above board," I explain. "Anyway, she threatened Carlota a few days before the murder."

"Seven husbands?" Eliza raises her eyebrows. "I can barely manage one."

"Poor Tom," Ritchie teases.

"Can we focus on the murder please?" I redirect. "Eliza, what do you think?"

"You already know what I think! I think you need to stop trying to solve a murder and just enjoy your retirement. It could be dangerous. I worry about you down here on your own."

"I'm worried about Mom, too, you know," Ritchie interjects. "But I also know that she has a lot more experience

148

solving crimes than the local yokels. The sooner the killer is caught, the safer Mom will be, right?"

"I'm still here," I feel the need to remind them. "Look, I'm not going to go busting in any doors or interrogating people. This is just us, sitting around a table, talking about a case like we used to do all the time with your father. Can we just do that?"

"Absolutely!" Ritchie exclaims.

"I suppose so," Eliza capitulates.

"At the moment, the people who have the strongest motives we know of are Stan, Astrid, and Selena."

"Technically, we don't know for sure if Selena has a motive," Eliza says. "Not until the Colombian police can confirm her identity, and that's taking longer than we expected."

"What's the delay? Do you know?"

"Someone stole Jesus Castillo's body—"

"They stole his corpse?" Ritchie asks.

"Yeah, it's a thing," Eliza explains. "If there's no proof that a drug lord is dead, you can inspire myths that they're still alive to shield the new guys behind the throne."

"Seriously?"

"Serious as a brain aneurysm."

"Not funny," Ritchie chastises Eliza. "Is he really dead then?"

"Of course, he's really dead! But they can't use him as a DNA reference, because his body is MIA. Anyway," Eliza continues, "Castillo's wife had an older sister. She died in a car explosion. But she had a daughter, who could provide a family link through DNA."

"Great," Ritchie says. "Where's the daughter?"

"That's the problem. They can't find her."

"That war on drugs seems to be going really well," Ritchie says.

"So, it could be a while before we know if Selena is involved in any way," I cut in. "That leaves Astrid, who wants to buy out Carlota's shares, and Stan, who could have lost everything if Carlota had ended his refrigerator contract."

"How is the fridge working now after Curt made his little adjustments?" Ritchie asks.

"Like a dream! We should loan him out to other residents who have problems."

"Child labor, Mom? Really?"

"It was only a joke."

"Would you guys be quiet for a second," Eliza shooshes us. "I think I heard something."

"What did you hear?" I whisper, wondering if I should double-check the locks on the kids' windows.

"Something next door, like a window breaking."

"Front or back?" I ask.

"Back, I think," she answers.

Ritchie goes to the patio door and slides it open without making a sound.

"Can you see anything?" I ask Ritchie.

"It looks like there's a light on in Carlota's house. Could it be on a timer or something?"

"No," I tell him. "All the lights have been turned off since Carlota died. There must be someone in there."

"Stay here and scream if you hear or see anything," Eliza instructs before getting up from the table and disappearing into my front office.

"Look, over there," Ritchie whispers.

"Is that a person?"

Just behind Carlota's house there's an unmoving shape, lurking in the shadows.

"It's hard to tell," Ritchie says, just as the shadow begins to move. Ritchie grabs my arm. "It's a person, it's definitely a person!"

The person rustles the leaves of the trees behind my house as they run, rather slowly, past us, along the lake path toward the river. It's a man, and his shape seems oddly familiar.

"Eliza, where are you?" Ritchie calls out.

150

"I'm right here," Eliza says. She's holding a handgun with a flashlight mounted on top. "Which way?"

"You brought a gun into my house?" I ask. "Why do you have a gun?"

"It doesn't matter. Which way did he go?"

"I don't know how I feel about this. What if one of the kids had found it? Your father always locked—"

"Mom! I had it locked up in your office! Now, can you focus? Which way did he go?"

"Lake path, toward the river," I tell her.

She runs out the screened patio door and off into the night. Ritchie and I stand in place, eyes on the lake, ears tuned for danger.

We're a bundle of nerves by the time Eliza returns half an hour later. Her weapon is holstered in the back of her jeans, and she's breathing normally.

"What happened?" I demand.

"I chased him to the fork in the path, and then I must have taken a wrong turn."

"As much as I hate to say it, we need to call Detective Fletcher," Ritchie says.

"We do," I agree. "Especially since I think I know who the man was."

"You do?" Eliza asks.

"And if I'm right, it's someone we haven't even considered as a suspect before now."

CHAPTER TWENTY-SEVEN

"The back window was smashed in, so someone was in the house last night, though nothing appears to have been stolen," Detective Fletcher explains.

The morning light coming in my living room windows accentuates the dark circles under Detective Fletcher's eyes. It looks like he has been awake all night, probably since Ritchie called about the break-in next door. Police officers had been securing the scene by the time I finally drifted off to sleep.

"How can you tell?" Eliza asks. We're lined up in a row on the sofa—Ritchie, then me, then Eliza—facing Detective Fletcher. He looks uncomfortable, his face set in hard lines against our interrogation.

A children's song can be faintly heard coming from my bedroom, where Eliza has turned on Saturday morning cartoons to entertain the girls. Curt won't be awake for another few hours.

"We cross referenced how the house looks now with the crime scene photographs and nothing appeared to be missing," Detective Fletcher says.

"Oh, that was very smart! Well done," I congratulate him on his initiative.

"Thank you." He smiles before clearing his throat and frowning. "Just part of the job. I am perfectly capable of doing my job."

Eliza coughs. Ritchie looks down at his phone.

"Of course, you are," I assure him. "We've never doubted you for a second."

He sits up a little straighter. "You said you recognized the figure that broke into your deceased neighbor's house?"

"Yes," I tell him, "It was dark, but I'm relatively certain it was Harold Small. He lives just up the street. Next to Roy Everhard, where we were yesterday."

A smile lights the detective's face. "Raging Roy. What a legend."

"So we've heard," Ritchie mumbles, then asks, "Have you spoken to Harold yet?"

"I'll be asking the questions, if you don't mind," Detective Fletcher says. "How well do you know this—" he consults his notepad, "—Harold Small?"

"Oh, I don't know him at all," I tell the detective.

"You've never met him?"

"No. I've seen his car. That's how I know who he is."

Detective Fletcher frowns. "You recognize his car? Was he driving away from your neighbor's house after the break-in?"

"No." I sigh, trying not to get impatient. "As Ritchie explained when he called the police last night, we saw him running out on the lake path, behind the house."

"Let me get this straight, a man you've never met, but whose car you recognize, ran past your house last night in the dark, and you're convinced it was him?"

"Well," I clarify, "he wasn't really running. He's in his eighties. Waddling quickly would probably be a more apt description."

"He got away from you when you chased him, didn't he?" Detective Fletcher baits Eliza. It's clear he feels some kind of competition with her. She barely acknowledges he's in the room.

"I lost him at the fork between the lake path and the river path. Once I doubled back, he was gone," she explains. "And, as a civilian, I wouldn't have been able to do anything anyway."

I feel Ritchie leaning back on the sofa so he can see around me to Eliza. I can't see his face, but I'm guessing he's rolling his eyes at her.

"Can we just step back a minute?" Detective Fletcher scratches his head. "There's one thing I still don't understand."

153

"One thing?" Ritchie whispers. I nudge his stomach with my elbow.

Detective Fletcher continues, "How can you be sure the person you saw last night was Harold Small? You've never even met him."

"His neck," I explain.

"I'm sorry, his what?"

"More the absence of one really," I clarify.

"The absence of a neck?"

"Precisely! It's very distinctive. His head is like an extension of his shoulders. I noticed it when he nearly ran Lucas off the road."

"What's this now? Who's Lucas?" Detective Fletcher seems to be getting flustered.

"Victor's son. He was in town visiting earlier in the week, before getting on his jet to fly back to Manhattan."

"And what does this have to do with Harold Small?" Detective Fletcher asks.

"Absolutely nothing, as far as I can tell," I say.

Eliza puts her hand on top of mine. "Big picture, Mom. Remember?" Then addressing the detective, she says, "Are you going to speak with this Harold guy? See what he has to say?"

"We are in the process of trying to locate Mr. Small. It doesn't appear he's been at home since the incident. His car isn't there either," Detective Fletcher discloses. "Can you think of any place he might have gone?"

"We just told you we've never even met the guy," Ritchie reminds him. "How would we know where he'd go to hide?"

"I had to ask." The detective shifts in his seat, then closes his notebook. "Well, I better get going. Unless there is anything else you think I should know?"

"I think we've told you everything we know," I confirm.

"I can show myself out. Always a pleasure Mrs. Delarouse," Detective Fletcher says, though it's evident he means the opposite.

As soon as he's out of earshot, Eliza lets out a frustrated sigh. "Well, that was useless. It's a wonder that detective can even figure out how to use his own pin code."

"Now, Eliza, that's not very nice," I chastise. "He did do well with the crime scene photo comparison! That's a step in the right direction!"

"Good gracious, Mandy!" Gina breezes into the living room. "Please tell me you're shacking up with some hot young police officer, otherwise I can't for the life of me figure out why you always have the law at your house!"

"Mandy?" Eliza raises a perfectly groomed eyebrow.

"Let it go," I whisper. "Gina, how did you get in?"

"That confused-looking detective let me in as he was leaving. What's going on? Has someone else been murdered?"

Ritchie gasps. "Don't even joke about that!"

"Sorry, kid," Gina apologizes. "At our age, you'd think we'd be used to people dying. But it's not usually this exciting."

"No one else has been murdered," I interject. "Just a little breaking and entering at Carlota's house last night. You haven't happened to see Harold Small around, have you?"

"No, why? Was it him broke into Carlota's?" Gina's eyes are gleaming.

"It appears so, but he hasn't gone back to his house, and his car isn't there either," I inform her.

"It wouldn't be, now, would it?" Gina says.

"What do you mean?" Ritchie asks.

"It got towed away yesterday, around lunchtime," she explains. "I saw it on the back of the truck. I know it was Harvey's, because every time I saw him in it, I thought he must be compensating for something."

Ritchie chokes on a sip of coffee. Eliza nods.

I frown. "Why was *Harold's* car towed away?"

Gina shrugs her shoulders. "Maybe the police took it? The way he drove around this place, it wouldn't surprise me if he had a bunch of speeding tickets."

"Or maybe Helen complained about the incident with Mitsy, and the board had it towed?" I suggest.

Gina shakes her head. "Leon hasn't said anything about it."

"How well do you know Harold?" Ritchie asks Gina. "Can you think of any reason he'd want to get into Carlota's house?"

"I can't help you there." Gina shakes her head. "I've never really had much use for the man. An old oil company exec, who got removed as CEO from his own company. He has a chip on his shoulder the size of Texas."

Yesterday, when Curt and I stopped to chat with Victor, Harold had pulled up in front of Stan's house. That must have been right before Harold's car was towed. If he was visiting Stan, maybe Stan knows something.

"Victor said Harold and Stan were best friends," I tell the group. "Maybe Stan knows where Harold is."

"Vincent told you that, did he?" Gina winks flirtatiously at me, while my kids groan.

"*Victor* and I were just having a conversation." I glare at her.

"Of course, hun. Whatever you say." She chuckles.

Eliza's phone begins to ring. She answers and walks into the guest bedroom, shutting the door.

Gina scratches her head. "For some reason, I thought those two had some kind of falling out, awhile back."

"Stan and Harold?" I ask.

"I don't know. I could be wrong." She frowns. "There's so much drama around here. It's like *Beverly Hills, 90210*, but with defibrillators. It's tough to keep all the storylines straight."

"Oh! Can I be Ian Ziering?" Ritchie asks. "I don't know if you've seen pictures of him lately, but he's aged *really* well!"

"Excellent!" Eliza's excited voice filters through the closed door. "Call me back as soon as you know." Moments later Eliza emerges from the room and heads toward the front door. "I have to head out for a little while. Ritchie, can you have Curt keep an eye on the girls while I'm gone?"

"Curt?" I ask. "What about your brother and me?"

"No offense, Mom, but Curt's the only one here with the good sense to run away from danger, not toward it." She smiles and shuts the front door behind her.

"You better show him where you hide the Reese's," Ritchie warns.

"Second shelf in the pantry," I tell him. "Can you show Curt, dear? Gina and I are going for a little walk."

"You are?" Ritchie asks.

"We are?" Gina echoes.

I glare at her. "I just thought we could take a few laps around the street. What do you think?"

"You really expect me to believe that?" Ritchie asks. "It's obvious you're going to talk to Stan."

"Would you try to stop me?" I ask.

"Eliza would kill me if I didn't," he replies.

"Like I said, Gina and I are just going for a walk," I repeat.

"Right." Ritchie sighs. "Just know, when Eliza finds out, I'm saying you slipped out the back door. It's every person for themself."

"Of course, dear!"

Taking Gina's arm in mine, we rush as fast as our hips will allow to the front door and into the sunshine.

"Oh, give me two seconds, Gina! I just need to go back for my hat."

CHAPTER TWENTY-EIGHT

"Stan, let us in!" Gina knocks loudly on the door. "We just want to talk to you."

"Go away. I have nothing to say to you two!" Stan calls out from the bowels of his technological dungeon.

"Let us in, Stan. We're your—" I struggle to remember the word he used to describe his little computer friends, "—homelies!"

"Homies!" He shouts back. "The word is homies! Stop trying to act dope. You can't hack it."

"What's he trying to hack now?" Gina asks.

"I don't know, but he really shouldn't be using a bladed weapon if he's high on dope," I worry.

Stan suddenly throws open the door. Gina stumbles. I have to grab her arm to keep her from falling.

"I'm not high on dope, and I'm not hacking away at anything! I just want you to leave me alone!" He yells and tries to slam the door, but I stick my handbag in the crack, so he can't close it all the way.

"We just have a few questions about Harold," Gina says. "It'll only take a minute."

"A minute? Last time, this one—" he points to me, "—ate up half an hour of my time—when I could have been playing Fortnite—installing an app on her phone! I mean, I have a four-year-old that can do that kind of stuff on his own!"

"You have children?" Gina asks.

"Kind of," he says. "I sponsor kids in Africa. We are the world, man. What's it to you?"

"Nothing!" Gina holds up her hands. "I just didn't think you had kids."

"Well, for your information, I communicate with dozens of kids online!"

I don't think he thought that sentence through before saying it. But he seems harmless enough, so I decide to let it slide. For now.

"Kids are so much better with technology than we are, though, aren't they?" I say. "They grew up with it, after all. Why, my six-year-old grandson fixed the little problems with your Fridge Friend app. It took him less than an hour!"

Stan laughs. "It's cute that you believe that. But there were no problems to fix!"

"Yes, there were!" I assure him. "Everything was going completely wonky, but then Curt played around with it, and now it's perfect. He even linked it up somehow with my coffee maker!"

"You're tripping," he says, looking at me sideways.

I look down at the ground. "I haven't even moved; how can I be tripping?" I ask.

He sighs. "Let me see your phone."

Reaching into my trapped purse with my free hand, I locate the phone by touch, then hand it to him through the crack in the door.

He sighs again, deeper this time. "You need to unlock it first."

The phone uses my face as the password, so all I have to do is turn the phone around and look at it. The nice young man at the Apple store helped me set it up. I wish I'd known ahead of time that the phone was going to save a picture of me. I would have gotten my hair done.

Stan emits a series of noises. *Huh. Oh. Duh.*

Gina and I glance at each other. My handbag is still stuck in the door. I hope the leather doesn't get ruined.

Finally, Stan looks up, a curious expression on his face.

"Is this grandson of yours still in town?"

"He is. Why?" I'm suddenly wondering if I should be more worried about his earlier comment.

"He knows his stuff. I don't really need his help, but, you know, if he's already found the glitches, maybe he could help me implement them systemwide." He blushes, embarrassed to be needing help from a child. "But, whatever, you know."

"I'd be happy to bring him by later on," I offer, "but only if you answer a few of our questions first."

He squints his eyes. "Are you trying to bribe me into helping you?"

"Yes," Gina confirms. "Yes, we are."

Stan seems to think about it for a minute, then opens the door wide. Such a shame I hadn't thought to offer up Curt sooner. There's a crease in my handbag that will probably never come out.

The house is dark again, minus the illumination from all the computer monitors coming from his office next to the entryway. There's a faint odor of stale pizza and overworn socks.

"What is it you want to know?" Stan asks once we're all inside. He doesn't offer us an opportunity to sit down.

"Do you know where Harold is?" Gina asks.

"I don't have a clue. Haven't seen him in a while. Next question."

"But I saw him pull up outside your house yesterday," I tell him. "Didn't he come by? It would have been just before noon."

Stan shakes his head. "I wasn't here. I was out at Best Buy, picking up an external hard drive. Why do you want to find Harold so badly anyway?"

"The police are looking for him," Gina says. "He broke into Carlota's house last night. Madeline saw him running away."

I give her a nudge with my elbow. I'm not sure Detective Fletcher would want us to be sharing that information.

"Why would he break into Carlota's house?" Stan asks.

"We were hoping you could tell us," I chime in.

Stan reaches his fingers under his black cap to scratch a thin patch of white hair. "He must have been looking for something. Maybe…" He pauses as a thought seems to cross his mind, then the lines of his face harden. "No, I don't know what he would have been looking for. You'll have to ask him when you find him."

Something about Stan's demeanor feels off. He knows something, but he's not going to come straight out with it. Perhaps he's just being loyal to his friend. Or maybe he worries the truth might implicate him in some way.

"Look Stan, you need to—" Gina begins to scold, but I put my hand on her arm.

"When was the last time you saw Harold?" I ask.

"I don't know. About a week ago, I guess."

"Before Carlota was murdered?"

"Yeah. Last weekend, I think. He came by to talk about—" Stan seems to stop himself mid-sentence, "—some personal stuff. Not important. But he did say he was worried about something he saw next door."

"Next door?" Gina asks, pausing to remember who lives on either side of Harold. "At Rob's house or Selma's?"

Stan looks confused. I decide to help him out. "Roy or Selena?"

"Oh, right. Selena. She really creeps Harold out."

That seems understandable. She's being investigated as the possible wife of one notorious drug lord and the mother of another. Not exactly the type of woman who's going to bring around a homemade apple pie, just because she was in the mood to bake.

"You said Harold saw something that made him nervous," I remind Stan. "What was it?"

"He said he got up in the middle of the night to, you know—" Stan winks, "—see a man about a horse."

"There was someone else there with Harold? Someone with a horse?"

Stan looks at me with a befuddled expression on his face. "No. It's an expression. He had to use the toilet. Are you for real?"

Gina turns to me. "Come on, Mandy, everyone knows what it means to see a man about a horse!"

"Sorry, I just got excited that there might be a witness," I explain. "Please continue."

Gina rolls her eyes. "What did he see when he got up to pee?"

Stan lowers his voice and leans in closer to us. "He saw a bunch of bulked-up dudes loading boxes into Selena's garage. The way he described them, they were built like brick poop houses. And he said he thought one of them had a gun tucked into his pants."

"Are you sure it was a gun?" Gina's tone is suggestive. "He wasn't just happy to see you?"

My elbow connects with her arm, and she lets out a little *oomph*.

"That's going to bruise, you know," she laments.

"You'll live," I tell her before turning back to Stan. "Any ideas about what was in the boxes? Was there any writing on them or anything?"

Stan thinks for a moment. "Harold didn't say. But even if it was something like guns or drugs, do you really think they'd be advertising it on the side of the box?"

"Probably not," I admit. "But why do you think there were guns or drugs in the boxes?"

I don't think the police have told anyone else about the possibility of Selena's secret identity.

Stan shrugs his shoulders. "Harold said the guys looked like goons. And if it was all legit, why were they unloading the stuff in the middle of the night?"

He has a point. Amazon never turns up at my door after midnight. If Harold saw something, could that be why he's missing now? And could it be connected to Carlota's murder?

"Do you think Harold would have mentioned it to Carlota?"

Stan snickers. "Hell would freeze over first. Harold and Carlota weren't exactly best buds."

This piques my interest. "Really? Why?"

"You'll have to ask Harold."

162

"If we could find him, we would!" Gina reminds him why we're here in the first place.

"And you haven't seen him since he told you about the boxes?" I ask.

Stan shakes his head. "I've heard him tooling around the neighborhood. He never has been able to handle such a flash car. I guess he almost ran over that maneater's dog."

"Helen? He told you about that?"

"No, she did." He rolls his eyes. "She came banging on my door, wanting to know where he was. Said Harold needed to 'answer for' what he almost did to her little ankle biter."

"Did she seem angry?" I ask.

"Oh man, she was stratospheric! You could practically see the smoke coming out of her ears." He chuckles.

One of the computers in his office starts to play a song. It sounds familiar. I think it's the theme song from *Miami Vice.*

"Oh, that's me. I got a call coming in. Nice chatting with you ladies," Stan says, pushing Gina and I toward the door. "I'll be around this afternoon if you want to send your grandson by. A deal's a deal."

Gina opens her mouth to say something, but by the time she catches her breath, we're standing on the other side of Stan's closed door.

"Well, I never…" Gina fumes. "He didn't tell us one useful thing! I don't think that deserves having Kyle come around to fix his little app thing!"

"Curt," I correct her as I take her elbow and walk her back toward the street. "Come on. I have to meet my kids for lunch."

On the walk back, as Gina chatters away, it occurs to me that Helen threatened two people in the last week. One of them is dead, and the other one is hiding out.

But then there are the boxes in Selena's garage. How do they fit in?

And if Harold and Carlota disliked each other so much, what was Harold looking for in her house? Is it possible he killed Carlota and that's why he's gone into hiding?

There's only one person who can say for sure, we just need to find him.

CHAPTER TWENTY-NINE

"Who me? Have an opinion? Would it even matter if I did?"

Eliza is furiously eviscerating the chicken nuggets the waiter just brought for the girls' lunch. If she doesn't stop cutting soon, Tory and Emmy are going to need spoons to eat them.

"Look, dear, I know you're upset…"

The knife freezes in Eliza's hand. "Upset? Why would I be upset? My mother is chasing after murderers, even though I told her it was too dangerous. But what do I know, right? I only work for the—" she stops and looks around at the other diners in the clubhouse, "—IRS."

"Gina and I were perfectly safe," I assure her. "And you seem convinced Selena is the killer anyway. So why are you so mad about us talking to Stan?"

"Yeah, if anyone should be mad it's me," Ritchie chimes in. "Mom's pimping out my son to some sketchy computer nerd! What were you thinking, Mom? How could you use your six-year-old grandson as a bargaining chip?"

Ritchie has lowered his voice, but there's no danger of Curt hearing him. My grandson excused himself to go to the toilet a few minutes ago. None of us were fooled. We all know he went to examine the kitchen to see if the health inspector missed anything on his last report.

"All I'm saying—" Eliza ignores Ritchie, "—is that I don't understand why you can't just act like a normal retired person! At least until we get enough evidence to arrest Selena. I swear, you're worse than my kids! Wait, where are my kids?"

"Hiding under the table." I know because, were it not for my arthritis, I'd be tempted to join them.

Ritchie lifts the tablecloth and calls to Tory and Emmy, "Come on, girls, it's lunch time!" Then to Eliza he adds, "Really? How hard is it to keep track of your own children?"

"Why would I? You're their uncle. You knew where they were," Eliza retorts.

"Grandma, I want to sit next to you!" Emmy exclaims, her blue eyes flashing. I push a strand of blond hair away from her eyes.

"I would love to have you sit next to me, sweetheart."

"Careful now, Emmy," Ritchie warns. "If your grandma asks you to sneak into someone's garage and go through boxes for her, just say no!"

Emmy looks at him with shining eyes and a big uncomprehending smile and says, "Otay."

"Come on, Ritchie, she's only three," Eliza chastens.

"Yeah, but that just means she's small enough to climb through air vents," he points out.

"Don't pay any attention to them, Emmy. You just sit up here next to me." I pull out the neighboring seat.

"Can I trust you not to interrogate my daughter during lunch?" Eliza glares at me while passing out plates to Emmy and Tory with what remains of their chicken nuggets.

My eyes scour the restaurant for our waiter. I wish our own food would arrive. My stomach is rumbling from all the morning's activity. Also, I forbid my children from talking when their mouths are full, so I'll finally get a little peace.

Just then I see Gina's husband, Leon, emerging from the side room that's reserved for board meetings and small conferences. He has on a plum-colored polo that compliments his dark skin and white hair. I wave to get his attention.

"Madeline. So nice to see you again," Leon says, after maneuvering his wheelchair around the other tables. "I've met your son, but there seem to be a few new faces at the table."

166

He goes around, shaking hands with Eliza and her girls, before coming to rest beside my chair. I take a deep breath, grateful for a reprieve from my children's harassment.

"I don't suppose you've seen my better half," he says in a deep bass that resonates from his chest. "She's not easy to keep track of."

Ritchie and Eliza stare pointedly at me. I pretend not to notice.

"We went for a walk before lunch. I imagine she's back at home now. Were you having another board meeting? On a Saturday?"

He shakes his head. "No. I was just preparing some notes for the meeting we have tomorrow. It's a holiday weekend, but decisions have to be made."

"That doesn't sound like a pleasant way to spend Veterans Day," I commiserate. "I've heard Astrid from Shady Palms is interested in taking over Carlota's stake in the community. Does that look like it's going to go through?"

Ritchie gently kicks me under the table. I ignore him.

"She is interested, but there are a few things that need to be addressed before we can seriously consider her proposal."

"Such as?" I push. Ritchie kicks me again.

"There are some changes she would like to make to the tenants' living agreements," he says. "But you're having lunch with your family. I won't bore you with the details."

"Yeah, Mom. We're just having a nice lunch," Eliza says, a fake smile plastered on her lips.

"Was the kitchen up to your standards?" Ritchie asks as Curt rejoins the group.

"While I did notice some shoddy applications of hairnets, overall, I feel comfortable eating in this establishment again today." Curt slides into his seat and notices Gina's husband has joined us. "Oh, hello, Luis. I was hoping to see you again. I was wondering if we could schedule a time to finish our discussion on the merits of HO versus N gauge models."

"What's that?" I ask.

"Model trains," Ritchie explains, adding, "and Curt, it's Mr. Wilson to you."

"But he told me I could call him Luis," Curt argues.

"You mean *Leon*," I correct my grandson, beginning to wonder if I've had him around Gina too much. Maybe being bad at names is contagious.

"Actually, he's right. My name is Luis," Leon says.

"But Gina said…" I pause while making my own argument. Surely Gina wouldn't get her own husband's name wrong.

"Yeah, no matter how many times I told her my name was Luis, she kept calling me Leon." He smiles. "After the first year, it didn't bother me so much. Leon suits me better than Luis anyway. Feel free to call me Leon."

"Your wife has been calling you by the wrong name for forty years?" Ritchie asks incredulously.

"More or less."

"Wow!" Ritchie says. "If I called Craig another name, the next call I'd be getting would be from his divorce lawyer."

Leon laughs. "You take the good with the bad, young man. And Leon's a good name. I've been called a lot worse, believe you me."

Eliza, who has been more relaxed since Leon joined us, suddenly tenses up when her phone rings. "Excuse me, I have to take this." She walks off toward the patio doors and the outdoor seating. With the sun sitting directly overhead, the tables out there are mainly empty.

"I heard you had some excitement at your house last night," Leon says.

I glance at Ritchie. He looks out at Eliza on the patio and shrugs his shoulders.

"Yes," I say, emboldened by Ritchie's acquiescence. "We saw Harold breaking into Carlota's house."

Leon clucks his tongue. "Such a horrible business. Breaking into a dead woman's house. It's unseemly. Not the kind of thing we want happening here at Egret's Loft."

I decide to road test something Stan said. "I heard Harold and Carlota had some kind of disagreement. Is that true?"

"I don't know of any altercations between the two of them, per se. It was more of a disagreement about who Harold should date."

"She was being possessive?" I ask, trying to imagine Carlota going out with Harold.

"No, nothing like that. Carlota didn't like that Harold was dating Astrid Roosevelt."

"Astrid? From Shady Palms? But she's got to be two feet taller than him!"

"Love overlooks all." The way Leon says it makes it sound like the chorus to a jazz song. Who can argue with jazz?

Apparently, Ritchie can. "If she was two feet taller than him, she probably looked over a lot."

It's my turn to kick him under the table. He lets out a very low *ouch*, which Leon pretends not to hear.

"Carlota and Astrid had some rivalry," Leon continues. "Carlota said it was because Astrid was trying to take credit for Egret's Loft. But, if you ask me, it goes back further. They'd known each other most of their lives, and I think they were very competitive with each other."

"Competitive about what?" Ritchie asks.

"Anything and everything," Leon says. "It got so bad, Carlota found a reason to kick Harold off the board when she found out he was dating Astrid. She said he violated some ethical rule she added in about 'intelligence sharing' with a representative of Shady Palms. It all felt petty, really, but Carlota had the majority share."

"Have you seen Harold?" I ask Leon. "Detective Fletcher said he's not at home, and his car is gone." I leave out that Gina told me it had been towed away.

"No, I haven't. But he's bound to turn up sooner or later."

The waiter appears, carrying a tray of plates that I assume is our lunch. Eliza nearly knocks him over in her zeal to get back to the table.

She looks at the waiter and orders him, "If that's ours, box it all up." Then she turns to us, her eyes wild. "Something's happening. We need to go. *Now!*"

CHAPTER THIRTY

"Can't those darn things move any faster?" Eliza slams her palms against the steering wheel.

We're all packed into Eliza's SUV, the only car on the streets as we make our way the mile back from the clubhouse. Not that the roads are empty. They're packed with golf carts carrying active elders to their holiday weekend activities.

"Mine can only get up to about twenty-five miles per hour," I tell her.

From the back seat Ritchie calls out, "Which is the posted speed limit, may I remind you."

"Then why are we only going five? Ugh, this is torture!" She runs a hand through her long blond hair.

"Yeah, real Guantanamo stuff," Ritchie jokes.

I ignore him. "Why are we in such a hurry anyway, dear?"

She turns, excitement in her face. "Don't you want to be there when they arrest Carlota's murderer?"

"Who?" I ask.

"You'll see!" She smiles.

I draw in a deep breath, unsure whether the feeling in my stomach is relief that justice will be served or sadness that the investigation may be over and the most exciting thing I'll have to look forward to is water painting with Serenity Karma.

The wail of a police siren approaches and, looking in the side view mirror, I can see golf carts behind us parting to make room for the emergency vehicle.

"Hallelujah," Eliza says as the cop car passes. She forces the SUV in behind it and sails past the golf carts that have pulled off to the side of the road.

We're stopped again at the entrance to Cypress Point Avenue by a uniformed police officer. He seems young and jittery. Beads of sweat line his forehead under a peaked police cap. He walks around to the driver's side window.

"This street is blocked to all non-residential traffic," he informs us.

"We are residential traffic. My mother lives just up the road," Eliza says while inching the SUV slowly past him.

He reaches in and puts his hand on the steering wheel. "I'm afraid I still can't let you through."

Eliza lowers her sunglasses so he can see the determination in her aquamarine eyes. She looks down at his hand and back up at his face. "No, you said only non-residents weren't allowed in. We're residents. Now move out of the way."

I can't watch. It's like the hunting scenes on those nature shows Clint used to like to watch. Eliza's going to eat him alive, and he knows it. I can smell the fear coming off him.

In the backseat, Tory and Emmy giggle. Their mother's children.

"The c-c-captain said..." he stammers.

"Look, you can let go of the steering wheel, or I'll drag you alongside the car for the next hundred yards to my mother's house. Because, make no mistake, I'm going in. Got it?"

His hand flies off the steering wheel. "Yes, ma'am. Have a nice day."

Eliza pushes her sunglasses back onto the bridge of her nose and puts her foot on the gas. Ten seconds later, we're parked in my driveway.

"I don't mean to criticize, dear, but was it really necessary to intimidate a police officer?"

"We're here, aren't we?" She asks in a way that makes it seem like a dumb question. "Can you get the kids inside and set them up with their babysitter? I have to go."

I turn to look at Ritchie. He shrugs his shoulders.

"Which one of us is supposed to be their babysitter?" I ask.

172

"Oh, neither. She meant the TV. We just need to turn on one of their shows," he says, unbuckling child seats. "Alright, everybody out."

Once all the kids are settled—Tory and Emmy with cartoons and Curt with some sudoku puzzles—Ritchie and I head out into the street and follow the sounds of activity.

Helen glares at me from her front yard as we pass, her arms clutched around her now-mute Pomeranian. On the other side of the street, Jinny chatters away to a woman leaning on a walker, whose hair looks like a dusky pink rose. I think it's Marjorie Higginbottom, who outmaneuvered an alligator with a frozen piece of chicken.

Running through the details of the case in my mind, I wonder who the police are arresting. Maybe they located Harold. His house is just up around the bend, and he did break into Carlota's house. Then again, Selena lives next door. Maybe they've uncovered some proof of her ties with the Castillo drug lords or evidence that she killed Carlota out of revenge.

Ritchie, who's been keeping his eye on the kids from his phone, turns to see what's taking me so long. I'm stalling. Maybe I'm trying to hold onto the moment—the brief flush of feeling alive—before settling back into meaningless routine. Because that's what will happen once the investigation is over. I'll just be another old widow in a quirky retirement community.

"Are you coming, lady?" Ritchie looks concerned.

"Cool your heels. My legs don't move as fast as they used to," I tell him, picking up my pace slightly.

We're just making our way past the path to the river, when I spot several police cars parked in a defensive semicircle. Officers and agents with DEA written on the backs of their jackets huddle behind the vehicles, guns drawn and pointed.

They're aimed at Selena's house.

"Well." Ritchie sighs. "Looks like my little sis was right again."

I scour the crowd of officers and agents, but don't see my daughter. "Where is she, do you think?"

He scoffs. "Are you kidding? She's probably the one putting on the handcuffs."

One of the police radios squawks, "*We're coming out.*"

Two burly men I don't recognize walk out of the house, Selena's large frame squeezed between them. She looks defiant, her multiple chins held high, and her colored caftan fluttering in the gentle breeze.

She turns to watch as her garage door goes up, revealing uniformed agents scurrying around stacks of unopened boxes in her garage. She says something to the men arresting her, but we're too far away to hear the words.

On the other side of the police barricade, I see Roy Everhard chatting with a deeply tanned older man, wearing only a Speedo with an American flag logo and sneakers. This must be Crazy Carl, who Carlota had warned me to watch out for on sunny days. Now I can understand why!

Roy and Carl are standing in front of Harold's house, but there is still no sign of the missing man.

Ritchie tugs on my arm, pulling me closer to an unmarked car. The agents flanking Selena are headed straight for it. One of them opens the back passenger door, while the other rests his hand on Selena's head so she won't hit the roof as she climbs in.

Just before they close the door on her, we hear her say, "*No entiendes que a las colombianas les encanta la sombra de ojos!*"

I turn to Ritchie. "What did she say?"

He scratches his head. "My Spanish is pretty rusty, but I think she said something about Colombian women liking eyeshadow."

"What? No, that can't be right. Are you sure?"

"Use it or lose it, right? Well, I guess I lost it." He sighs.

"It looks like my work here is done." Eliza's voice comes from behind, making us both jump.

"Eliza, dear, where did you come from? Were you in the house?"

"It doesn't matter." She drapes one of her thin arms over my shoulder. "All that *does* matter is you're safe now, Mom."

"But what happened? I didn't think they could do anything until the DNA match came through."

She smiles, revealing little dimples in both cheeks. "All those calls I had to take today? They were from Coronel Arturo Sánchez with the Colombian National Police. He asked me to say hello to you, by the way." She winks. "They were finally able to track down the niece. They ran the test this morning and just got confirmation. Selena Fuentes *is* Selena Castillo. And there's evidence she wanted revenge on Carlota's son, Juan Carlo."

"You knew and kept this from us all day?" Ritchie fumes. "What the heck, Eliza?"

She shrugs. "Need to know, Ritchie. You didn't."

Richie turns to me. "Well, I never would have kept it from you, lady. That's probably why I'm your favorite child."

"Oh, give me a break, Ritchie," Eliza moans. "You wouldn't be her favorite even if I'd never been born."

Having long since learned to tune out the sound of my children's squabbling, I'm thinking about what Stan said about men unloading boxes in Selena's garage. I can see the boxes now, medium-sized, and with pink writing on the side. It's hard to tell from this distance, but I think the boxes say "Mary Kay."

"Dear, do you know what was in the boxes? The ones in Selena's garage?" I interrupt my kids' ongoing competition for my affection.

"On the surface, they appear to be women's makeup, but the DEA guys think it was probably a cover to transport drugs. They're taking everything back to the lab to have it tested. Why?"

"Do they think Selena could have been selling drugs in Egret's Loft?" Ritchie asks.

"Unclear," Eliza admits. "Either way, she won't be selling anything here ever again. Once she confesses, the case will be officially closed."

"Does this mean I can go back to DC?" Ritchie asks Eliza as we make our way slowly back to my house. "Craig has been on me to fix some loose tiles in the bathroom."

"Yeah, I'll probably be headed out tonight as well," Eliza says. "The girls were invited to a birthday party in Indian Creek tomorrow. I can't name names, but it's being hosted by the daughter of a former president."

"And you still want to go?" Ritchie asks.

"I just want to see the house. Apparently, it has its own petting zoo."

"With her father's reputation, just make sure you don't end up in one of the cages."

"Gross." Eliza makes a fist and punches Ritchie's arm.

As he berates her for the bruise he'll get as a result, my mind wanders. I can't stop thinking about Harold and why he broke into Carlota's house.

Had Carlota figured out who Selena really was? Maybe Carlota had some kind of evidence against Selena and that's what Harold was looking for. After witnessing the boxes being unloaded, Harold might have started doing some digging of his own.

From the sounds of it, the kids will be heading back to their respective homes tonight, confident that Carlota's killer is safely behind bars. That leaves me free to continue the search for Harold.

Because no matter what happens with Selena, I can't shake the feeling that, somehow, he's the key to finding out what really happened.

CHAPTER THIRTY-ONE

An undercurrent of excitement sizzles through the Saturday night crowds gathering for a special pre-Veterans Day concert at the River Club. A procession of golf carts pulls up alongside a skid-resistant red carpet, where women, dressed in their finest capris, emerge from under their carts' plastic canopies.

The Egret's Loft PR department has all hands on deck for the event. One young intern takes pictures of the female guests as they disembark, sporting their most stylish orthopedic shoes. After their paparazzi moment, another intern escorts the women to a nearby bench, where they can drink water as they wait for their husbands to return from parking the carts.

Ritchie and Eliza left a few hours ago. Curt, disappointed about not getting to have his chat with Leon about model trains, made Ritchie promise to bring him back soon. Tory and Emmy, in their smiley treachery, managed to steal all the remaining Reese's I had in the house.

Even Gina, who I'd been on the phone with earlier, gossiping about Selena's arrest, said she had other plans. Which leaves me to attend the breakout musical act of the season alone.

Observing the pageantry from the parking lot, I decide to skip the main entrance and go in through a side gate near the swimming pool. As I'm resecuring the childproof lock on the gate, I literally bump into Serenity Karma as she sips a flute of champagne.

"Oh, dear me, I spilled your drink," I say. "I'm very sorry."

"It's all groovy, Madeline. How can it harsh my mellow when I have more?" She pulls a half empty bottle of bubbly from the cloth purse draped across her shoulder.

"You certainly came prepared," I admire. "Are you excited for the concert?"

"Oh yes!" She undulates her body, her long silk skirt swaying. "Stealers Wheel is totally out of sight! One of my absolute favorites."

"Really?" I ask. "Didn't they just have the one hit song?"

"Stuck in the Middle with You" had been one of the top songs of the early 1970s and got a second life two decades later thanks to a John Travolta movie that both my kids loved. I found it a little too violent.

"Oh, I never actually listened to any of their music." Her lips curve into a catlike grin and she practically purrs. "But I did have a vibrant and electrifying few days with Gerry Rafferty. I painted him once, you know. He had the most amazing p—"

"Oh no," I interrupt her, "you must have been so sad when he died."

She cocks her head, questioningly. "Why? None of us ever really die. We just become something else. Maybe Gerry is now in this flower." She points to a ruby-colored hibiscus tucked behind her left ear.

"That looks like the flowers Carlota grew in front of her house," I point out.

She looks annoyed and says, "No one can ever own nature, can they? It's not like flowers belong to any one person."

The American Horticultural Society might disagree with her analysis, but fortunately, I'm drawn away from the bizarre exchange when Victor waves at me from the other side of the large outdoor patio.

"If you'll excuse me," I say to Serenity. "I hope you enjoy the show."

She nods and I take that as my cue to depart.

Drawing nearer to Victor, I can see he has a guest; his son Lucas is back in town.

"Madeline, I'm so happy you came," Victor gushes. "You remember my son, Lucas? He just flew in from New York today."

"Of course. It's nice to see you back here visiting your father." I shake his hand. "How is everything in Manhattan?"

"Cold, dark and miserable." He laughs.

"I know what you mean," I agree. "I always thought I liked the snow, but after moving here, I'm reconsidering my position."

"Lucas knows he's always welcome here, as long as he leaves his work behind at the office." Victor playfully ruffles his son's hair. "Madeline, can I get you something to drink?"

"A glass of white wine would be nice," I tell him.

Victor leaves us to get in line at the crowded bar.

"If you haven't noticed, my dad is the more fiscally conservative type. We don't talk about my work because he doesn't believe in investments that deliver profits without hard work."

"Money for nothing? How can anyone not believe in that?" I joke.

"Exactly." Lucas's eyes twinkle. "I just got on the ground floor of a company that's going to revolutionize the home vacuum market. It's called Dytson. If you're interested, I might be able to convince the board there's room for one more investor."

"Dytson? Isn't that too much like Dyson?" I ask. "From a marketing perspective, that could be confusing to consumers."

"You know marketing?" He asks.

"I only spent thirty years doing it." I smile.

"Really? You would be a great addition to the team!"

"Lucas, are you talking about work?" Victor hands me a glass. He's smiling, but his face is red. He must have had to fight his way to the front of the line. "That's enough about your investment deals, do you hear me?"

Lucas looks at me and smirks. "Yes, Dad."

Taking a sip of wine, I scan the crowd. I can feel her eyes on me before I see them, laser focused and angry. Helen, fifty feet away, wearing a low-cut top and a high-cut skirt, glares at me. In her tight-fitting blouse, one breast appears slightly larger than the other. She probably has a little swelling after the surgery.

She's not alone. A very tan and toned older gentleman stands beside her, his hands practically petting her blond hair. He looks familiar, but it takes a moment to reconcile the distinguished-looking man in linen pants and shirt to the eccentric character talking to Roy outside Selena's house, when he was dressed only in a patriotic Speedo. It's Crazy Carl and he clearly thinks he and Helen are on a date. But she can't take her eyes off Victor and, by extension, me.

When Lucas steps away to refill his drink, I turn my back to her.

"There was a lot of activity on my street earlier today. Police and the DEA arrested Selena. Did you hear?" I ask.

Victor takes a sip of his drink. "It did come to my attention, yes. Sad business."

"Very sad. Have you heard anything about why she might have killed Carlota?" I'm careful not to divulge any information Eliza might not want public at this point.

"From what I've been told, the police think it was an issue of revenge. A kind of feud involving family members in Colombia."

I have the sense he knows who Selena really is, and her connection to not one, but two, Colombian drug lords, yet he says nothing. His discretion reminds me of one of the things I admired most about Clint.

"Did you also hear about Harold breaking into Carlota's house?" I ask.

"I heard a rumor, but it strikes me as being highly impractical."

I put my hand on his arm. "It's true. I saw him running away."

Victor looks down at my fingers resting on his sleeve. I quickly withdraw my hand, my face suddenly feeling very warm.

"I'm sorry, Madeline." He puts his hand on *my* arm now. "Had I known it was you who reported it, I never would have doubted it for a second."

My heart beats a little faster. "Thank you, Victor. I do know what I saw. Can you think of any reason why Harold would do that?"

Victor takes a sip from his highball glass, thinking. "It just doesn't make any sense to me. I haven't a clue what he could have been looking for."

"I thought maybe it had something to do with Selena, since she lives next door to Harold. Maybe Carlota had evidence of something that Selena did, and Harold found out about it? Maybe he was trying to blackmail Selena?"

Victor chuckles. "You do have the most vivid imagination! Do you have any proof?"

"Well, no. Of course not. I'm just trying to make sense of the facts we do have. Do you know if Harold had any money troubles?"

Victor, who had been taking a sip of his drink and glancing in Helen's direction, begins to cough. "Sorry," he chokes out, "wrong pipe."

"Oh, I do hate when that happens. It really is so painful." I follow the direction of his glance and see Helen, smoothing down her shirt and smiling triumphantly. I pull the edges of my wrap dress closer together and shake my head. People brought their grandchildren here!

"I'm sorry for the interruption," Victor says when his coughing subsides. "You were saying?"

"Do you know if Harold was struggling financially?"

"Why do you ask?"

"Gina said his fancy car was towed away yesterday. It just made me wonder."

Victor shakes his head. "I'm afraid I really don't know anything about Harold's finances."

"Whose finances?" Lucas asks, having returned with a fresh drink.

"It's nothing, son," Victor replies, putting an end to my interrogation. "The music's about to start. How about you go save us a spot, and we'll be with you in a minute?"

"Sure thing, Dad." Lucas gracefully weaves through the crowd, trying to find available space near the stage. One of the musicians walks out to start a sound check.

"Would you like another drink before the concert begins?" Victor inquires.

"No, thank you. I'll be sipping this glass for the next forty minutes." I laugh.

"Have you given any more thought to my dinner invitation? Lucas leaves Monday morning. I could have you over in the evening."

Victor must be able to sense my hesitation, but his eyes remain expectant. After spending nearly forty years married to the same wonderful man, it's still hard to believe that he's really gone. But he is. And it is only dinner.

"That sounds nice," I tell him and watch his face flush.

"Great. Just great." His voice is upbeat. "Now what do you say we go join my son for some music?"

As he takes my hand and pulls me toward the stage, I look back to where Helen was standing. Her date is handing her a glass of something red with a drink umbrella, but Helen only has eyes for me and Victor. And if looks were cruise missiles, I'd be dead.

CHAPTER THIRTY-TWO

The room smells like mothballs.

That's my first thought as I walk into the Golf Club ballroom early Sunday afternoon. It's been set up to host a Veterans Day buffet for anyone who served in the military and the families of former servicemen and women.

Several attendees have poured themselves into their old uniforms, all of which must have been in the closet for decades, next to little spheres of pesticide. The pungent aroma reminds me of my own grandparents' house, and it pains me to think my grandchildren might begin to associate that smell with me.

Ritchie recently bought a little device that uses natural oils to make his own place smell nicer. I'll have to remember to ask him to get me one for Christmas. Lost in my own thoughts, I don't hear Dom Skellig approaching until he's right behind me.

"Hello, Madeline. I haven't heard of any new golf-related injuries, so I trust all is well with you."

He's once again wearing knee-length shorts, but, for the occasion, he's donned a short-sleeved button-down shirt with embroidered Hawaiian flowers. It's white, and you can see the dark hairs on his chest through the material.

"Dom, you startled me!"

"It's a good thing you didn't have a club in your hand."

My face falls, thinking of Carlota, and he seems to belatedly realize the connection. "Oh, that just slipped out. I didn't mean anything, you know, about…well, you know. I just meant people get hurt when you play golf."

I inhale deeply, drinking in my embarrassment.

"Oh no, shoot. I'm sorry. I didn't mean that!" He seems so flustered and on edge I can't help but take pity. It's also hard to deny that he has a point.

I rest my hand on his shoulder. "Are you doing alright, Dom?"

He exhales slowly. "I've had better weeks."

"Has the board made a decision yet about keeping you on?"

He points to the conference room door. "It's being decided as we speak."

"I hope it all goes well for you, Dom. I really do." I squeeze his shoulder before dropping my hand back down to my side.

"Thanks. Are you here for the Veterans Day buffet?" He asks.

"I am. It seemed right to come."

He raised one bushy eyebrow. "Were you in the military?"

"No, not me. My husband, Clint, served. He was drafted to go to Vietnam. We met not long after he came back from his tour."

It's almost impossible to imagine my life before Clint. We shared so much joy and laughter in our thirty-nine years of marriage, not to mention having two extraordinary children together. Which makes it even harder to come to terms with life after him.

As I've been silently reminiscing, Dom has shifted his focus to the conference room door. He's probably desperate to know what's happening behind it.

"I've been meaning to ask you—" I try to distract him, "—what was it like being on the PGA Tour?"

Dom looks back at me. A smile chases the worry from his face before he settles into a casual stance that feels rehearsed. "It was alright," he says nonchalantly. "Hard work though. Tiger and I would be out there practicing every day for hours on end."

"Are you good friends with Tiger Woods? You mention him quite a bit."

184

"Do I? We used to be really tight, but we don't see each other as much these days. I still send him a Christmas card every year though."

I don't ask if he gets one in return. His day seems rough enough. Instead, I ask, "Do you want to grab something to eat? They're just starting to put out the food."

A worried expression returns to his face. "I'm not really that hungry."

We're not that far apart in age, but I am tempted to deliver a mom lecture on the benefits of a hot meal. Before I can, the door to the conference room flies open with such force it bangs against the wall.

"You'll come crawling back, mark my words!" Astrid practically screams. Her back is to us, blocking our view of the board members.

Her body whips around, but her short hair, strangely, doesn't even flutter. I must find out what kind of hair products she uses. Now is not the right time, though. Her face is bright pink and the veins in her long neck are so prominent they resemble a topographical map.

Seeing Dom, Astrid uses her middle finger to push her round glasses further up her nose. She strides in our direction, her long legs carrying her across the room in a few short steps.

"Well, Dom, it looks like you'll get to keep your job after all," she hisses. "At least for now."

"You're not joining the board?" He asks.

"Bravo, genius," her lips snarl. "I wasn't good enough, apparently. Because of you!"

"What did I do?" Dom asks. "You're the one who came to me!"

"I've been labeled as someone who likes to cause conflict. Me! All because I had the ridiculous notion that I could trust you."

"But you could trust me! I didn't tell a living soul that I was designing your golf course!"

She leans her head back and laughs, though it sounds more like a rabid dog barking. "Did you seriously think I'd have trusted *you* to design a course? Grow up. Anyone with half a brain would have seen right through me, would have known I just wanted to stick it to Carlota."

Stricken, Dom's jaw and shoulders drop. Astrid certainly isn't making a very good impression on me, but I don't think I know Dom well enough to come to his defense. Especially after all the mishaps I've had under his tutelage.

I choose another tactic that I hope will put a stop to Astrid's bullying, at least for now.

"What a beautiful keychain," I say to Astrid, pointing to the plastic rainbow with a pot of gold that's clutched between her bony fingers.

Her head pivots, and she's staring at me now, her dark brown eyes narrowing.

"Did anyone say anything to you?" She asks. "Who the heck are you anyway?"

"My name is Madeline. I just moved here."

"Well, woopty-doo for you. Now if you don't mind, grandma, we're in the middle of a conversation here."

Vanity urges me to point out that, close up, she actually seems quite a few years older than me, but I refrain. One of us is already being petty and spiteful. Even that is one too many.

"Where did you get it?" I ask instead.

"Really? You're still talking?"

"My lips are moving, and words are coming out, so, yes. I am. And I'm really interested in where you got that beautiful keychain. My granddaughter just loves rainbows. She'd be so happy if I got her something like that."

"It's cheap plastic." She looks skeptical. "Seriously?"

"Seriously! Do you remember where you got it? It really would just make her day."

She snorts. "Impeccable taste here at Egret's Loft, I see. But best of luck. My partner won these in one of those claw games at a traveling fair last year."

"These?"

"Yeah, there were two. He kept the other half." It's on the tip of my tongue to ask if Harold has the other half, until she adds, "Not that it's any of your business."

Leon, Victor, and some of the other board members start to filter out of the conference room. They stop when they see Astrid.

She makes a rude hand gesture at them, then turns back to Dom.

"I wouldn't get too comfortable if I were you," she warns, then swivels on her heel and storms out of the clubhouse.

"If I were you, Dom, I'd be grateful I didn't have to work for her," I tell him.

"She used to be so nice to me. But I'm certainly seeing the other side now." He sounds regretful. "Hey, did you really want that keychain, or were you just trying to get her to lay off of me?"

"Emmy does love rainbows, but she's three. Why would she need a keychain?" I give Dom a wink. "I just didn't think it was very nice of her to treat you that way."

"Well, thank you. I think that earns you a private lesson, on the house."

"Brave man," I tease. "But I'm very happy that you'll get to stay."

A toothy smile emerges from under his mustache. "Yeah, me too."

As I walk to the buffet table, I think about my list of murder suspects. Selena's under arrest, and maybe Eliza's right. Selena could well be the killer. If she's not, it seems two of my other suspects—Dom and Astrid—might have hypothetically killed Carlota for nothing. Neither of them got what they wanted.

And then there's no-neck Harold. If he gave Astrid that keychain, and she's still using it, they must still be a couple. Was he breaking into Carlota's house to retrieve something for Astrid? Or did it go even deeper? Did he kill Carlota at the request of his lover and go back for something he left behind?

Holding my plate out for a serving of Eggs Benedict, determination settles in me. I must find Harold.

CHAPTER THIRTY-THREE

Two blocks from home, lights start flashing on my golf cart's dashboard. They flicker between yellow and red, colors which normally mean something bad is about to happen.

The problem is, I can't read the display without my reading glasses. I feel the top of my head, which is where I frequently find them, but the only thing on my head at the moment is my sun hat. I must have left my readers at home.

My foot eases off the gas, and I feel my speed drop to two miles per hour.

Years ago, Eliza made me watch that Sandra Bullock movie about the bus that would blow up if it went over a certain speed. Or was it if she slowed down? I can't quite remember. Either way, whenever something goes wrong in a vehicle I slow down. Blowing up seems like such an awful way to go.

Marjorie Higginbottom saunters from behind to pull up alongside me. She's out for a late afternoon stroll with her walker. She lifts one hand to wave and then continues on, outpacing me and the cart.

Finally, I arrive at my driveway to find Roy sitting on my stoop.

"Roy, could you help me?"

He makes a move as if he's going to jump to his feet, but his knees seem to slow his progress. "You betcha! What do ya need?"

"I think something might be seriously wrong with my golf cart!"

He's next to me in three strides. "Let me have a look-see."

He looks at the dashboard, then leans back and squints his eyes slightly.

"I see what the problem is," he says, chuckling softly. "She's almost out of battery. When was the last time you plugged in the old girl?"

"Just to be clear, you *are* talking about the golf cart?" I ask.

He lets out a short whoop of laughter. "Sure am. Did you remember to charge her last night?"

"It's been a couple of days," I admit. "If I plug it in, that'll solve the problem?"

"She'll be right as rain." He offers his hand to help me disembark from the cart. Grabbing my little dented purse, I take his hand and step out onto the driveway.

"Thank you. I'm afraid I'm not the best with electronics."

"You and me both. I usually rope in the grandkids to do that kind of stuff for me."

"Oh, you have grandchildren?"

"Sure do. Twelve of the little rugrats."

My eyes widen. "Twelve?!"

"Yeah, a whole football team and one substitute! Course now, seven of 'em are girls, but sports are much more progressive than they were in my day."

"Seven granddaughters?" I shiver, imagining Tory and Emmy, with five more just like them. "How many children did you and your wife have?"

"Oh, I've flown solo my whole life. Never took on the old ball and chain. Did have five kids though. All of 'em had different mothers," he says.

I'm trying really hard not to be judgmental, when Roy shifts his large frame. Behind him I see a big, circular bouquet of white carnations, with a red sash that reads *With Sympathy*, sitting next to my front door.

I point to it. "Is that yours?"

He follows the direction of my finger with his eyes, as if he doesn't know what's there, then recognition dawns. "That's for you! Remember how you told me you wanted a proper funeral for Egretta? Well, here it is!"

"Egretta?"

He shrugs. "The vet needed a name to put on the urn."

"You had her cremated?"

"I did!" He walks to the front door, where an urn sits next to the funeral bouquet. He picks it up and turns to me smiling. "Solid marble with a little gold statue on top. It's a parakeet, but it was the best they could do on short notice."

He hands it to me, but it's so heavy my arms nearly collapse from the weight of it.

"I'm impressed with the effort you put into this," I tell him, handing it back to him. "Poor little Egretta."

"Well, hold on to your hat, cause there's more!"

"More?" I scan the hedges, hoping a bugler won't pop out to start playing "Taps."

Roy pulls an envelope out of the back pocket of his shorts with the hand not holding the urn. "It's a donation to wildlife rescue and rehabilitation. Got a plaque with your name on it and everything."

He hands me the envelope and I open it. He's donated $10,000 to a local charity!

"Roy! This is too much!"

He shakes his head, the smile vanishing from his face. "Naw, I was being an idiot. You gotta believe I meant well. But it was stupid, and I felt really bad for the little thing. I hope this does a little toward making it up to you."

I look up at his face. He's a big oaf of a man, and there's no question he's a sore loser, but it also seems like his insides are part marshmallow.

"You want to carry that urn inside for me? Maybe help me pick a spot for it?"

His expensive veneers glisten in the sunlight. "At your service, m'lady."

I open the front door, and we walk inside, both uttering a small sigh of satisfaction when we feel the air-conditioning hit our skin.

"How about over there?" I point to the mantle above an electric fireplace in the living room. It doesn't give off any heat; it just lights up and crackles like a real wood fire.

"You got it," he says, effortlessly transporting the twenty-pound urn across the room.

I hand him a glass of iced tea, which he gratefully accepts. Before taking a sip, he lifts his glass. "To Egretta!"

"Egretta!" I echo and we both drink.

"Ya know, having Egretta cremated really got me thinking about Carlota," he says, staring intently at the condensation on his glass. "She didn't deserve to go like that."

"The last time we spoke about her, it didn't seem like the two of you were friendly," I say, stopping short of reminding him he said it wasn't worth ruining a golf club on her head.

"My blood was boiling already because of the bird thing, ya know? I didn't mean what I said. She was alright. Darn good Scrabble player too."

"When was the last time you spoke with her?"

"Lemme think." He scratches his mostly bald head. "She died on the Monday night, so it must've been Saturday the last time I saw her."

"Do you remember what you talked about?"

"She came round my place asking if I'd seen Selena or Harold. Said she had some business with each of 'em."

This was the first I'd heard of this! Carlota had been seeking out two of my main suspects right before she died. It must mean something.

"Did she say what she wanted to talk to them about?"

He shakes his head. "She didn't say, and I didn't ask. None of my business what goes on in their huddle."

"Of course," I agree. "Speaking of Harold, have you seen him around lately? He seems to have gone into hiding."

He slaps his thigh. "You clocked that too? I've been thinkin' it's right weird. Him just up and disappearing. Haven't heard the dreadful racket from his car in a couple of days!"

"He didn't say anything to you about where he was going?"

"Heck, no. He hasn't been himself lately though."

"What do you mean?"

He thinks for a minute. "Just real jumpy-like. On edge. Something has him rattled, that's for sure."

"You think he might be scared of something?"

One side of his face contracts in contemplation. "Not so much scared. More anxious. Kinda like he's worried about something."

"How long has that been going on?" I think of Astrid and wonder if she might have pushed Harold to do her dirty work for her.

"Just the past few weeks or so," Roy says. "But I don't know the guy that well. We don't talk much. He's not into sports."

"I see. It is very curious, though, don't you think? Carlota was asking about Selena and Harold. Carlota's dead, Selena's under arrest, and Harold is nowhere to be found. I wonder if it's all connected somehow. Did Carlota say anything else? You know, the last time you saw her."

"Small talk mostly. Oh, she did ask me if I knew anything about Stan gettin' scammed on some fake cryptocurrency. I told her I couldn't help her. My accountant handles all the finances for my crypt—all marble, with space for all my kids and grandkids!"

"That's…something," I say. "But I thought cryptocurrency was sort of like poker chips that you trade online, like money."

"What? Naw, that can't be right."

We both shrug our shoulders, neither swayed by the other's opinion. I take a sip of my iced tea, thinking. "I wonder why Carlota didn't go to Stan directly to ask about the scam, if it was a scam."

"Oh, she did," Roy tells me. "But he slammed the door in her face."

"That does sound like something he would do," I say, remembering my own visits to Stan's house. I belatedly realize that I never took Curt by his house to help sort out the Fridge

Friend app. If I want any more information out of Stan, I may have to have Ritchie set up a video call with Curt first.

A loud ping sounds from the kitchen, startling Roy. Ritchie insisted on turning up the ringer volume on my cell phone before he left, so I'd be sure to hear if he or Eliza were trying to get ahold of me. He set it so loud, though, it sounds like it went off next to my head, even though the phone is buried at the bottom of my purse on the kitchen counter.

The refrigerator chimes in to tell me I have a new text message.

"Probably my kids," I apologize to Roy. "I should check to see what they want."

He takes the hint. "Right, sure. I'll leave you to it. I wanted to ask though…any chance you'd like to go out on my boat with me? The river behind my house leads right into the bay. Good fishing. If you're into that."

I remember the way he checked out Helen's posterior earlier in the week, which puts me off accepting. But, after all he just did for Egretta, it seems rude to refuse. "That sounds nice."

Only when his shoulders relax, do I realize he'd been tensing up his muscles. "Great. I'll check the forecast and let you know what days might work."

"Perfect."

"Cool," he responds, smiling.

"Roy?"

"Yes?"

"My kids are probably waiting for me to respond."

"Oh, right." He sets his empty glass on a coaster. "Well, I'll see you soon then."

He shows himself out as I dig through my purse for the phone. It wasn't my kids trying to reach me after all. It was Gina. The message reads: *Selman stelling droogs. On my waze over soon.*

CHAPTER THIRTY-FOUR

"Thank goodness, you're alright! I thought maybe you were having a stroke or something." I hug Gina as soon as she arrives an hour or so later.

"A stroke? What are you talking about?"

"Your text message. It was so erratic, I felt sure you were having an episode!"

"An episode? I'm fine. Maybe your eyes are the problem." She pulls her phone out of her pocket and checks the text. "There's nothing wrong with…oh. No, I see what you mean."

"What was the text supposed to say?"

"I was trying to tell you that Selma wasn't selling drugs after all!"

"You mean Selena?"

"Yeah, sure. But did you hear what I said? It really was just makeup in all those boxes. She had loads of the stuff!"

"She could probably stand to lose a few pounds," I admit, "but she has a very pretty face. Such a shame she feels the need to wear so much makeup."

"It wasn't all for her, Mandy. Jeez. She was one of those…what do you call them?" Gina snaps her fingers. "Mary Kay people."

"Mary Kay? They used to sell a foundation that was just divine! Heavy enough to cover my little bouts of rosacea, but not so heavy it made me break out. I wonder if they still make it."

"Are you listening to me or doing a Mary Kay commercial?"

"Yes, sorry. I'm listening!" Though in the back of my head I'm wondering if I could get products from Selena. Only if she's not a murderer, of course.

Gina uses the back of her hand to wipe off beads of sweat that have formed on her forehead. "Are you going to invite me in? It's hot out here."

I step out of the way to grant her access. "Would you like something to drink?"

She pulls a bottle of wine out of a canvas shoulder bag. "Way ahead of you. Do you have ice?"

"You want ice for your wine?"

"It's not cold, and I'm impatient. You got any better ideas?"

I pour her pinot grigio into two stemmed glasses with ice and hand one to her, checking the time on the refrigerator. It's just after six o'clock. At least I'm not turning into a day drinker.

"So how did you find out about the makeup? Did Detective Fletcher tell you?" I ask, surprised Eliza hasn't texted me with the information.

"My security guard friend told me," she says, after taking a long sip of her iced wine. "A cop friend of his came over to check the vehicle entry logs, and they got to chatting. Anyway, turns out she didn't have guns or drugs stashed in her garage."

"But why were men delivering the boxes in the middle of the night? That does seem odd."

Gina shrugs. "According to my guy, those were her gardeners. She pays them extra to go pick up boxes for her from time to time at a PO box in town. They were just running late."

"You don't think Selena could have outsmarted the police?"

She contemplates the question. "Not out of the realm of possibility. Let's be honest, it'd be harder to outsmart a goldfish than the police around here. Why? What are you thinking?"

"I don't know. Maybe Selena knew Carlota was onto her, so she switched out all the drugs in her garage for cosmetics! Then she killed Carlota to protect her identity and threatened

196

Harold. That could be why he's gone into hiding! What do you think?"

"I think you may have watched too many episodes of *Murder, She Wrote*, but what do I know?" Gina says. "Does that mean Sam, Holly, and Ashley are in the clear?"

I take a minute to think before answering. "*Stan* is hiding something, that's obvious. But I don't know what it is."

"I know he was hiding his air fresheners. His place smelled awful."

I ignore her and continue my train of thought. "Helen was mad about Mitsy, and she does have a temper. But would Harold go into hiding for days just to get away from her? It seems unlikely."

"Maybe if more men hid from her, she wouldn't have seven dead husbands," Gina adds.

"You're terrible! Though that is a lot."

"My mother always used to say the best husband is a dead husband," Gina says, winking. "But what about Ashley? You think she's clean?"

"*Astrid.* I don't know. She was in a relationship with Harold, and she wanted to get control of Egret's Loft. If Harold was helping her to do that, maybe he ran away because he worried he might get caught. Especially after I saw him breaking into Carlota's house."

Her glass empty, Gina goes to the fridge to pour more wine, asking, "What's our next step?"

Getting my thoughts together, I wait until she's done replenishing our beverages to respond. "Would you agree that, right now, Selena and Astrid are our best suspects?"

She nods. "Sounds about right to me."

"So, we're agreed on that. And they're both tied to Harold, who's missing. I really think finding him is the key to this whole thing."

"Fine. How do we go about doing that?"

A thought occurs to me. "Can you see into Harold's house from the back?"

"I think so. All the houses over there face onto the river…real pretty views. Only an idiot would put up something to block them. Why?"

"I'd just like to take a little peek in his house. Not break in or anything, just look in through the windows. See what we see."

I wait for Eliza to text me to stay out of the case. She never did take those infernal cameras down. But no message comes. She must have stopped spying on me now that Selena is in jail. I find myself surprisingly disappointed.

Gina claps her hands excitedly. "I knew I put on my good walking shoes for a reason! Let's go!"

Turning right out of my driveway, we pass Helen's house on the left. Mitsy perches on a sofa to stare out the window but doesn't bark as we pass by. If you ask me, Harold did Helen a favor with that. Little dogs are adorable, but often have the lung capacity of Satan himself.

Before getting to Jinny and George's house, Gina and I hurriedly cross the street. Without speaking, we both agreed we didn't want to get cornered into having a long conversation if Jinny saw us passing.

Marjorie lives across the street. Her house smells vaguely like cookies.

Luckily, we're the only ones out on the street. All our neighbors are probably just finishing their dinners. Which means we only have about an hour of daylight left.

Picking up the pace, we turn left to cut between Marjorie and Selena's houses, where there's a concrete path, just wide enough for a wheelchair, leading to the river. Despite its obvious handicap accessibility, there's a certain raw savagery to the wild foliage chipping away at the pavement from both sides and partially blocking out the sun.

We hear rustling emanating from the thick branches and a rather loud splash from the water's edge up ahead.

"Maybe we should come back tomorrow," Gina suggests, her voice shaky. "There'll be better light in the daytime."

I'm tempted to agree, but it won't work. "I can't. Ritchie signed me up for a day-long evaluation with the fitness instructor."

"Oh, wow, you have to spend the whole day with Mary?"

"The flier said Molly, but yes. Why? Is that a bad thing?"

"Let's just say you'd be safer here with the gators."

"There are gators here?" Curt's earlier warning springs to mind, and I suddenly wish I'd paid more attention.

"You're in Florida, hun. They're everywhere."

I struggle to remember the statistics he'd rattled off. From what I can recall, the chances of a horrible death were rather slim…weren't they?

Suddenly our plan is starting to feel a little reckless.

We're behind Selena's house now. She's planted tall hedges around the back of her property, creating a cocoon of privacy for her screened-in patio. Stepping past the hedges, onto Harold's property, a deep, throaty growl paralyzes us in our tracks.

"What was that?" I ask.

Gina points a shaking finger, her voice barely above a whisper. "There. Across the river."

I squint, trying to peer into the shadows. "Where are you pointing?"

"The mangroves!" She whispers more adamantly.

"It's all mangroves!" I whisper back.

"A…A…A…alligator!"

I can't believe I missed it—the dark green scaly body, the beady, soulless eyes, and the teeth, tinged red with blood. I start to scream. Then Gina starts to scream. The alligator, annoyed by our sudden wailing, slides under the surface of the water, leaving whatever it was eating behind on the bank of the river.

Gina tugs insistently on my arm, already backing toward the path between the houses. "Would you come on! We gotta get out of here before that gator comes for us!"

Focusing on the opposite side of the river, I can't help but notice that the meal the gator had been feasting on is wearing pants.

Just then, the carcass shifts, a human head rolling to the side, its vacant eyes staring back at me. Recognition dawns. I'm looking at the dead body of Harold Small.

Someone, or something, found him before I did.

CHAPTER THIRTY-FIVE

"In almost seventy-five years, there have only been twenty-three fatal alligator attacks in the state," I recite the stats that Curt texted at my request. "I'm just asking if you're really sure that's what killed him."

"And I'm just asking you to stop trying to play detective and let me do my job!"

Detective Fletcher, his wide nose flaring slightly, challenges me. He's working so hard to be authoritative, but I detect a slight quiver in the dimple on his chin, and his bald head is slightly redder than normal.

He arrived early Monday morning to interview me after spending a good portion of last night trying to safely retrieve the body. The gator, apparently, had not taken kindly to the forensics team trying to steal its food.

I take a deep breath and adjust my strategy. "The last thing I want to do is undermine you, Detective. Quite the opposite, in fact! You've come quite a long way since we first met."

His shoulders relax. "Thanks for saying that. It's been a pretty steep learning curve."

"I'm sure it has!" I assure him. "But you're handling it wonderfully. And you're becoming much more intuitive. When I asked if you thought anything was off with Harold's death, I had the impression you already felt that way. So really, I just verbalized the question I sensed you already had in your own mind."

I'm slightly embarrassed to be so blatantly leading the detective, but what choice do I have? A full autopsy needs to be done on Harold and, for Detective Fletcher to request one, it's going to have to seem like his own idea.

He scrunches his eyes. "Why, exactly, did you think that's what I was thinking?"

Oh boy. I'm going to need to spell this out for him. "I was thinking that's what you'd be thinking because you're far too clever not to be thinking it! As you know, better than anyone, this is the second suspicious death at Egret's Loft in the past week."

"Well, of course, I would be thinking that," he defends himself. "But wouldn't I also be thinking that death here isn't exactly surprising? I mean, it's a nursing home. Everyone here is old." Then, as an afterthought he adds, "No offense."

"None taken," I tell him. "But, technically, it's a retirement community, not a nursing home."

"Is there that big of a difference?" He asks.

"Just humor me here, alright?"

"Whatever." He shrugs. "But the fact is, mortality rates are higher in places like this."

I swallow my impatience like it's the chalky cocktail you get before a colonoscopy. "That's true. But usually, those deaths are caused by heart attacks or diabetes or cancer. That's not quite the same as a golf club to the head or an alligator mauling!"

He tilts his head. "Fair point. But I don't have any evidence Harold was murdered. And autopsies are expensive. Or so my boss tells me. I've never had to ask for one before."

"Yes, you poor man. Carlota's is your first murder, isn't it?" I ask him.

He sits back, slightly surprised. "You make that sound like a weird thing…not being exposed to homicidal violence on a regular basis!"

"Yes, I suppose because my Clint was a detective in DC, I heard about violent death a lot more than most people would consider normal," I grant him. "But, back to the autopsy, I'm sure you've considered the break-in at Carlota's house. I provided a statement for the police report, pointing the finger at

Harold. That was three days ago; now suddenly he's dead. You must have thought that was a little suspicious…"

Detective Fletcher ponders this train of thought before deciding to disembark. "Or…" he lingers on the single syllable, "the alligator got him after he fled the crime scene. It was dark. Maybe he took a wrong turn and…*bam!* He's gator bait. Oh—" he warms to his theory, "—maybe that's why your daughter lost him in the chase. The gator had already dragged him underwater."

"That is possible," I acknowledge. "Though you wouldn't be able to prove that *is* what happened without an autopsy. And you must have Selena's situation in the back of your mind."

"Of course, I do," he snaps, then leans forward in my direction. "What part of her situation do you think I'm thinking about?"

I remind myself to be patient. If you treat people like they're idiots, they'll think you're a jerk and ignore anything coming out of your mouth. That's what Clint always used to say. If you talk to people as if they're smarter than they actually are, they're more inclined to believe it and listen to what you have to say.

With that in mind, I playfully swat the detective's hand. "No need to play coy with me! It's obvious you're worried about Harold's time of death. If he died when Selena was in jail, she wouldn't have been able to kill him."

"Why on earth would I be worried about that?" Detective Fletcher's face is a mask of confusion until, once more, he gets a hold of himself. "I mean, hypothetically speaking."

"Well, if Selena is charged with Carlota's murder…which I don't think has happened yet, has it?"

"Not yet," he confirms.

"Precisely. So, if she *is* charged, any good defense attorney would argue that the deaths are connected in some way. As unfair as it might be, her lawyer would pick apart the case, and likely stir up some trouble for any officers who worked the case, if Harold's death looks like it wasn't handled properly. Or, even worse, they could say that was intentional! Some kind of police conspiracy to protect the *real* suspect!"

Detective Fletcher flinches as if I've slapped him. "But that's ridiculous! And not true!"

"I know that, but the jury won't. Especially if the lawyer points out that there were other possible suspects in both murders."

"Other suspects?" He seems to choke on the words.

"Yes, of course! You don't have to pretend with me," I tell him, fully realizing he isn't pretending. "You must be talking to Astrid about her plans to take over Egret's Loft—which she put into motion pretty much as soon as Carlota died. Not to mention, she was in a relationship with Harold."

"Carlota was?"

"No, Astrid. Oh, and then there are Stan and Helen. They both had run-ins with Carlota before she died. Helen also had an issue with Harold nearly running over her precious dog. And Stan was supposedly Harold's best friend, but something feels off about their friendship, wouldn't you agree?"

"Uh-huh," he practically whimpers, looking like Bambi in the headlights of an oncoming car. He's staring at me, but I get the impression he's looking right through me, wondering if his career is going to be the next casualty of Egret's Loft.

My phone rings. The refrigerator tells me it's Eliza. I ignore her call for now.

"Detective Fletcher?" I decide to intervene after he's spent several minutes gazing blankly out the window. I'm genuinely starting to worry about him.

"What's that now?" He asks, getting back his bearings.

"Just making sure you're alright. You've got a lot on your mind, trying to solve this case."

He nods. "To be honest with you, this is a lot harder than I thought it was going to be without a partner. Mine retired right before all this happened. My new partner starts next week, but that doesn't help me now."

As out of his depths as I know he is, I truly believe he wants to be a good detective. He just hasn't had the practice necessary to get there.

He closes his notebook, not having taken a single note in the past fifteen minutes and picks up the glass of water I poured him earlier. He takes a long sip, sets the glass down and reopens his notebook.

"Is there anything you'd like to add to your statement?" He asks. "Anything else you remember about finding the body?"

The shift back to my statement catches me by surprise, but perhaps he's trying to reestablish his professionalism after coming off as a little insecure.

"I think I told you everything already," I assure him. "We only saw the body for a few seconds. The alligator that was…oh dear, how should I say this…eating Harold, had us pretty spooked."

"Understandably. If you happen to think of any other details, ma'am, don't hesitate to give me a call."

He stands and starts walking toward the door.

"Detective?"

He pauses but doesn't turn around. "Yes?"

I point to the sofa. "It's just that your gun must have fallen out of its holster."

He whips around, his face an uncomfortable shade of red. "Oh shoot! That's the second time that's happened. I guess I need a new holster."

He walks over and grabs the gun, shoving it into his holster with such force I fear he might accidentally shoot one of us. Then he turns around and stomps back toward the door.

"Detective?"

He whips back around. "What now?"

"I was just wondering…are you going to ask for that autopsy?"

"Maybe. Probably." Loosening his neck muscles, he blurts out, "Yes! Yes, I am! Happy now?"

Without waiting for me to respond, he throws open the front door, walks through it, and slams it behind him.

I'm left trying to predict what the autopsy might say, when the doorbell rings. I wonder if Detective Fletcher left something else, like his badge, behind.

But when I open the door, Victor is standing there. And he looks frantic.

CHAPTER THIRTY-SIX

"I just heard that you and Gina found Harold dead! Are you alright?"

"I'm fine," I assure a concerned-looking Victor. "So's Gina. We had a bit of a shock, but at least the alligator didn't try to chase us."

"Alligator?"

"Yes, the one chewing on Harold's body when we found him."

"Goodness gracious! An alligator? Is that how he died?"

I shake my head. "I don't think so, not that my opinion counts for much. But the police are going to do an autopsy to figure it out."

"An autopsy?" He clears his throat. "That sounds serious. Did that detective say why he thought Harold was murdered?"

I glance away, cognizant that his blue eyes will be searching mine for weakness. "He had a few theories…"

Victor squints his eyes. "His own theories? Or did you, by any chance, loan him some of yours?"

My eyes lock on his. "Am I that obvious?"

He nods with a little too much enthusiasm. "I'm afraid so. You're a smart lady, but a terrible liar. And, not to be unkind, but Detective Fletcher doesn't seem like the sharpest knife in the drawer."

After the detective's earlier vulnerability, I feel a maternal desire to defend him. "He's learning a lot and genuinely seems to want to get better."

"Learning a lot? From you?" His voice sounds heavy with an emotion I can't place.

"Oh no, I don't feel comfortable taking credit for that—"

"Madeline!" He interrupts, clearly frustrated. "Can't you tell I'm starting to really worry about you!"

"You're worried? About me?"

"You bet I am! It sounds like you're saying there may now be two murders at Egret's Loft in the past week! And you keep putting yourself right in the middle! Do you realize how dangerous that is?" He's breathing heavily, and the veins in his neck are throbbing at an alarming rate.

"Don't you think you're being a bit unfair?" I ask as we face off in the doorway. "I mean, it's not like I planned on finding Harold's body! Nor did I plan to catch him breaking into Carlota's house, for that matter!"

"Alright." He folds his arms across his chest. "What were you and Gina doing behind Harold's house when you *just happened* to find his body?"

I suddenly feel sixty years younger and back in the principal's office, trying to convince Sister Susan that I didn't pass notes in class. She could always see right through me and, I suspect, so can Victor right now.

"We were trying to find Harold," I admit.

His arms unfold and he throws his hands up in the air. "Exactly what I thought! Don't think I don't know you've been going around asking people questions. Trying to learn everyone's secrets. Don't you see what you're doing?"

"Trying to solve a murder?"

"No…but, actually, yes!" He corrects himself. "You *are* trying to solve a murder, but you're not a police officer. You're going to either get yourself killed or arrested!"

I exaggeratedly roll my eyes. "That sounds a little overly dramatic, don't you think? Why would I get arrested?"

"It's interesting you chose being arrested as the more unlikely outcome, but okay. Let's explore that, shall we?"

"Go ahead," I dare him.

"If there are now two dead bodies…two murdered people here…how long do you think it's going to take people to realize all of this started to happen right after you arrived? And then,

208

you go digging into their personal business? It wouldn't take much to convince them you're the killer."

"Well now, that's ridiculous. I could never kill anyone!" I argue, adding, "But can we continue this conversation inside, because my ankles are swelling up from all of this standing."

Victor lets out a sigh of relief. "I thought you'd never ask. This darn osteoarthritis. My knees are killing me."

"You have osteoarthritis too? My kids thought the weather here would be good for managing the pain. Do you think that's true?'

"It is better most days," he says.

I stand aside to let him enter, and we both make our way into the living room.

"Can I get you something to drink?" I offer.

"No, thanks. I had a lot of water with my morning pills." He sits down on the sofa and waits for me to take the chair opposite him. "Now back to the point. There's a decent chance you could become a suspect in this mess if you're not careful."

I swat away his worry like it's an annoying fly. "Detective Fletcher wouldn't arrest me."

"You're probably right. I'm sure you'd find a way to talk him out of it," he grudgingly concedes. "But what about the fact that there may well be a serial killer on the loose? Do you want to make yourself a target by asking too many questions?"

"I'm not a target," I argue. "And, anyway, my kids had a state-of-the-art security system installed, so I'm perfectly safe."

"Security systems only work when you use them. You just let me in. What if I was the killer? You're so busy trying to get answers from everybody, you'd probably volunteer the murder weapon the killer would use on you!"

My phone beeps. Thinking it might be Eliza calling back, I glance down, but she's only sent a text.

I really like this guy! If you won't listen to me, at least listen to him!

Oh, now she's paying attention again? I glare up at the camera above the cupboard that she's still using to spy on me.

"Madeline? Are you alright?" Victor asks, probably wondering if I'm hallucinating, based on the way I'm staring up toward the ceiling.

"I'm fine," I assure him. "It would just be so nice, in my old age, if my children would treat me with a little more respect."

Another ping of the phone. Another text, which simply reads: *Oh, cry me a river.*

Victor appears confused and I don't blame him.

"Sorry about that. Where were we?" I ask Victor, while trying to figure out how to turn my phone onto silent.

Victor, seeing me struggle, leans over the coffee table between us until his face is mere inches from mine. He smiles, looks down, and flips the lever on the side of my iPhone that turns off the ringer. His cologne tickles my nose.

The joint in his knee makes a popping sound as he sits back down.

"Look, Madeline. It can't come as a surprise when I tell you that I like you. I've liked you since we first met. You were so poised and elegant as the detective tried to grill you about Carlota's death. I knew right away that I wanted to spend more time with you."

"That's very…sweet." My response isn't what he was hoping for. I can see that right away. But I'm only recently widowed and, if he's as interested as he claims to be, he'll have to have the patience and sense to wait.

Which could prove to be a problem. We're not getting any less old.

"All I'm trying to say is, I want you to be safe." his eyes beg for understanding. "Aren't you a little scared yourself? I heard there was a dead bird left at your door."

I hold up my hands to stop him. "Oh, no, *that* was a misunderstanding."

"Does it matter? What was your first thought when you saw it?" He asks.

210

"That someone left it there as a message for me. Phyllis thought so too."

"Phyllis?" He points toward the front door. "The woman across the street?"

"Yes, why?"

"She talked to you?" He asks, his voice disbelieving.

"She did. Why is that so odd?"

He shakes his head, as if to erase his thoughts. "Sorry. She's just kind of like a myth around here. Like a chupacabra or a banshee. No one ever sees her. She just occasionally leaves broken mailboxes in her wake. Stan thinks she's been dead inside that house for years."

"I assure you, she is very much alive."

"Huh. Good for her. Anyway," he says, "you admit that you thought someone was threatening you. How are you sleeping?"

Darn, he's got me again. "Not great. But my doctor recently prescribed some new beta blockers, so that's probably why I haven't been sleeping as well lately."

"Just hear me out, here," Victor requests. I nod my acquiescence. "The cops think Selena killed Carlota. Quite frankly, so do I, after learning who she really is. And Harold probably just had a terrible accident. Maybe there's no crime left for you to solve, and you're just making people around here angry by asking all your questions."

His logic doesn't wash. "If you think the police already have their killer, why are you so worried about me?"

He considers his response before speaking. "I could be wrong. I don't think I am, but if you're right, and there is still a killer on the loose, I don't want you to be putting yourself in any danger. I'd hate to see anything happen to you. And we need to be practicing for the scramble in a few weeks. I need your head in the right place."

He winks. I know he's teasing me, but he does make a fair point.

"Alright."

He raises an eyebrow. "Yeah? You'll stop trying to play Nancy Drew?"

"I'm impressed you know who she is, but yes. I'll back off and let Detective Fletcher handle things from here," I say, quickly adding, "but if Harold *was* murdered, I reserve the right to change my mind."

"I guess that will have to do. Are we still on for dinner at my place tonight?"

"We are," I confirm.

"Great! I'll see you this evening. Try to stay out of trouble until then. If you can."

CHAPTER THIRTY-SEVEN

Sauvignon blanc or pinot noir? The two bottles sit like unanswered questions in my hands, as I kick myself for not asking what Victor would be preparing for dinner.

As soon as Victor left, I decided to try out the small grocery store at the very edge of the Egret Loft property, not wanting to arrive at his home empty-handed.

The shelves in the small shop are fully stocked but, fortunately for me and my indecisiveness, the options are significantly more limited than you'd find at the Publix on the other side of the complex's gate.

The unmistakable clacking of shopping cart wheels on linoleum alerts me that someone else has just entered the wine/beer/pre-made pina colada section.

"Fancy meeting you here, Madeline!"

I recognize Jinny's voice. Turning around, bottles still in hand, I see her decked out in solid pink. It's hard not to think she looks like she belongs in one of those Hello Kitty stores that Eliza loved so much when she was a toddler.

"Hello, Jinny. How are you?"

"Oh, I can't complain. Can't complain. Not that I couldn't, don't you know. But what's the use in complaining? It takes just as much energy to be happy as it does to be sad, which doesn't seem like much of a choice when you put it like that, now does it?"

"I suppose not…" I begin speaking, but Jinny was merely pausing for breath and, like a car with faulty brakes, can't stop the trajectory she'd already set herself on.

"I see you're looking at wines! I like a good Moscato, myself. George thinks they're too sweet for him, but he says, for me, it must be just like drinking water, since I'm just as sweet. He really does go on sometimes! But is there a special occasion? It's always nice to have something to celebrate, though I don't think many people around here feel like celebrating…not after what happened to Harold. Can you imagine it? Attacked by an alligator? Holy Jesus Murphy!" She puts a hand in front of her ballet slipper pink lips. "Oh, pardon my French. I don't normally swear, but this whole thing just has me so worked up. I heard you were the one found his body! That must have been just awful, eh?"

"It was awful." I take advantage of the opening. "Poor Harold. I feel so terrible for his family." As I say it, I realize I don't know if Harold had any family.

"Oh, no, Harold didn't have a wife or kids." Jinny seems to read my mind. "I think he had a sister somewhere out west, but I don't think they were very close, don't you know. Now, he and that woman from Shady Palms were quite the item, if you know what I mean. Until she broke it off, or maybe she didn't after all. It's so hard to say. It seemed very on again, off again. All drama. But then I always got the sense she was using him a little. So, good riddance to her. But, no, Harold didn't have any real family to speak of. Even Stan fell out with him at the end. Those two used to be thick as thieves, but then Harold asked Stan for that favor, and the friendship was over. Which makes me so sad for Harold, having no one there to help when times got tough. But look at me gabbing away when I just popped in to pick up some homo milk and KD!"

My mouth hangs open, trying to process everything she has just said into questions that my brain begs to have answered. The first seems the most obvious.

"Homo milk and KD?"

When she laughs, it reminds me of a tinkling waterfall with pink strobe lights underneath.

"Oh, dear me, I do forget that people down here say things different than we do up north. Homogenized milk and Kraft dinner." She holds up a cardboard box of Kraft macaroni and cheese. "My George just can't get enough of the stuff. He could eat it for breakfast, lunch, and dinner if I let him. So, I can't keep it in the house, no I can't. With his diabetes, I have him on a very strict diet most of the time. Just when he's feeling a bit down and needs a bit of pep, I make him his KD. He's so broken up aboot what happened to Harold, I decided to pick up a box to surprise him."

"Such a shame about Harold," I agree. "You said he'd fallen on some tough times. Did he tell you that?"

"Oh goodness me, no!" Jinny adamantly states. "He would talk to George and me from time to time, but he would never talk aboot money with us. No, I heard it from the tow truck operator that took away his big fancy car!"

It's not hard to picture Jinny, all sweetness and bubble gum, striking up a conversation with the tow truck driver. And while it might seem like Jinny does all the talking in conversations, I get the sense that she hears, and more importantly remembers, everything people say.

"Apparently," she continues, "he was behind on his payments. It was the darndest thing though, the tow truck operator asked for my help! As I was passing by, out on a little walk before lunch, I saw the tow truck, and the driver waved me over. Said he wondered if I would be able to help. He couldn't find Harold's keys. They weren't in the car, and Harold wasn't answering the front door…thinking back on it now, maybe Harold was already dead and that's why everyone thought he was missing! It does make you think, eh? Aboot living alone. He could have been dead for days. You read stuff like that happening sometimes. It just makes me——"

"Yes. Being widowed myself, I don't like to think about things like that too much." I attempt to soften the blow of my interruption. "Did you ever find Harold's keys?"

"Sure didn't. Maybe the police will find them inside Harold's house, if they ever get around to looking. Or maybe they don't need to look, because it was just an accident after all, eh? George and I were never so happy to have bought a house on the lake side of the street, don't you know. We originally chose it because I was worried aboot all the bugs, so many of them coming off the river. George is like a bug magnet. He's had every kind of bug bite you could ever imagine. It really is the most peculiar thing."

She stops to take a breath, and I take the opportunity to get in another question. "You mentioned Harold and Astrid had a somewhat tempestuous relationship?"

She rolls her eyes so far back, all I can see are the whites of her eyes. For a second, I worry they might get stuck like that. Fortunately, they don't. "Did they *ever*! Harold was more of a keener, don't you know. Oh, I can see by your face you don't, so I'll just go ahead and tell you, that's someone who's keen to make everyone like him, a real people-pleaser type. Astrid was the opposite, a real hard nose, that one. When she wanted something, there was nothing getting in her way. And she had no trouble hurting other people if it got her what she was after."

Dom experienced a similar type of behavior with Astrid. She asked him to design a golf course, only to hang him out to dry once the plan was discovered. Part of me wonders if she wasn't the person who leaked the information about Dom's treachery to the Egret's Loft board.

Jinny has continued talking as I've been thinking.

"From what I heard," she continues, "she asked Harold to do something or other for her and, quite out of character for him, he refused. She didn't like that one bit, no she didn't. They were out at lunch, don't you know, because Astrid isn't welcome at Egret's Loft in the daytime, though she would sometimes sneak in at night to see Harold. Anyway, one of my friends just happened to be in the restaurant and heard them fighting. Well, her. Apparently, *he* didn't say much. But *she* was saying enough for the both of them, don't you know. Then she stormed out of the restaurant, saying she'd had enough, and it was over."

"Sorry to stop you Jinny," I say, "but did your friend happen to hear what Astrid asked Harold to do?"

"She…my friend, I mean…didn't say what Astrid had asked for. But she did hear them talking aboot money, at one point."

I hold up my hand and ask, "You said Harold was late on his car payments. Did he seem to be having cash-flow problems before then?"

"Not that we ever suspected, until more recently, I guess. See, about a year back, Harold seemed to come into a lot of money. Bought that flashy car, started dressing in designer clothes, would pick up other people's tabs at the River Club. It was a bit over the top, truth be told, but you wanted to be happy for him. But then, not long ago, he stopped going to the River Club altogether. The only time you'd see him out was speeding past in that ridiculous car of his. George thought maybe Harold made a bad investment. It happens a lot to older people in Florida, don't you know. They get suckered into something and then, before they know it…*poof*…their life savings are gone. I knew someone who got caught up in one of those internet scams out of Nigeria. Horrible business that was." Jinny shakes her head at the memory.

"I was curious about something you said earlier," I say, thinking that Stan never mentioned having a fight with Harold. "You say Harold asked Stan for a favor. Do you happen to remember what the favor was?"

"Money, don't you know. The root of all evil. George got me a magnet that said that once. And then at the bottom it said that all women need roots. Get it? All women need money! We got quite the laugh out of that, don't you know. But we were talking aboot Harold, weren't we? Yes, apparently, he asked Stan for some money. Said he wanted to hire a lawyer for something and needed a retainer. See, Harold had been real good to Stan when Stan had some money trouble of his own, so Harold must have thought his old friend would return the favor. But Stan said no. Which seems mighty callous to me. But, to each his own, that's what I always say."

Mentally, I'm kicking myself. I have so many more questions for Stan now, but I never did set up that call with Curt about the Fridge Friend app. I doubt Stan will talk to me before I make good on that.

Then I remember, he lives right next door to Victor. Since I'll be headed there in a few hours for dinner, maybe I'll find a way to "accidentally" bump into him.

In the immortal words of Desi Arnaz, Stan has some 'splainin' to do.

CHAPTER THIRTY-EIGHT

"Is everything alright, Madeline?" Victor asks.

"Of course, I'm having a wonderful time!"

"I'm glad to hear it. But I can't help but notice your attention seems a bit diverted."

We're sitting out on Victor's back patio, at my request. He opened the bottle of wine I brought, and we've been enjoying a few pre-dinner drinks, but he's right. I've been finding it hard to focus on the conversation. I keep glancing over at Stan's house, hoping he'll make an appearance.

After the talk we had earlier about ceasing my investigation, I can hardly be honest with Victor about my true intentions. So, I concoct a little white lie.

"I'm sorry, Victor. I'm worried I might have forgotten to turn off the stove after lunch."

"Oh." He seems relieved. "That's happened to me before too. You know you could always check on your Fridge Friend app."

"Of course! How could I forget about Fridge Friend?" After all, its inventor has been on my mind all evening. It strikes me that I have been rude; I need to relax and enjoy the evening. I can stalk Stan tomorrow.

"Tell me a little bit about yourself." I attempt to make amends for my earlier conduct. "What kind of law did you practice? Before you retired, I mean."

He chuckles. "You mean before the dawn of time?"

I laugh. "You know that song 'Were You There When They Crucified My Lord'? Every time my kids used to hear it they would respond, 'No, but Dad was.'" Clint would pretend to be offended, but even he thought it was funny. Especially as I was the older of the pair of us.

The memory makes me smile.

"There's no respect from kids these days," Victor agrees. "But back to your question, law was, actually, always a side thing for me. My main job was running a Fortune 500 company. Well, it was just one store when I started it. Now there's one in pretty much every American city."

"Would I know it?"

"Have you ever heard of Dollars and Sense?" He speaks with pride, but also a touch of humility.

"Of course, I have! There's one two blocks from my house in DC! I used to go there all the time. Does that make me a shareholder?"

He smiles. "Not exactly. But I do appreciate your business."

"Wow, you *founded* that company? I can't believe it. That's very impressive, Victor! I thought you said you used to be a lawyer!"

"In the early days, when I was still trying to get the business off the ground, I decided to go to night school and get my law degree. It's come in surprisingly handy over the years."

"I bet it has. Does your son Lucas run the company now?" I ask, knowing full well that Victor told me Lucas works in finance. It just seems impolite to ask straight out why his son doesn't work for one of the biggest companies in the country.

Victor shakes his head, some of the happiness leaching from his face. "No, I wanted him to take over, but I told him he had to do something of his own first. It didn't have to be much, just something to teach him the value of a dollar."

"And sense," I quip.

"Precisely. Long story short, he got seduced by the high-flying world of finance. Quick money and get rich quick schemes. Too risky for my blood, but it's what he enjoys. All we want is to see our kids happy and safe, am I right?"

"Well, you're definitely not wrong," I agree. "Is Lucas your only child?"

"He's my pride and joy." His words don't quite match their delivery. "His mother, my late wife, had some complications during her pregnancy. After Lucas was born, the doctors said we shouldn't plan on having any more children. We still tried, thinking the doctors were wrong. After three miscarriages, we agreed to stop trying."

"Oh, Victor, that must have been so hard on you both," I sympathize, unable to imagine losing one of my own children.

"Suffice it to say, Linda, that was my wife's name, focused all her attention on Lucas. And don't get me wrong, he was always a good boy, but I could see he was getting a little spoiled by the attention. That's why I didn't hand over the company when I retired. I wanted to give him a taste of what it was like not to have everything handed to you. It was the only thing I ever denied him, but I had to do it."

"That's very admirable," I say, meaning it. "On my late husband's detective salary, our kids never had to worry about being spoiled. I've been lucky, though...now they're spoiling me. They pay for this place. I never would have been able to afford it without them."

"From what I can see, you are very lucky indeed." He lifts his glass. "To our kids!"

I look down at my own glass. "I'd love to share in the toast, but I'm afraid I'm empty."

He stands up, holding out his hand. "You must think me the worst host, letting your wine glass run dry. Give me a few seconds, and I'll have you topped up!"

"Take your time, I actually need to use the ladies' room," I tell him.

"Of course! It's past the living room, down the hallway, and on the left. If you get to the billiard room, you've gone too far."

"The billiard room?" I ask. "I thought that was only a board game invention! People actually have rooms in their house just to play pool?"

"Don't make fun! You have to allow a man a few indulgences."

"Fair enough," I teasingly concede. "Excuse me."

We both walk to the sliding glass doors, which he opens, bowing theatrically to let me through first. Once inside, we split off—he goes left toward the kitchen, and I turn right into the hallway past the living room.

Taking in the decor, I don't have to be reminded that he chose the Picasso package. While cubism had been the focus of the living room, the hallway appears to have more of an influence from the painter's primitivism phase.

The bathroom appears on my left, as described, but I halt outside the door. At the end of the hall, there's a guest room that seems decorated to reflect Picasso's Blue Period, which is my favorite. Surely Victor wouldn't mind if I take a quick peek.

There's a lovely reproduction of *La Vie* on the powder blue painted wall. The floors are hardwood—pine, I think—and there's a large plush white rug at the base of the bed. The room seems at once peaceful and melancholy.

I'm turning to leave, when a splash of vibrant orange catches my eye. It seems so out of place in the environment. There's something just under the bed, nearly out of sight. Moving closer, I gingerly kneel, wincing as I hear my bones creaking. Unable to lower myself further, I reach under the bed and pull out the item.

Glancing down, my head fills with so many questions it feels like they're squishing my brain, making further thought impossible. In my hand, I'm holding a rainbow keychain just like the one Astrid had.

She said it was one of a pair.

Jinny said Harold's keys appeared to be missing.

But why would Harold's keys be in Victor's spare bedroom?

222

"Madeline? Is everything all right?" Victor calls out from the living room.

I tiptoe quickly back to the bathroom and close the door before calling out, "I'll be out in a minute."

I flush the toilet, because he'll be expecting to hear a flush. Then, turning on the faucet, I splash my face with cold water. I need to get my thoughts in order, but there's no time. Victor is waiting for me and will get suspicious the longer I take.

There must be an explanation, I tell myself. I just need to figure it out.

"Sorry, I didn't mean to bother you while you were in the ladies' room," Victor says when I return to the living room. "I just wanted to make sure you found it." He hands me a fresh glass of wine.

"Oh, yes. I had no trouble finding anything," I say, sounding far too chipper. "I love the hand soap you have in there. Where did you get it?"

A groove appears between his eyebrows. "It's one of our own brands."

"Fabulous! And are there any Dollars and Sense around here?" I try, unsuccessfully, to keep my voice from shaking. "I haven't seen any, but then I haven't been off the grounds since I arrived."

"Are you alright, Madeline? You're acting very strange."

"Me, acting strange? I don't know why! Maybe it's the wine. At my age, I should know better than to drink on an empty stomach." I try to laugh, but it comes out more as a cackle.

My phone pings with a message from Eliza.

Mom, you were right. Harold was murdered. Friday night. He was poisoned with weed killer.

Victor uses weed killer on his garden. He'd gotten some on his pants when Curt and I saw him during our walk along the lake. My mind searches for a reasonable explanation, but I'm suddenly agreeing with Eliza—that I should never have tried to solve this case on my own.

"Oh, I'm so sorry. It's a message from my daughter. She decided to come stay the night," I lie. "It doesn't look like I'm going to be able to stay for dinner after all." I stand up and look around for my handbag.

"She just showed up at your house unannounced?" Victor doesn't sound convinced.

"She can be like that sometimes. Not much of a planner, my Eliza." I'm walking toward the kitchen, where I think I might have left it.

My heart is beating too fast. I hope this isn't what the start of a stroke feels like!

Standing next to the refrigerator, I search the counter for my bag. It's not there!

"Madeline?" Victor calls from across the room. The handles of my purse are perched on the tips of his fingers, and he's swinging it very gently. "Do you want to tell me what's going on?"

I try to smile, but my lips are trembling. "What do you mean?"

I look at Victor. He looks back at me.

I swallow the lump forming in my throat.

He was right. I am a terrible liar.

"Why, Victor?" I blurt out. "Why did you kill Harold?"

CHAPTER THIRTY-NINE

"I can see you're upset, but be reasonable. You know I'm not a killer!"

"Oh really? Then why are Harold's keys in your spare bedroom?" I demand, realizing I won't be able to bluff my way out of Victor's house.

"I don't know, maybe he dropped them when he was over at some point," Victor says. "We don't even know for sure that Harold was killed! The autopsy—"

"Just came back," I interrupt him. "He was poisoned with weed killer."

"Oh."

Just the one word—oh. Then he seems to shrink into himself as his body sinks into the loveseat. Neither of us says anything for a solid five minutes. He must be thinking that he's caught, unless he kills me, of course. I'm thinking that I don't want to die.

One of us is going to leave this house disappointed.

"All of this has to do with your son's investments, doesn't it?" I finally break the ice.

His eyes grow wider, but he says nothing. I take it as confirmation.

"Am I right to assume your son scammed Harold out of his money?"

He nods, but doesn't look up at me, just continues to stare at the purse dangling on his fingertips. "How long have you known?"

"Honestly, I only put the pieces together just now. But why Carlota? How was she involved?"

Victor sighs. "She was going to report Lucas to the attorney general and the SEC for scamming elderly people. Harold told her everything, and she went on the war path. She came to me, offering to give Lucas a chance to turn himself in before she went public with the information. Lucas flew down to meet with her himself, but the conversation didn't…go well."

"Lucas killed her! That night, with her own golf club. If you knew, why didn't you turn him in yourself? Or convince him to surrender. It's not like he cheated on his taxes! He killed a woman for goodness' sake!"

"When he came back to the house and told me what had happened, I didn't know what to do. He's my only son, Madeline. My only child," Victor pleads with me. "He was scared and crying. Said if only I'd given him the company when I retired, none of this would have happened. I felt like it was all my fault."

"But it wasn't your fault! You didn't kill her!"

"No, my son did. And, God help me, I'd rather turn myself in for a crime I didn't commit than see him spend one day in jail." He passionately implores me to understand. "But I'd really hoped it wouldn't come to that."

"I don't understand why he killed her! White collar criminals are usually treated leniently. And if it was just the one incident, he'd have been out of jail in no time."

He doesn't say anything.

"It was just the *one* incident, right?"

His eyes meet mine. His look tells me all I need to know.

"Stan," I realize out loud. "Lucas scammed Stan, too, didn't he? And you gave him the Fridge Friend contract to shut him up."

"Lucas promised me it was a one-time thing," Victor laments. "I didn't think it would be an issue. I thought we'd handled it."

"But if you gave Stan the contract to compensate for the money he lost, he wouldn't have gone behind your back and squealed to Carlota, would he? So how did she know about that?"

"You're right. Stan refused to talk to Carlota about it. She found someone else. Lucas's business partner, Jeremy. She said she would try to get him immunity in exchange for testifying against Lucas."

"Wait a minute, didn't Lucas's partner die in a car accident recently?"

Victor hangs his head.

"Oh, Victor! Lucas killed his business partner too? And you've known all along?"

"He's my *son*! What was I supposed to do?" His voice lacks its earlier conviction.

"And Harold? Oh my gosh, of course! That's why he broke into Carlota's house. He was trying to find the paperwork that implicated Lucas. He was planning to hire a lawyer and needed proof. Did he come to you for help?"

"He did come to talk to me, when you and Curt were in the backyard, but I pretended I wasn't home. Then I ran into him on Friday night. On the lake path. He asked if we could talk, and I invited him back here for a drink. Lucas never meant for him to die."

Something about the dates isn't adding up in my mind.

"Harold died on Friday night," I think aloud. "But Lucas didn't get into town until Saturday. He couldn't have done it. Oh no, Victor. You didn't!"

His ice blue eyes mist over. "He's my son. I had to protect him. Harold was going to ruin everything."

"You put weed killer in his drink and watched him die?"

"It all happened so fast! He asked if he could lie down, said he wasn't feeling well. I sent him to the guest room. You have to believe me! I changed my mind right after he finished his drink. I was about to call for an ambulance, but when I went into the bedroom to check on him, he was already dead."

I have a flashback of Harold's head, rolling to one side to stare at me after the alligator had released its grip on him.

"And the alligator?"

"That wasn't us," Victor vehemently insists.

"Us?"

"Lucas helped me move the body to the river."

"On Saturday night? After we went to the Stealers Wheel concert?" I groan.

How could I have been so blind? How did I not pick up any of the deception coming off both Victor and Lucas that night? They were about to move a body! Unless they're psychopaths, they had to be feeling a bit jittery!

"I asked you not to get involved! I begged you to leave it alone!" Victor practically shouts. "You were never supposed to be part of this. I like you, Madeline! I was really hoping we could try to find some happiness together!"

"Before or after you'd been implicated in the deaths of three people?" I ask calmly.

He squints, the lines on his face becoming more pronounced as his features harden into a scowl. "You know I'm not a killer," he growls. "Not really. Everything I did, I did to save my boy."

"Maybe your *boy* didn't deserve to be saved."

He stands up, my purse dropping to the floor as he balls his hands into fists.

"What?" I ask, my voice not as steady as I would have hoped. "Are you going to kill me now too? Dump my body in the river to have alligators feast on me too?"

"I told you to stay away from the investigation." He speaks so softly I can barely hear him.

"You'll never get away with it!" I threaten. "My daughter is on her way right now. She knows I'm here with you!"

"I thought your daughter was already here." Victor refers to my earlier bluff. His face looks almost resigned as he begins walking toward me.

He's going to kill me.

Eliza was right. I should have kept my nose down and out of trouble. Now, my kids will lose both their parents in one year. I hope Curt and the girls remember their grandmother. I wish I had one more chance to tell them how much I love them.

"I'm so sorry, Madeline," he says, picking up a bronze statue from a side table. "I never wanted to hurt you."

Then I remember, I'm in the kitchen! Fridge Friend! I hustle over to the refrigerator, activate the touch screen and press the button that reads: "Life Alert: In Case of Emergency Press Here."

The phone rings, and the wall speaker comes to life. "Please remain calm. Help is on the way."

Victor freezes less than five feet away.

"Now why did you have to go and do that?" He asks.

"You were going to kill me!" I shriek.

His face reflects his conflicting emotions—disappointment and relief.

Then we hear it. The sound of a siren racing up the street. Not the tinny sound of Jimmy's emergency golf cart. This is the real deal.

Victor turns to face the front door. The bronze statue falls to his feet.

The sirens stop just outside. I can see the flashing blue and red lights through the windows. A door slams. Footsteps. Then banging.

"Victor Collins, this is Detective Fletcher. We have you surrounded. Come out with your hands up!"

It sounds like a line from a movie. The detective probably borrowed it from one, in fact. But I don't care. All that matters is that I'm not going to die today.

Only then does it occur to me, I never actually used the ladies' room.

CHAPTER FORTY

"How many fingers am I holding up?" Detective Fletcher asks, his hand inches away from my face.

"Really, Detective, I'm fine," I assure him. "Victor never touched me, so I can't possibly have a concussion."

"An ambulance is on its way, just in case. Are you experiencing any chest pain?"

He has me seated on Victor's couch as he fawns over me. He's already taken Victor out of the house. He's probably sitting in the back of a police car, waiting to be taken in for booking. I know Detective Fletcher will have to take my statement, but for now, he seems to be too worried I'll drop dead from the shock of it all.

"How did you know where to find me?" I ask.

He puts his fingers down and sits next to me. "Your daughter called me. When you didn't respond to her text, she hacked into your phone to see where you were. She heard the whole confession."

Good old Eliza. Maybe I shouldn't be so bitter about her spying on me after all.

"She's on her way now," Detective Fletcher continues. "She said your son will be flying in as well. I just want to make sure you're alright until they arrive." He pauses, debating whether to indulge his curiosity. Eventually, it gets the best of him. "How did you know it was Victor?"

"To be perfectly frank, I didn't. Not until I found Harold's keys in his spare room. Then all the pieces started to fall into place."

Detective Fletcher shakes his head, embarrassed. "I should have listened to you. I was so convinced it was Selena."

I rest my hand on his shoulder. "Don't be too hard on yourself. When we found out who she really was, I think we were all a bit blinded."

"But you knew. You could tell something wasn't right."

"Or maybe I'm just an old busybody." I chuckle. "In the end, you caught the murderers. Just in the nick of time, too. I can't thank you enough for that."

"Really you should be thanking your daughter," he demurs.

"Oh, I will. But you were the one who saved me. I won't forget that!"

We sit on the sofa in silence, listening to the chatter of the crowd that's begun to congregate out in the street.

"I hate to ask," Detective Fletcher says. "Is there any way you could do me a favor?"

"You saved my life, so I can hardly say no, can I?" We look at each other and smile.

"I just feel like I could learn a lot from you," he admits. "And you were right. I did write *A Sunny Day to Die*."

I playfully punch his shoulder. "I knew that was you! It was a really good book."

"I have another one I just finished. I was wondering if maybe you would read it? Point out any mistakes with the investigation?"

The eagerness on his face melts my heart. "It would be my honor."

A paramedic walks through the front door and, with Detective Fletcher in tow, escorts me out to a waiting ambulance. I insist I'm fine. The paramedic insists on checking my pulse and blood pressure anyway. He sits me on the ambulance's bumper and begins setting up his equipment.

I look out at the crowd that has assembled. Jinny and George are there. So are Roy Everhard and the elusive Stan Polotski. Closest to me is Helen Richards, a contrite look on her face and a silent Mitsy clutched in her arms.

She leans in toward me as the paramedic pumps the vise wrapped around my arm.

"Listen, sugar, I want to apologize for the way I acted. I was havin' a dying duck fit over thinkin' you were trying to steal Victor away from me. Turns out you did me a big ole favor."

"Don't mention it, Helen," I say, really hoping she'll never mention it again. "How's Mitsy doing?"

Helen looks affectionately down at her dog. "Oh, she's hangin' in there like a hair in a biscuit. Bless her heart, she gives me a lot less headaches these days."

"Helen, can I ask you something?"

"Whatya wanna know, sugar?"

Even after all that I've just been through, I can't seem to help myself. "I heard you had a fight with Carlota shortly before she died. What was that all about?"

Helen looks confused at first, but then her lips purse as she seems to recall the fight. "It started out with Carlota trying to tell me to keep my distance from Victor. I guess now she was only tryin' to help, but then she came out with some harebrained notions about my Donald."

"What did she say?" I push.

"Implyin' she'd say I put him in an early grave if I didn't leave off Victor. Well, clearly saying I had anythin' to do with Donald's death was a dog that don't hunt. Still, it made me madder than a possum eatin' fire ants."

Helen has a lot of colorful ways of describing anger. I guess with her temper, she'd have to.

"But hearin' about Victor bein' a killer and all, it's made me rethink some things. Carl has been asking me to marry him for years. I think it's about time I made his day and tole him yes." She grins, all her perfect teeth gleaming.

"Carl?" Crazy Carl? The one who walks around in American flag Speedos?

"The very same!"

"But are you sure? I mean, it seems kind of sudden," I say, wondering why I care what mistakes she might make in her own personal life.

"I reckon he's got three qualities that are really important."

"Yeah? Such as?"

"He's nice to me. He's got plenty of money. And he's never killed no one as far as I can tell."

"I hope you'll be very happy together." I mean it.

She blushes slightly. "I'd really be tickled if you would come to the weddin'."

I smile, realizing that the crazy characters at Egret's Loft, for better or worse, are becoming my new family.

"I wouldn't miss it," I assure her.

"You're all checked out," the paramedic announces, stepping in front of Helen so he has my undivided attention. "All your levels are good, just make sure to let someone know if you start having any heart palpitations or difficulty breathing."

"Yes, alright. I will."

Madeline?" A familiar voice cries out from the back of the crowd, then a muffled, "Don't you dare try to stop me, young man. I'm going up to that ambulance whether you like it or not!"

Gina's petite frame boulders through the small group of onlookers. She sees me, relief flooding her eyes, and moves as quickly as her hips allow to come join me on the edge of the bumper.

"Lordy, you gave me quite a fright." Her voice is laced with emotion, but she maintains her distance. "Vincent? Can you believe it?"

"Victor," I correct her, then nod. "Considering he was about to crush my skull with a statue when Detective Fletcher showed up, yes. Yes, I can believe it."

"Poor Carlota. No one stopped him from killing her." She makes a remorseful clucking sound with her tongue.

I don't bother to tell her just yet that it was actually Lucas who killed Carlota. There'll be plenty of time for that when we sit over glasses of wine, reliving the details.

But there is one thing that's been on my mind.

"Why is it you can remember Carlota's name, but you forget everyone else's?" I ask.

"What do you mean? I don't forget other people's names!"

I tilt my head down in an expression of disbelief. She starts to laugh.

"Alright, I do. It's a curse. I've always been horrible with names. Except after a person has passed. I guess calling them by the right name is my way of honoring them."

Touched by the unshed tears I hear behind her words, I reach out and take her hand in mine. She squeezes her appreciation.

"What do you say we find something fun to do tomorrow?" She says. "Maybe we could finally finish that bocce ball game we started?"

"That sounds wonderful. Maybe you and Leon can come over for dinner too. My kids are on their way back. We can make a little party out of it."

"Sounds good to me. As long as we have a few days without talking about murder. Deal?"

I sigh in relief that she won't immediately ask me to recount all the events of this evening. "Deal. I think I've had enough murder for one lifetime."

"You and me both," she agrees.

Little did we know then, another murder was just around the corner for one of the residents of Egret's Loft.

ACKNOWLEDGMENTS

This book is dedicated to my father. Dad, you're missed every, single day.

I want to begin by expressing my deepest appreciation to all my family members and friends who listened to my story ideas, read my early drafts, and sweated with me over selecting the best book cover to launch my Egret's Loft murder mystery series. You're the best friends a girl could have and, depending on how well this series sells, I owe you all several rounds of drinks.

It is with deepest humility that I also thank the amazing team of professionals who helped me launch this novel. I'd especially like to give credit to my editor, Shannon Cave, for her meticulous attention to detail and spot-on feedback. This book is better because of you, Shannon. And huge thanks to cover designer extraordinaire, Joe Montgomery. I'm so grateful for your patience, kindness, and talent.

Last—but polar opposite of least—I want to thank Steve for his steadfast encouragement and support throughout this entire process. You shared in my enthusiasm and carried me through my self-doubt. I wouldn't be here now without you, sweetheart. Thank you.

Read on for an excerpt of T.E. Harkins next
Egret's Loft mystery,

THE DEAD MEN'S WIFE

CHAPTER ONE

Gorgeous November day in the tropics? Check.

Multi-tiered red velvet cake frosted and delivered? Check.

White dress for a decidedly un-virginal and post-menopausal bride? Check.

The hot, steamy Florida air hums with excitement as the elderly residents of Egret's Loft, so recently rattled by the murders of two of their own, gather for the wedding of Helen Richards and Carl Hancock.

"At least we know it's not a shotgun wedding," my new friend Gina whispers to me, stepping out of the way of an anxious-looking young woman struggling under the weight of an enormous flower arrangement.

"True, it would be physically impossible for Helen to be pregnant," I concede. "But Carl's got to be in his eighties. He can't be sure how much time he has left, so I suppose the same urgency applies."

The pace of the wedding planning had been nothing short of frenetic. The groom's niece, Tiffany—who also happens to be the activities director at Egret's Loft—has put the entire wedding together in less than a week.

The River Club banquet hall has been magically transformed into a kind of fairytale kingdom. On steroids. It's so over-the-top Disney themed, I can't help but wonder if I'll be charged $7 for a soda here too.

"I don't know that he should be quite so anxious to walk this particular bride down the aisle. The odds aren't exactly in his favor," Gina points out.

She's not wrong.

Helen's been married seven times already, but never divorced. All her husbands died, though I can't say whether the circumstances were suspicious or not. Given that I moved into the upscale retirement community less than two weeks ago, it seems a bit forward to ask the bride-to-be how all the past Mr. Richards met their ends.

Having already been on the receiving end of her temper, it's not a stretch to imagine her bumping off one, or even two of them. But it's her wedding day. Not the right time to debate whether she's a homicidal lunatic. So, I keep my mouth shut.

After bumping her head on a particularly low-hanging balloon, Gina reaches up to adjust the royal blue, lace fascinator perched like an exotic bird on her shoulder-length gray hair. The hat perfectly matches her tailored skirt-suit, both of which pop against her mocha-colored skin.

"Why did Holly want to see you before the ceremony anyway?" She asks, battling the string from the balloon that assaulted her.

"Helen! Her name is Helen. Can't you at least try to get it right today?"

Gina has a habit of forgetting the names of everyone she meets, including Leon, her own husband of forty years. She remembers *a* name, it's just never *their* name. In the short time I've known her, I've grown to accept that I will always be "Mandy" to her, even though my name is Madeline.

Still, a woman should be called by her own name on her wedding day.

"Helen. Holly. What's the big deal?" Gina waves off my concern. "What I don't understand is why she asked to see you before the ceremony. Just two weeks ago, she wanted to skin you alive!"

"Well, to be fair, I did pop one of her breast implants," I remind Gina. It wasn't intentional, just an unfortunate golfing accident. Understandably, Helen hadn't taken too kindly to me after that first meeting. All was forgiven, though, when I saved her from dating a sociopath.

"She seems to think I'm the reason she and Carl ended up together," I say, though I'm not particularly eager to claim credit. "She asked if she could borrow something blue for the day. That's why we're going to see her now. I need to give it to her."

Somewhere behind us a musician runs through the scales, warming up on their harp.

"Something borrowed *and* something blue?" Gina scoffs. "That's kinda lazy, don't you think? Asking you for both."

"Not at all, I'm happy to help."

"You know your problem, Mandy? You're too nice. She's only asking you because she's not exactly spoiled for choice when it comes to friends."

"Shhhh!" I shoosh her. "You're not supposed to speak ill of the bride!"

"The dead."

My heart beats faster. "Who's dead?"

Gina rolls her eyes. "No. The saying is not to speak ill of the dead. Which, given her track record, would mean I shouldn't speak ill of the *groom*," Gina says, loud enough that one of the flower arrangers sends a disgusted frown in our direction.

I stop walking, partially because someone is relocating a large, flowered arch in front of us and partially for dramatic effect. "If you can't play nice, I'm going to have to leave you out here while I go in to see Helen."

"Fine, I'll behave." Gina pouts. "What are you going to loan her anyway?"

"That was a problem since most of my things are still back at my house in DC. All I have here that's blue are my lisinopril pills."

"Oh, I used to take those. They made my tongue swell, so my doctor switched me to Lotensin," Gina says. "But really? Your something borrowed is blood pressure medication?"

"No, of course not! I had my son Ritchie go by the house and pick something up for me. He sent it with that overnight delivery. The price was on the box. It's highway robbery what the post office charges these days!"

4

Gina shakes her head. "I remember when it cost six cents to send a letter."

"Here we are!" My hand rests on the handle of the door leading to Helen's makeshift dressing room. "Be good!"

Gina sticks her tongue out at me but quickly retracts it as I open the door.

Helen stands in front of a full-length mirror, turning this way and that, trying to get a view on all her angles. She's not alone. In the corner, a woman is packing up a makeup case, and a vibrantly dressed young man rolls up the cord of a curling iron. Both give me wan smiles as I enter.

"Madeline! Bless your heart, you're just in time!" Helen gushes after spotting my reflection in the mirror. Turning around, she sees my companion and adds a curt, "Oh, hi there, Gina."

"Congratulations, Holl…en," Gina corrects herself mid-word.

"Oh, Helen! You look…beautiful!" I say.

And she does. Her long bleached-blond hair is curled and partially pulled back. Her gown is a vibrant white silk-and-lace creation that clings to her hourglass curves. It would all be so tasteful, if only the bodice wasn't so low-cut you can practically see the scars from her breast implants.

But as my late husband Clint always used to say about women who opted for plastic surgery, if you've bought it, flaunt it.

"Thank you, sugar," she purrs in her thick Southern drawl. "Though I may be getting too mature for all this wedding nonsense. I've got a few more lines on my face this time around."

"Stop now, you don't look a day over forty-five." I exaggerate. Her numerous face lifts and Botox injections have certainly done wonders, but they're still no match for gravity. "How are you feeling?"

5

She picks up one of the wedding programs Carl's niece had printed for the occasion and starts fanning herself. "I'm so nervous, I'm sweatin' like a sinner in church!"

Gina opens her mouth to speak but, afraid of what she might say, I quickly cut her off. "There's no reason to be nervous! This is a happy day! Just try to relax and enjoy it. Oh! Doesn't Mitsy look precious!"

Helen's Pomeranian sits quietly at her feet. Mitsy has on her own silk-and-lace gown with a pillow perched on her back. Strings hang loose from the cushion, likely where the wedding rings will be attached for the ceremony.

"Doesn't she just?" Helen beams, then turns to the young woman in the corner. "Tanya, would you be a peach and pour me and my friends a glass of champagne?"

"Ummm…sure," Tanya replies, looking longingly at the makeup case she seems eager to depart with. "But if you want me to stay longer, we'll go into overtime."

"Fine, fine!" Helen waves a perfectly fake-tanned hand. "Not a problem. Now, Madeline. Do you have something for me? Nothing too fancy, though, I hope!" It's clear she means the opposite.

"I do! My Clint bought it for me ages ago to wear to a policeman's ball. I really hope you like it!"

I reach into the little silk handbag I bought for this occasion and pull out a hair clip studded with blue and white sapphires. Clint had saved up for months to buy it for me. He loved my then-natural blond hair and said it deserved only the finest adornment.

"Well, butter my butt and call me a biscuit!" Helen exclaims. "It's gorgeous! Will you put it on for me?"

She turns around and I clip the barrette into her hair. By the time my arthritic fingers manage to secure the clasp, the woman named Tanya, who's clearly been waiting for me to finish my task, practically shoves a flute of champagne into my hand. Gina and Helen are already holding theirs.

"To you and Carl!" I announce, before Gina can congratulate the wrong couple.

"Yes, congrats!" Gina chimes in, her dark eyes glistening.

There are still a few sips left in our glasses when a knock comes on the door, and Carl's rotund niece pops her head in the door.

"Only me, only me!" Tiffany practically sings the words with theatrical enthusiasm. "It's nearly time! Are you ready to do this?"

Helen smiles. "Ready as I'll ever be!"

"Great! I'll go now and make sure the groom is in place. You don't have bridesmaids or groomsmen, so as soon as the theme song from *Beauty and the Beast* starts playing, you walk down the aisle. Walk slowly, though, because I want to sing the whole song before you get to the altar!"

When she pauses to catch her breath, Gina and I excuse ourselves to find our seats.

As we join the crowd of people now gathered in the banquet hall, Gina bumps her head on another balloon and whispers, "You know, for all the murders at Egret's Loft, someone could have done us a favor and killed the clown who turned this place into a Disney cartoon."

In the throes of celebratory fervor, neither Gina nor any of the other guests assembling would have ever imagined that, by the end of the day, another one of us would be dead.

Printed in Great Britain
by Amazon